Nowhere to hide...

During the week she'd cared for him, she'd taken special care not to touch him unless absolutely necessary. She had been too affected by the sight of the hard muscles of his chest and arms. But what ploy could she use now? They were face-to-face.

"I need something else right now." He touched her chin, taking it in the palm of his large hand. Her heart hammered, her blood pounded, her face grew hot with humiliation. Transfixed, she could only stand and watch him lower his head toward her.

"Princess." His mouth brushed across her lips, touching gently, seeking entry. "Open up. Let me taste how sweet you are," he cajoled, his voice rough, deep and seductive . . .

DIAMOND WILDFLOWER ROMANCE

*A breathtaking line of searing romance novels . . .
where destiny meets desire
in the untamed fury of the American West.*

Night Train

Maryann O'Brien

DIAMOND BOOKS, NEW YORK

If you purchased this book without a cover, you should be aware that this book is stolen property. It was reported as "unsold and destroyed" to the publisher, and neither the author nor the publisher has received any payment for this "stripped book."

This book is a Diamond original edition, and has never been previously published.

NIGHT TRAIN

A Diamond Book / published by arrangement with the author

PRINTING HISTORY
Diamond edition / November 1994

All rights reserved.
Copyright © 1994 by Maryann O'Brien.
This book may not be reproduced in whole or in part, by mimeograph or any other means, without permission.
For information address: The Berkley Publishing Group, 200 Madison Avenue, New York, NY 10016.

ISBN: 0-7865-0058-1

Diamond Books are published by The Berkley Publishing Group, 200 Madison Avenue, New York, NY 10016.
DIAMOND and the "D" design
are trademarks belonging to Charter Communications, Inc.

PRINTED IN THE UNITED STATES OF AMERICA

10 9 8 7 6 5 4 3 2 1

To my friend, my mentor, my "big sister,"

Barbara Benedict

for her encouragement, for her insight, for her willingness to stay the distance with me.
Thanks, Barb.

This one is for you.

AUTHOR'S ACKNOWLEDGMENTS

A special thanks to Nancy Wagner, who taught me to look into my characters and see their souls.

Thanks also to: Pat Teal, my agent, for her heartfelt encouragement; Meryl Sawyer, Olga Bicos, and Debbie Harmse for those early weekly sessions; Meridith Brucker, who encouraged me to join RWA and write a romance; Pat Beharry, Marcy Rothman, and Marilyn Mitchell, my present Thursday night Glendale gang, for their well-rounded insights; my husband, Jack, and my daughter, Alisha, for their love and understanding; Jean Brainerd, Senior Historian of The Wyoming Historical Society, for all those special pieces of research material; and Dorothy Garlock for acting as the godmother of my "baby."

Night Train

PROLOGUE

October, 1866
247 miles west of Omaha, Nebraska

Drake Lassiter eased his body into the warm bathwater, sighing as he stretched his tall frame out as far as possible in the short tub. Not much room for a man his height. With his knees poking up through the water, he raised his right arm and lifted a glass to his lips. Four fingers of good Kentucky disappeared, washing away the dust that had settled in his throat after days on the trail. He repositioned himself. The dirt slid from his flesh, leaving a layer of mud on the bottom of the tub.

Steam rose from his bath, mingling silently with the noises of music, vaudeville acts and fireworks that drifted on the breeze. The applause of the audience of one hundred forty visiting dignitaries shattered the quiet prairie night. Maybe Thomas Durant was right about this extravagant shindig at the end-of-track. It seemed the perfect way to advertise the Union Pacific Railroad's need for additional backers.

"Ahhhh," he sighed, his voice loud in the small, enclosed bathhouse. Let the dignitaries delight in their cases of vintage wine, imported whiskey, champagne and other liquors.

He reached for his own magical elixir, refilled his glass and relished the fire and warmth that spread through him, a needed balm to soothe his weary body.

Only a few hours off the trail, he hadn't expected private bathing facilities. Drake had passed the unposted bathhouse but a teamster had pointed it out to him. Durant, Vice-President of the U.P.R.R., had ordered a western camp set up with tents complete with floors for his visitors from the East and England. The fancy accommodations were a nice touch and Drake never looked a gift horse in the mouth. He could almost smell the smoke floating on the wind from the expensive Havana cigars and the choicest pipe tobacco. He had to settle for rolling his own cigarettes.

Throughout the war he'd been a part of the United States Military Railroad, formed by the federal government and dedicated railroad men who directed, managed, operated, built and rebuilt the badly damaged lines under wartime difficulties. They moved troops and supplies in record time, then tore the track up and laid it again. Now as chief engineer for the U.P.R.R., his task was to construct a road that would join a nation and heal its wounds.

If only he could handle his own pain as easily.

By God, if he could speed the joining of track with the Central Pacific by one day he would move heaven and earth to do so, even if it meant kowtowing to lofty English lords and rich American nabobs.

Thomas had musicians and entertainers aboard the finest train cars available. He even had a skull reader moving from car to car interpreting grooves and bumps on guests' heads for signs of wisdom and statesmanship, who was a particular hit.

Whatever it damn well takes to complete the railroad, Drake swore.

He rolled his shoulders, stiff from his lengthy ride. Now all he needed was a hearty meal and a soft woman. The thought of curvy, feminine flesh pressed against his rough frame gripped the lower part of his body with a new rigidness. With all the visitors in camp, not to mention the camp followers, he'd have no trouble finding a little lady of the evening.

In camp only a short time, he'd heard there was a real lady among the visiting dignitaries whom the men called "Princess." She was the daughter of a British investor and they called her the princess because she led such a pampered life. He didn't want so much as a peek at this aristocrat. Society women got under his skin like a burr, causing a lifetime of misery and discomfort. He'd have his bath, an evening's enjoyment, and restock his provisions, then hightail it out to one of the construction camps at first light. Peace of mind would return when miles separated him from any association with a lady.

Dry from just the thought of being in the same camp with that sort of woman, Drake swallowed the last of his liquor, leaned over, and picked up the bottle sitting on the small table next to the tub. With his attention on pouring another drink, he didn't lift his head as he heard the squeak of the door's leather hinges.

"Dammit, Hardy. Can't a man get privacy around here?" He chastised his partner and banged the empty bottle down on the table. In the process of lifting the refilled glass to his lips, his gaze shifted to the door. He sucked in his breath.

It had been more than six years since he had beheld such a vision. Tall and regal, a woman dressed in a ball gown of black watered silk, shot with gold and silver, leaned against the canvas, her eyes half closed as she attempted to catch her breath and at the same time discover who had spoken to her in the semidarkness. A small light near the door gave him the advantage, for he was hidden in shadows. She held her chin high and made a movement to exit. He knew the instant her eyes locked on his that this beautiful woman was Georgiana Radcliffe, the "Princess."

"Who are you running from?" Drake's words broke the silence as she began to pull the door open.

"I'm not running," she answered quickly, her hand

pressed against her throat. Her skirts swished as she spun around, her gaze roaming sections of the room, looking anywhere but at him.

"Then you always enter a bathhouse unannounced?"

"And who would announce me in a frontier shack?"

Her words amused him. Deep in his chest Drake felt a chuckle building. Totally preoccupied, the princess failed to realize how socially scandalous her impromptu actions were. "Spoken like a true English aristocrat, Princess."

She shot him a condescending glance before looking over her shoulder, her blonde curls swinging across her alabaster skin. "Good night, sir." In an instant, fear and panic shadowed her face as the door to the bathhouse opened, preventing her escape.

"I've been worried out of my mind, Georgiana. I thought you had wandered away from the camp." A stout, dark-haired Englishman dressed in black evening attire grabbed her upper arm.

"I'm fine, Lawrence. You've had too much to drink. I told you I can find my tent alone." She lowered her gaze to his hand and, in a voice used by the rich to dismiss servants, she said, "Let me go."

The stranger shrugged, unaffected by her demands and she cringed when he pulled her closer. Angered by the woman's distress, Drake reached on the floor next to the tub and found his holster. He stayed seated while he drew the revolver. "Mister, take your hands off the lady," he ordered.

Disconcerted at first, the man squinted and located Drake. "Someone should teach you better manners, sir. A gentleman never interferes in private family matters."

"Family?"

"Yes. I'm Lawrence Fowler, Viscount Beeton. Georgiana is my stepsister." Beeton moved to the door and attempted to pull the woman along. "I'll take you to your tent, Georgiana. This is no place for you. For God's sake, the man's naked," he admonished her.

The princess jerked her arm out of the man's grasp and

glanced toward Drake, his naked body shrouded by the water and the semidarkness of the room. "Under the circumstances I prefer his company."

Looking at the viscount's angular features, Drake saw something uncomfortably familiar. During Sherman's march to the sea the enlisted men had worn similar demonic expressions when they went wild, attacking the women they found hiding in the woods. They left a trail of lusty carnage alongside the destruction of land and beasts. All at once, Miss Radcliffe's earlier flight made sense.

Drake stood, tall, angry and naked. "Worried about gentlemanly behavior?" The water ran in streams down his body, splashing the floor as he stepped over the edge of the tub. He moved to the middle of the room. "You're in America, Mister, where men protect women and children."

The Englishman stood his ground. "I am Viscount Beeton. You'll address me properly."

"The introductions are being made by Mister Colt. This makes us equal." Drake lifted the gun a few inches, catching more of the light. He wanted the stranger to get the full meaning of his words. "I don't care if you're the Prince of Wales. The lady doesn't want your company. Leave."

The viscount glowered at Drake.

"Lawrence, that's enough! Or shall I inform Father of your sudden interest in my welfare?"

Beeton's face paled at the mention of her father, his gaze straying to the gun pointed at his chest. Drake didn't know which had given him the most leverage, her mention of her father or his drawn gun.

Nonchalantly, the princess walked over to Drake, placing her hand on top of the revolver, her palm grazing his thumb, triggering a deep, hot need for her to touch another part of his body.

She's a cool one. She hasn't flinched at my nakedness, Drake thought.

Standing only inches away from her now, he saw that the color of her eyes was a shade that would match a blue heron's egg. His nostrils, so used to the smell of sweat, horses, dust and dry prairie wind, drew in the fresh clean scent of her body. Her unbound blonde hair fell across one shoulder, thick and luxuriant.

Without a sign of distress over his lack of clothes, her gaze shifted toward the viscount. It was shadowed with anger. "This isn't necessary. My stepbrother is leaving. Aren't you, Lawrence?"

"He doesn't have a choice, ma'am," Drake retorted.

"Why, you bastard!" The Englishman's precise diction disappeared as his irritation increased. He clenched his hands and made a movement as if to lunge at Drake.

Gripping Georgiana's fingers, Drake pulled them from his gun hand and moved her to the side, away from any possible harm. His Colt possessed an international form of language, for within the count of three heartbeats, the viscount slapped his hands against his thighs and marched toward the bathhouse door. "I won't forget you, sir," he said in the dark, his voice steel-edged.

"Then remember the name," Drake called out. "Drake Lassiter."

"Lassiter." Beeton rolled the name around on his tongue and repeated it under his breath. "Goodnight, Georgiana." The viscount exited the bathhouse.

Drake listened to the footfalls until they finally faded. The brisk fall air blew in the open door and chilled his body. In his haste to protect the woman he hadn't cared about his nakedness. When he turned to replace his gun in its holster, he felt her eyes burning a path down his spine and across his buttocks. He grabbed a towel, tied it around his waist and swung around, marvelling that she hadn't swooned.

Her indifference, he soon discovered when his hands touched the knot on the towel to verify its sureness, was all a façade. Her eyes widened. Above her neckline, her pulse pounded erratically.

He took a step closer. Looking at him, she clearly studied

his almost naked body, flags of crimson whipping at her cheeks. He grinned and hoped she was enjoying the show.

When he lifted a hand to smooth her loose hair from her face, she inhaled sharply at his contact. "Don't faint now, Princess." Drake placed his hands on her shoulders to steady her. "Don't worry about your stepbrother. You're safe now."

But not by much, he thought.

He felt a familiar ache, the demand for the soothing touch of a female companion. Hadn't fate dropped a fair-haired princess into his arms? Pure instinct took over. He tightened his rough palms on her softly rounded shoulders and eased her closer. Her scent again. Like a blanket of prairie wildflowers in spring. Feeling her stiffen, he slipped his hands down her arms and hesitated a moment at her elbow where his fingers tangled in a loose strand of silken hair.

"You've been a perfect gentleman. Don't spoil it now," she said shakily. "You may catch cold standing around like that." She made a quick inventory of his body above the waist, cleared her throat, and turned on her heel, her wide skirts swishing across his ankles. "Good night, Mr. Lassiter," she said, her opal and pearl earbobs brushing across her shoulders. A "thank you" was added almost as an afterthought as she hastened from the bathhouse, the rustling sound of her silk petticoats and the scent of wildflowers an overwhelming reminder of her presence.

With the towel still wrapped around his waist, Drake leaned against the door. He kept his eyes glued to her back until she halted at the entrance to the large canvas tent directly across from the bathhouse. She stopped, a flicker of apprehension touching her soft features as she took in the encampment. When she turned and faced him, her expression was illuminated by the massive bonfires ringing the campsite. He stood in the shadows but she accurately picked him out with her gaze. Briefly, mystery shimmered, excitement flared between them.

Out the side of his eye, Drake saw Lawrence Beeton

move into the copse of cottonwoods outside the light of the camp. Evidently she, too, noticed the viscount because in an instant her eyes were blue ice, cold as a frozen mountain lake. She entered her tent hurriedly, pulled the flaps back, and tied them closed for the night.

Rolling a cigarette, Drake's pulse quickened as he speculated how long it would take to warm the cool princess and how many petticoats he'd have to peel off before he found the white flesh of her soft thighs. Her nearness had affected him and he knew it would linger with him for a long time.

Far off, beyond the camp music, the muted noise of the prairie with its animals making their rounds, rose in the night. All the powerful sounds roared around him, but not one played in his mind over and over as did the sweet, sensuous tone of that woman's voice.

He rested his forearm against the canvas wall, taking deep, soothing drags of tobacco. He'd ridden the long hard trail from construction camps to the end of track on many occasions, his body tired and disoriented, but he'd never felt like this.

He lifted his hand. A sense of restlessness clung to him as strongly as the smoke swirling around him. The lingering feel of her soft skin against his calloused palms had created an ache in his soul. What little bit of peace he'd etched out for himself in the last six years had been shattered in one moment when he'd touched a strand of the fair princess's golden hair.

CHAPTER 1

February 17, 1869
Southwest Wyoming Territory

Georgiana stood on the platform outside the private railcar attached to the Union Pacific train. Black smoke from the funnel-shaped locomotive stacks shrouded linen-like clouds and then floated into the blue prairie sky. Her perfect day would not be destroyed by the cinders, soot and dust that filtered down and clung to skin, hair and clothes. Happy to be back on the American frontier, her joy was marred for only one reason: her father had not lived to return with her as he had pledged when they'd left the Nebraska prairie almost two and a half years ago.

"Come inside, Georgie. Please." Siobhan Ryan, Georgiana's redheaded traveling companion, stood at the door, holding tightly to the rail to keep her balance. "I'm afraid you'll fall off the train." The ship from Liverpool, the jostling trip by rails from Baltimore and then the riverboat trip to Omaha had kept Siobhan nauseated most of the time and her fair complexion was pale, her freckles like drops of ink on thin parchment.

"Isn't it beautiful, Siobhan?" Georgiana took a deep

breath and smiled. "I wish the train would stop so I could run through the ocean of grass."

"And what would a lady be doing lifting her skirts and playing like a hoyden? Have you forgotten your upbringing?"

"For once I'd like to forget..." Wishfully, Georgiana looked at the open sky, the puffy layer of white clouds. "Are you too old to remember how to enjoy yourself?"

"Maybe I am. I'm fifteen years out of the schoolroom." Siobhan pursed her lips and stared at Georgiana. "Now. Let's get back to my question."

For a moment Georgiana's mind spun like a whirlwind. A picnic, she thought. Years ago, she had shared many a happy one with her father, but his second wife, Edythe, had discontinued them. Her stepmother had said it was unseemly for a young girl to be out in the sun like a common laborer. No lady allowed her nose to turn red, she had scolded John Radcliffe. Well, Edythe can no longer tell me what to do, Georgiana reminded herself, her face opening in a brilliant smile. "I'd go on a picnic."

"Alone?"

"Of course not alone," she sighed. *With a handsome frontiersman,* she added silently. Someone who wouldn't question her about not wearing shoes while she walked through the tall, cool grass. Someone who wouldn't worry about naked toes.

Or naked bodies!

Unbidden, Drake Lassiter's image popped into her mind, his broad tanned chest and his strong lean hips as clear as that night two and a half years ago. Seeing again that area below his narrow waist, her heart stopped and she had to draw in deep gulps of air to calm herself. Enough, she told herself. She was tired of being haunted by that vision.

Siobhan narrowed her gaze, shook her head in exasperation and held her hand out. "I want to know who then, but come, talk to me inside. A nice cup of tea will help my nerves, not to mention my digestion." Her mouth was clenched tight and she looked as if she might lose the fragile control she held on her stomach.

Sympathy overcame Georgiana's desire to watch the passing landscape. She'd have time for that later. Now Siobhan needed her.

They moved through the doorway and down the paneled passageway, passing the well-provisioned galley, two bedrooms and private bath. The plush Brussels carpets muffled the sound of their heels as Georgiana held on to the silver mounted iron handrails with one hand and assisted her friend with the other. Once in the lavishly appointed saloon, Georgiana eased Siobhan onto one of the rosewood chairs and placed her legs across an ottoman.

"I should be doing that for you. I'm *your* companion," Siobhan quibbled.

"You can. Later, when you're feeling better."

Georgiana pulled the cord for the porter. With wire-rimmed spectacles perched on the middle of his nose, a giant bald man entered the saloon. Dressed in a pristine uniform of stiffly starched cotton, the man was as much a fixture as the china and linens aboard the private car.

"Washington, would you bring us a tea tray?" Georgiana requested.

"Yes, ma'am. Shall I add a little something for Miss Chiffon's ailment?" he asked, a mischievous glint in his eyes. He pronounced Siobhan's name like the sheer piece of fabric.

"Yes. Thank you, Washington."

The man's quick attention amazed her. He knew of Siobhan's fondness for a little nip with her tea and he catered to their every whim. When she thanked Thomas Durant for the use of his extravagant private car, she'd have nothing but praise for the efficient porter. He had made their journey to the American frontier very comfortable.

Siobhan sat with her feet up and rested her head against the back of the chair. "Now that my head has stopped spinning, I would like to hear more about this picnic?" she insisted, her eyes sparkling. "I know. You wanted me to forget to ask," she said, color finally seeping into her cheeks again.

"Ever since Father died, you've become quite the scold. Very well, if you must know, once I see the railroad and finalize my plans for my inheritance, I plan to take time for a picnic. Maybe I'll find a handsome cavalry officer and let him show me the beautiful countryside."

That wasn't entirely true. She liked to think that Drake Lassiter still worked for the railroad. That he would be in Bear River City, the railroad's base town, when they arrived. If she asked him, would he take her on a picnic? Shivers raced along her spine. She took a deep breath to control her untoward reactions to the thought of seeing the man again.

"Is that all?" Siobhan smiled.

"Yes, it is, stubborn witch."

"*I'm* stubborn?" She stared at Georgiana with a wounded look. "I'd be careful throwing accusations." Siobhan rolled her head, her eyes glazed with pain. "You knew Lawrence was planning a trip to his Wyoming ranch. It would have been safer to wait for him to travel with us."

"When we received the letter telling us he had been delayed on the Continent I wanted . . ." she halted. *I needed to go to America now.* "The rails will be joined in only a few months. A delay would have interfered with my plans."

"Lawrence has plans also."

"He doesn't have any say in my investments. I take care of my own business matters. Father made certain of that in his will."

"I'm still not sure about his decision to leave the railroad stock in your name. I've had too many strange dreams about this godforsaken place."

Georgiana narrowed her eyes. "Siobhan! America is beautiful. It's a new land. Anything can happen here."

"I know. That's why I told you of my vision."

"But you told me you didn't understand the vision, only

that you saw the hand of a man stroking my hair as I'm lying in bed. That doesn't sound frightening to me."

If Drake touched me again with his large calloused hands as Siobhan has suggested, I wouldn't be frightened.

"It's the feeling I get that follows the sight. I wish I'd been with you when you first set foot on this cursed land," Siobhan continued.

"Being with your mother when she died was more important."

"I feel I let you and your father down because I wasn't able to be with you."

"That's nonsense. You've always been loyal. After Mother's death you stayed on and handled everything for Father and me. You've always been there when we've needed you. That's why Father left you a good-sized bequest." Georgiana sighed, extending a hand to grasp her friend's arm. "I'm glad you're my companion. I don't know what I'd do without you."

Siobhan's tentative smile was cut short as the train jostled around a sharp curve of track. Luckily, Washington returned moments later with a silver tea service with delicate china piled high with bite-sized sandwiches and cakes.

Georgiana poured two cups of tea from the pear-shaped silver pot. Siobhan accepted hers, sipped, and smiled at the porter as he left the room.

"Your solicitors could have handled all the inquiries about this railroad and also about the canal at Suez. Cutting through an immense pile of sand so ships can sail from one body of water to another makes no sense to me." Siobhan drank deeply of the liquid, sighing.

"I think it's a very interesting theory. It may very well help bring products from the East to market sooner than ever before. There isn't anything amiss in my decision to personally travel to America and then onto Suez to look at the other construction site." *If luck is with me, I may also have another look at the man who has inhabited my thoughts for almost two and a half years.*

"Then why have you done your best to get around questions about this trip?" Siobhan asked.

Because I don't know all the answers, Georgiana mused, her thoughts traveling back to when she had accompanied her father to America. There was great promise in this land and its people, he had told her before their first visit. That was why he had invested money in the Union Pacific Railroad.

On that trip with her father, she had met many Americans. But only one stood out in her memory. A man in a bathhouse who had set her heart to flutter and her skin to flame.

Normally Georgiana would tease Siobhan about reading her mind, but at this particular moment she didn't want anyone invading her private thoughts. Anxious to be alone, she rose from the settee. "I think you're feeling better. I'm going outside to enjoy the fair weather."

When Siobhan offered no objection, Georgiana retraced her steps and returned to the rear platform. She couldn't break the habit of slipping out of her shoes at every opportunity. Now, she flexed her stockinged toes on the warm metal. Breathing in the fresh air, she watched the ever-changing scenery, more wild, more rugged, more grand than what she had seen on her last visit to America.

Over the rear of the caboose she viewed the eastern horizon behind the speeding train. From reading the travel books she knew that the American Plains started far to the east and stretched to the west a thousand miles, the great height of the Rockies a halting wall of solid rock. One could feel isolated in the middle of such beauty and scope, if not for the procession of wildlife—bison, antelope and prairie dogs—along the tracks.

She laughed at the playful antics of a family of prairie dogs that ran from mound to mound. They'd dive into their holes and up again farther down the line, only to jump in midair, spin and disappear once more. She enjoyed her own laughter, something she hadn't done in a long time.

Twelve hours of travel would bring the train to the latest

base town of the Union Pacific Railroad, Bear River City. Once there she knew she'd no longer be able to deny to Siobhan or herself the real reason for her journey. Six thousand miles seemed a short distance to travel to discover if seeing Drake Lassiter again would affect her so strongly.

Drake rubbed his forearm across his sweaty forehead and replaced his hat. From high on his saddle he took in the far-stretching high plateau overlooking the desolate Wyoming and Utah border. Sagebrush, creosote bush and cactus, but damned little else. A gulp of water from his canteen wet his lips but didn't assuage his thirst.

They'd ridden for two days to reach the circular basin at the crest of the Promontory Mountains. After spending forty-eight hours surveying the land and verifying its grade and curvature, they'd almost completed their reconnaissance for the grading crews. Drake didn't like the route that had been chosen. The elevation was too high on the proposed road and he knew that it could not be maintained and operated economically. Regardless of his expertise and objections, the line was coming through here. He stared blindly at the horizon, mapping the area in his mind.

"It's too damn hot, Captain."

Drake grinned at Hardy Anderson's use of his military rank. They'd experienced hell together during the War, and on too many other occasions, then and since, Hardy had saved Drake's skin. Partners stayed together and accepted each other's quirks, he knew. For better or worse.

"You complaining again, Hardy?"

"You heard me. Even when your mind's a workin', your ears always hear what's goin' on. I watched you durin' the War. Folks thought you were dreamin', but you always knew exactly where to put those rails and when to take them up again."

"This isn't the same, Hardy. This time we're building a railroad to last for generations."

"Not if we don't do somethin' about those bridges we're puttin' up."

"The bridges are safe. I'd let my own mother travel across them."

Now where the hell did that thought come from? Drake silently fumed. He hadn't spoken a word about his mother in eight years. Nor had he had any contact with his family since then. Eight miserable years of wandering, of not admitting or even really knowing who he was, or where he came from. Never going home.

Far above them, a golden eagle flew, its wings spread as wide as a man was tall. Drake watched, shielding his eyes from the intense rays of the sun. He envied the bird's flight of freedom. His own had been shattered when his mother, after a sordid accusation by his fiancée's family, had freed her heart of a long-kept secret.

Damn! What was eating at him? He didn't have time to dwell on the past.

It was time to work. Time to forget.

Drake forced himself to make notes about the rock formations and the topography for the grading teams that would bring the ribbon of iron rails farther west and nearer a meeting place with the Central Pacific. Hardy took one last reading of his surveyor's compass and they were ready to ride.

The Great Salt Lake stretched across the southern horizon. Eastward, the town of Bear River City offered them a hearty meal, a soft bed, and a willing woman. One last glance at the golden rays of the late-afternoon sun started him remembering a woman with hair the color of fool's gold.

You're insane, Lassiter, he mumbled, for dwelling on Georgiana Radcliffe. Forget her hair and how it slipped through your fingertips like Oriental silk. Forget her scent. It ensnared your head, not your heart or soul. There will be a girl at the dance house or at the new saloon. He might as well forget the princess, for she was six thousand miles away and a lifetime removed from the prairie.

"Somethin' wrong, Captain?" Hardy asked. He stood on Drake's left, holding the reins for their horses.

"Yeah. We're crazy for staying out here. Let's ride. We got the information I need for the directors. I've got a hankering for some nice-smelling company tonight."

"You complainin' about the way I smell, Captain?"

"After days with you, I know how badly I need a bath." For effect, Drake sniffed his sleeves and his vest.

"What are we waitin' for? Last one to town buys the whiskey and women," Hardy yelled as he jumped on the pinto's back. He slapped his reins and headed out, leaving Drake eating his dust.

Drake awoke to the pain of an anvil chorus ricocheting in his head. Were they laying track this late at night? No. He gingerly rubbed his aching eyelids with his thumb and index finger. The sound was coming from inside his head.

Pressed snugly to his side, a woman mumbled in her sleep and settled closer as she wrapped her arms around his waist. Now, he remembered how he'd spent the evening. After he'd won the race back from the summit, Hardy had bought them the tastiest meal, too many bottles of the best whiskey in the saloon and the easiest ladies money could find. Hours later he now found himself alone with one of the women.

"Are you ready for me to be your princess?" She yawned and stretched against him, her full breasts stroking along the side of his chest. "Everybody has a little problem sometimes. You were tired. I'll make it good for you now, sugar. I promise." The rouged face of a woman came into focus, surrounded by a mop of blonde hair and lit with a pair of pale blue eyes. The woman's hands crept along Drake's leg.

"I think it's time I left." Drake's voice sounded gritty from too much liquor.

"You kept talking about a princess when we was in bed. Honey, I won't charge you extra. I'll be glad to play the part for you." She pulled herself up on her knees and dropped her head toward his flesh.

He couldn't deal with this. "Not now, sweetheart." He stayed her by putting his hand under her chin. The poor kid looked brokenhearted. "It's okay. I'll still pay you. I guess you expect more activity from your customers." He tried to smile and rubbed his knuckle along her cheekbone. She pouted a moment, searched his face and then sat next to him waiting patiently for further instructions.

He shifted his body as pieces of the evening came charging at him like a herd of buffalo. He'd failed in his attempt to bed this woman. All because she had pale hair and a pair of dull blue eyes. A shadow of the beauty that his real princess possessed.

The walls of the tent seemed to close in on him. Drake pushed his legs over the side of the cot and surveyed the tiny area, seeking a fast exit. His clothes lay in a tidy pile at the foot of the bed. Can't take the boy out of the man, he grumbled. When he was a child he had been taught to fold his clothes neatly in his room.

Within moments he was dressed and ready to depart. He shook his head and ran his hands through his unruly hair. The barmaid sat on the cot, a devastated expression on her face. "You can't leave, honey. We got hours 'til daylight."

"Sorry. I've got to go." He pulled out some bills, more than enough to cover a few nights in bed with her. "Buy yourself something special."

Her blue eyes lit up at his grandiose gesture. "Come back any time, honey. I'll play the princess for you."

He laughed. "Maybe it's only a macabre torture to make me lose my sanity." Thirsty, with no water in sight, Drake lifted the near-empty bottle of whiskey to the filtering light. Taking a gulp, he stalked out into the night, weaving along the track.

Restless and unable to sleep through the volley of gunshots interrupting the peace and tranquility of Bear River

NIGHT TRAIN 19

City, Georgiana stood on the railcar's rear platform and stared out at the tracks that formed a siding for the Union Pacific Railroad. Uneasy, she ran her hands up and down her arms, listening to the cacophony. Mixed in with the rustling of the tall grass was the scurrying of small prairie animals. Alert to the new sensations, she heard a human groan.

Close by, an owl hooted.

Momentarily, she wondered if she had mistaken the earlier moans.

She'd heard that the railroad workers drank each night and fired willy-nilly into the sky and kept shooting into the wee hours until they fell into their beds. The gunshots she heard now were closer than they had been before.

She jumped as Washington appeared behind her. Holding a lamp, he joined her on the platform. "Come in, Miss Radcliffe. It's unsafe out here. Too much shooting for my peace of mind."

"I believe you're right, Washington." But as she turned to enter the car, Georgiana thought she heard a voice call out for help. "Is anyone out there?" she called. She turned back to the railing, staring into the darkness that surrounded the lone siding that held the railroad car. A night breeze fluttered her thin nightgown and robe, curling her hip-length hair around her waist.

Then she heard it again in the silence. A deep groan.

"Someone is hurt, Washington." Sensing she couldn't waste time, she stepped down the metal stairs to the ground.

"Are you sure you want to go out there, Miss Radcliffe?" Washington's eyes were bright behind his spectacles. He hadn't moved off the platform.

"What's going on, Georgie?" Siobhan came through the doorway of the car and pushed her way past the porter.

"I think someone has been hurt," Georgiana called over her shoulder as she hurried away from the safety of the railroad car.

"Wait for me," Siobhan hollered and took the lamp from the porter's frozen hand.

Treading lightly across unfamiliar terrain, Georgiana quickened her step. Some unknown power pulled her into the darkness. She never stopped until Siobhan reached her with the light. A few feet ahead a body lay sprawled face-down in the dirt.

Hesitating briefly, Georgiana proceeded to step over the track and draw closer. She knelt down on the hard ground next to the man. With Siobhan standing over them, the light casting eerie shadows through the darkness, Georgiana touched his shoulder and felt something sticky and warm. As she pulled her hand back, she saw blood stuck between her fingers. She gasped.

"Bring Washington. We need help."

Siobhan took the lamp to find her way back, leaving darkness in her wake. Adjusting her eyes to the faint light of the full moon, Georgiana leaned closer to the injured man. She wiped the blood on the hem of her gown and touched his cool neck. Under her fingertips she felt a strong pulse. She breathed a sigh of relief. At least he was alive.

To make sure her vigil wasn't in vain, she placed her two hands on his right shoulder, pulled him over on his back and listened to a short grunt of pain.

"We've come to help you," she spoke softly, encouraging him to trust her.

Hatless, the stranger's hair fell low on his brow. Georgiana wrapped her fingers in the thick hair and pushed it back off his forehead. With the help of the bright moon she was able to see his eyelids flash open. Smoky gray eyes stared up at her. Eyes that had sparkled with the muted light of a bathhouse on an autumn night more than two years ago. For a moment Georgiana's heart fluttered erratically.

Drake Lassiter.

She forced herself to breathe slowly. In these last months she hadn't forgotten how the man had saved her from Lawrence's drunken advances. Given a lifetime, she'd still remember the perceptive gleam when Drake Lassiter had told her she was safe. Safe from Lawrence, perhaps, but what of her own secret desires?

"We've come to help you." She stroked his cold, damp brow.

"Who the hell are you?" he demanded with a hoarse voice. He held her wrist in an iron-banded grip, his eyes storm clouds of questions looking up at her. Before Georgiana could reply he grabbed her other wrist and pulled her down across his chest.

"Really, Mr. Lassiter. If you're not careful you'll injure yourself even more."

His incredible strength amazed her. Just a few minutes ago her hand had pressed against him in an attempt to keep him from bleeding to death. Evidently the man had a well of power deep within from which to draw. As she pulled away from his grasp, Georgiana dug her elbows into the man's stomach muscles only to find them as hard as steel.

When she lifted her head, Drake Lassiter focused his eyes on her face. "Princess?" he whispered. He drew her closer, holding her tightly against his body. A huskiness lingered in his tone when he said, "If this is a dream just like all the other times"—a lopsided smile opened his grim face—"kiss me before I wake up."

"Mr. Lassiter, you've been shot. We can't—"

Georgiana's words were lost in the savage sweep of Drake Lassiter's lips as he crushed her against his chest. He wrapped his hand in her hair, holding her securely in place as he began to kiss her.

CHAPTER 2

Until now, Georgiana had held certain illusions of being kissed for the first time. It would be springtime at home in Yorkshire. A handsome beau would hold her gently as they sat on a stone bench under the shade of a flowering arbor and whisper words of love.

Instead, Drake Lassiter ravished her with his hard mouth. He pulled her down across his chest, her own fragility and womanhood a poignant counterpoint to his overriding male strength, the stubble on his chin scratching her tender skin. Holding the back of her head, he continued to kiss her as he murmured undecipherable words against her lips and smelled like . . .

Cheap whiskey and cheap perfume!

Injured or not, he was incoherent and she had to stop such insanity. Georgiana pushed against his hard chest, her palms aching from the strain, feeling the powerful drumbeat of his heart. Then all at once his incredible strength faded, his hands fell against his sides and his head hit the ground, stirring up dust around them.

"Mr. Lassiter? Can you hear me?" She felt an icy panic as she looked down at his still form. "Lord! Don't die on me."

"I'm still hanging in there, Princess."

His low husky voice was music to her ears. But when he didn't move or speak again, she leaned over his prone body and laid her hands on the solid muscles of his chest. His heart now thumped a slower beat against her palms.

"Keep doing that, Princess. There's nothing like a woman's touch to bring life to a man."

"Please, don't talk. Conserve your strength."

Moving her hand gently across his shirt, Georgiana slipped her palm under the open collar. His flesh was warm to the touch, a warmth that saturated her fingertips, rushed to the pit of her stomach and made her dizzy as she knelt in the dirt.

An image flooded her senses. Naked from his bath, a gun drawn in her defense, Drake had stood with his formidable expanse of chest, its fine mat of soft hair covering his powerful muscles, an image that dissipated as she moved her fingertips and discovered a small stream of blood flowing from his shoulder.

His heart beat faster, as if his blood hurried to ebb from the wound. She knew she had to stop the flow in order to keep him alive. In her pocket she kept two handkerchiefs, always ready to offer one to Siobhan, who had the habit of forgetting hers. She folded them, placed the material between his shirt and skin, and pressed down. Her actions induced a groan from the injured man. Minutes passed. Looking over her shoulder, she mumbled a silent prayer for Siobhan's swift return.

Relief washed over Georgiana when she saw the light break the darkness. Washington and Siobhan raced toward her. They crossed the tracks and the light from the lamp poured over Georgiana. She looked down at Drake, lying in darkness and shadows. His breathing now held an exaggerated rhythm. He had to be moved as soon as possible. His wound needed attention.

"What took you so long?" Georgiana brushed her palms over her flushed cheeks. If Siobhan had arrived moments earlier... Her cheeks flamed anew as she remembered Drake's kiss.

"Sorry... ma'am... spectacles... I dropped... my glasses." Washington moved closer. "Is he going to die?"

"No," she shouted too loudly. *Not if I have anything to say about it.* "We must move him quickly. Can you carry him, Washington?"

"Don't give it a second thought, ma'am." The porter pulled his trousers higher on his waist, tightened his spectacles across the bridge of his nose and pushed the sleeves of his shirt up a few inches.

Still kneeling next to Drake, Georgiana tugged at his heavy gun belt and removed it. Across the other side of the tracks, she spotted a Stetson. She rose from the dirt and retrieved it.

One moment Drake lay in a puddle of blood, in the next instant he rode on Washington's shoulder like a sack of potatoes. Holding the light high, Siobhan led the way along the tracks. Georgiana walked last in the small procession and watched Drake's head sway back and forth. Laying a comforting hand on his shoulder, she prayed he was unconscious, for the jiggling of his wounded shoulder must hurt terribly.

Silent the entire time of the journey, Siobhan tilted her head twice in Georgiana's direction. Georgiana could sense her friend's turmoil over the decision to take Drake Lassiter back to their private car. More times than she wished to remember she had been the recipient of Siobhan's speculative gaze.

Minutes later, inside the safety of the railroad car, Georgiana helped Washington lay Drake on her bed, and for a moment memories of caring for her ill parents haunted her. *They* had both died. Please, God, don't let me lose this man, she prayed. Deftly she unbuttoned his vest and shirt to the waist. Fleetingly, she remembered the railroad bathhouse, the way he rose from the tub as he cavalierly attacked Lawrence, totally naked, but for his Colt revolver. If she breathed deeply, the phantom scent of his damp flesh washed over her.

His uneven breathing echoed in the bedroom and when she leaned close to him, his eyes opened. "Princess," he whispered, his breath hot against her ear.

Glad of the semidarkness of the room, she delayed turning around and facing Siobhan. She'd blushed more times than she wanted to recall since she'd found Drake Lassiter in the dust. How could an injured man, flat on his back, bring a flush to her body so easily? She'd best be the one to care for him. "I'll take care of cleaning his wound." She looked over at Siobhan. "We'll need plenty of hot water." Before she turned her attention back to Drake, she addressed Washington, "We'll need a doctor. Maybe the railroad has one in attendance."

"Yes, ma'am," they both echoed before leaving to see to their assignments.

Georgiana resumed undressing the top half of Drake's body. She gently pulled the damaged shirt away from his wound. Blood flowed afresh, with a stream of mumbled words and a rash of agitated movements.

"Please. You must stay still."

"Where . . ." At the sound of his voice, she bent closer to him. He licked his lips before continuing. "Where am I?" he managed in no more than a hoarse whisper.

"We've taken you to my railroad car. You're safe."

"Doctor," he said, his voice thick and unsteady.

"Yes. Soon. He'll be here soon."

Siobhan reentered the sickroom and handed Georgiana additional pieces of linen. "Later we'll have a nice talk and you can tell me all about the stranger." Siobhan had the maddening habit of speaking to Georgiana as if she were a child in the classroom. "He needs our attention now. We don't want him to die. Do we, Georgie?"

Shaking her head, Georgiana lowered her gaze, a strange emotion washing through her when she thought of Drake Lassiter lying dead before her eyes. Composing herself, she studied the American's face unhurriedly, feature by feature. His black hair fell over his forehead, split side to side by a widow's peak. His cheek lay on the snow-white sheet, looking paler than when she had first come upon him on the ground. When her gaze found his mouth, she touched her own with her fingertips. His lips looked so soft, yet she had experienced how demandingly hard they became with passion. A strange connection to the rough frontiersman budded to life within her. It grew at an alarming speed and encompassed her.

But Siobhan's soothing caress on her shoulder reminded her that she wasn't alone with Drake. The man needed her clinical ministrations now, not an emotional female.

Moments later, Georgiana was relieved when Siobhan helped her attend to Drake's wound. Georgiana lifted her chin, aware that her blue eyes were aglow with her growing emotions. "Thank you, Siobhan." She could hardly lift her voice above a whisper.

The railroad doctor arrived soon after. He cut the bullet out of Drake's shoulder, sewed him up and applied a bandage. After dosing him with laudanum, the doctor told Georgiana he'd return in a few days, unless she notified him sooner of any complications.

After all, there was still a great possibility of fever. After giving her a bottle of laudanum for pain, telling her to keep the patient as quiet and comfortable as possible, the doctor left without asking if she had a desire to nurse the injured man.

She most certainly was not prepared emotionally to nurse anyone back to health. The years she'd spent taking care of her parents had left her disturbed and fearful of the process. Still, considering how he'd once come to her rescue the very least she could do was share her hospitality.

With the doctor gone, Georgiana fussed over Drake, pulling the covers up to his chin to protect him against the chill of the night. He lay on his left side and before she could walk away he threw his arm out from under the covers. When she lifted the blanket over him again, his hand grasped her wrist and held it. She swayed when his scratchy chin grazed the soft skin, but his lips pressed against her pulse only briefly before he dropped her hand on the bed.

His breathing slowed perceptively. With shaking hands, she tucked the sheet up across his chest. Freed from his shirt, his tanned skin looked vibrant against the pearly-white counterpane and sheets. He rested comfortably and didn't move again.

After a few minutes, Georgiana left the room and found Siobhan waiting in the passageway. "Let's have a cup of tea, Georgie," she said, leading Georgiana to the saloon.

As they passed the galley, they found Washington preparing a tray of refreshments. For the first time since the porter carried Drake Lassiter aboard, Georgiana breathed easily. The man's injury had been tended. He was strong and vital. He would be as good as new in a few days.

"Please sit with Mr. Lassiter while Miss Ryan and I have some tea. We'll take the tray ourselves."

"Of course, ma'am."

Siobhan lifted the pot of tea and Georgiana carried the small tray with the rest of the tea service and little cakes. When they settled in the saloon, Georgiana decided to waylay Siobhan's suspicions by explaining how she'd first met the American.

She told about Lawrence's drunkenness the night of the prairie party, and how Drake Lassiter had helped her. She failed to mention that the American had been naked at the time. "Why didn't you tell me this sooner?" Siobhan asked, bridled anger in her voice.

"Because I knew you would go to Father. I worried about his health. He took sick on the trip to America and never really recovered his strength after our return to England. Besides, Lawrence has never approached me like that again."

Disbelief clouded Siobhan's gaze. "Now I understand

why we left England without waiting for him to travel with us, why you're not even going to his ranch in Wyoming for a visit."

Georgiana shifted her attention to the window. "He thinks he can control me. At least my fortune. I wanted to send him a clear message that I can take care of my own affairs."

The interior temperature of the railroad car was comfortable but she shivered, a strange foreboding slipping up her spine. "He's always trying to interest me in a new investment scheme. But he outdid himself recently. I read through a different prospectus and found out by accident about the Suez Canal. When I asked questions about de Lesseps's project, Lawrence told me it wasn't worth my time. Later I found out if I invested in a company that he suggested, he would get a commission."

"Didn't your father's will leave Edythe and Lawrence with enough money to live respectably the rest of their lives?"

"Yes, but Lawrence wants to live like a member of the landed gentry. In America, no less. Before I left England I heard that he's had a run of bad luck with the cards. Then Edythe asked me for more money."

"And of course you gave her what she wanted."

"I don't mind. After all, she was my father's wife."

"Not for the last few years."

"Oh? How would you know that?"

"Servants' gossip. You must realize they know everything that goes on abovestairs."

"Really? Then they must have had a grand time talking about the size of the bequest Father left you." Siobhan turned a paler shade. Was she sick again? "You could be in your own home. You wouldn't need to worry about traveling sickness."

"I know. But it's not safe for a young woman to travel alone. You need a companion." Siobhan's demeanor changed dramatically, her eyes sparkling with bedevilment. "Especially now with a man in your bed."

"Siobhan!" Georgiana covered the hot patches on her cheeks. "Please. I've had experience in nursing. What was I to do when the doctor said to keep Drake in bed?"

"Evidently nothing," Siobhan said too nonchalantly.

"Exactly. I owe Drake Lassiter my gratitude for his help during my last visit. I'll care for him until he's capable of leaving his bed, then he'll be on his way to the next town. He's a railroad worker. He follows the rails."

Uneasy with the reminder that Drake would indeed be on his way when he healed, Georgiana rose and looked out the window at the darkened night, the landscape of canvas tents and shanties bereft of civilization's refinements. No soft light of gaslamps, no gardens or stands of shade trees. Where was the heather on the hillside? The stables of fine horseflesh? Where were the giggling girls ready for their Season on the arm of a handsome beau?

She missed them all, yet she was strangely drawn to this countryside despite its fleeting spots of dismal frontier towns that changed from week to week according to the distance of rail laid. The temporary buildings rode along on the railcars with the workers and their tools. These towns sheltered vagabonds, thugs, gamblers, men who walked the wrong side of the law. These travelers stopped briefly, long enough to earn a few dollars, then they were on their way once more. This was home to Drake Lassiter.

Uncomfortable with leaving Drake alone all night so soon after his injury, Georgiana kept a vigil at his bedside. Raising her eyes from her cross-stitching to check his condition, she found his breathing still steady, steadier than her own. She realized that flat on his back with a gunshot wound, Drake Lassiter was still the most virile man she'd ever met.

She hadn't realized how late it had become until she studied the dial of the gold and pearl watch she held in the palm of her hand. Only a few hours until dawn.

She finished the last stitch of a pattern, folded the material, and placed it on the commode table next to the chair.

Her eyelids were heavy, her arms stiff, and her body sluggish. She dimmed the lamp on the table and settled against the cushioned chair, resting her head on the high back.

"Have I taken your bed?"

Drake's voice, thick and unsteady, startled Georgiana. She raised her eyes to find him watching her through thick eyelashes. For a moment she was privy to an unguarded pair of gray eyes.

"You need it more than I," she gently reminded him.

His gaze focused and a faint light twinkled in the depths of his eyes. "We could share." He grabbed the covers, pushed them aside as if to make a spot for her close by his side, and paled from the exertion.

"You must not move, Mr. Lassiter."

Fearing he would open his wound and start the bleeding anew, she moved the short distance to physically restrain him if necessary. He stared up at her as she towered over him, his expression hypnotizing, the warmth of his flesh intoxicating as he casually grabbed her wrist. She was his prisoner.

His grip tightened and his color returned as his attitude became more serious. "I thought you were a dream. But you're real. Aren't you?" His drugged voice sounded husky. He quirked his mouth in an off-center smile; his eyes darkened as he held her gaze.

She offered him a wry smile in return. "I'm very real."

Or am I? Georgiana thought to herself. Maybe this is all a fantasy and I'll awaken to discover Drake Lassiter is only a dream. Georgiana pulled away from his hold and wandered restlessly around the room; his gaze followed her every movement. "How are you feeling?" she asked as she stood at the bottom of the large bed, pulling at the white cotton quilt that spread across its edge.

Drake took some moments to answer as he looked down the length of the bed and took in his appearance in the gilt-framed looking glass hanging over a console table. He touched the large bandaged area on his shoulder and grimaced. "I guess I'm lucky to be alive. The last thing I remember was falling on my face in the dirt and thinking I was going to meet my maker." He focused his eyes on her. "You found me?"

"Yes. I was outside on the rear platform when I heard gunshots. Soon after I heard you moan. We investigated the sound and found you lying in the dirt."

"We?"

"My companion and porter helped to bring you to the railcar for care."

Drake shifted on the bed; his eyes took on a stormy look. "That's very commendable—being a good samaritan. But weren't you warned about the antics of my workers? You should take cover when you hear shots. You're not supposed to go looking for trouble."

"Are you trouble?"

"I could be," he warned her.

He slipped his legs out from under the covers. Georgiana rushed to his side. "Where do you think you are going, Mr. Lassiter?"

"I need to find my trousers so I can go back to work." He grunted in pain as he moved his legs farther over the edge of the bed.

She knew he wasn't going far. His strength would give out shortly. Still, his determination fooled her. He flattened his palms on the mattress in an attempt to push himself up. When she set her hands on his broad shoulders to ease him down on the bed, he clamped his arms around her waist, tugged her, and they both fell back onto the mattress.

The outrage of lying face-to-face with Drake Lassiter in her own bed served her well in her effort to roll off his naked chest. Unfortunately, she was then pressed against the length of his hard torso with only a thin sheet separating them. She felt his warmth as heat leapt between them, engulfing her nerve endings, growing hotter until her fingertips burned against his skin. Between gulps of air, she berated him, "You are much too forward, Mr. Lassiter."

He had the audacity to laugh.

"You're not going anywhere until the doctor says you can leave." His hands had begun to wander up her ribs and she grabbed his wrists, holding them at her sides.

"Are you a betting female? No one tells Drake Lassiter when he moves or stays. Bet the ranch on that one, sweetheart." His voice had deepened, resonance strong and true in the tones. But as he struggled with Georgiana his color paled under his deeply bronzed skin. His words were strong but his strength needed some shoring.

"Well, now. Is this a new form of nursing that I need to know about?" Siobhan stood in the doorway of the bedroom.

"The man is impossible," Georgiana told her companion. "He wants to leave his bed."

"And you decided to sit on him to keep him here?" She made a clucking sound with her tongue. "Georgie, if the man wants to leave, you shouldn't stop him." Siobhan's green eyes widened a fraction as she stood on the far side of the room. "At least let him have his trousers."

For a moment Georgiana was stunned that Siobhan would allow the wounded man to leave. Then she looked at the mischievous glint in her friend's eyes and understood the game she played. "I agree. Two grown women can't possibly tell a stubborn, mule-headed man to stay in bed if he doesn't want to."

She pushed away from Drake and slipped to the other side of the bed. Once on her feet, she brushed her hands and smoothed her skirt. "We'll leave you alone to dress, Mr. Lassiter." Georgiana retrieved her cross-stitching and followed Siobhan through the doorway. "Please shout if you need any help with your shirt."

Georgiana stopped outside to listen and wait. Siobhan continued down the passageway. A strange mixture of sounds flew from the room: creaking bed straps, distinct swear words, a burst of laughter, followed closely by coughs and then a groan.

"You win. You can come back in now," he said, his voice huskier from his exertions. As she reentered the bedroom, he mumbled, "You two females have got me hog-tied. I've got no choice but to stay put." He raised his eyes to hers and said, "I need to contact my partner."

"That can be arranged. Anything to set your mind at ease." She watched him struggle as he lifted his legs back on the bed.

This time she gently coaxed him backward. She held his back, her palm sliding across the firm flesh to his right shoulder. Weakened from his ordeal, Drake's renewed strength surprised her. When she exerted more pressure to help continue his descent onto the pillow, his body stiffened and he refused to be pushed farther.

"When my mother put me to bed, she would lie down next to me." He smoothed the sheet next to his legs with his big hand. "I offered before. There's plenty of room."

"Mr. Lassiter! No gentleman would imply such improprieties."

"Princess," he whispered in her ear. "It's about time you found out the truth." He grabbed her wrist. "I'm no gentleman."

Off balance from his warm lips pressed to her sensitive skin, he tugged her closer. Their eyes met and held. As she breathed, his musky scent enveloped her. For a moment she thought their lips would meet, but he lifted her hand and kissed the soft skin at her wrist below the lace trim of her sleeve. "Thank you. Again," he whispered. Her head spun and her stomach felt as if she hadn't eaten for days.

You set my pulse to racing, Drake Lassiter, she thought to herself, but I'm too sensible to become serious about your sort of man. My life is in England, not in a frontier town in the American West.

Physically, she drew herself away from Drake's touch and left the room. Emotionally, she carried him with her into the railroad car's saloon.

Early the next morning, Washington delivered a telegram for Georgiana and a visitor for Drake.

Georgiana leaned over the oblong, walnut, marble-topped table that separated her from Siobhan. Lifting the piece of paper in the air, she waved it at Siobhan. "Thomas Durant sends his regrets. He has been detained. He suggests we contact his chief engineer, Drake Lassiter."

"Yes, ma'am. That's the captain." Their visitor, Hardy Anderson, held his hat politely while shining the tops of his boot on the back of his pant leg. His spurs dug into the deep piled Brussels carpet.

"Captain?" Georgiana narrowed her eyes and squinted her nose. "I thought he was a civilian."

"He is ma'am, but he was the captain of our squad durin' the War. We've been together ever since. He was determined to build this railroad. I promised to help. Can I see him now, ma'am?"

"Certainly. Mr. Lassiter's down the hall. I'll take you to him."

When they entered the bedroom, Drake was awake, his hands cupping his head as he stared at the ceiling.

"The men are mighty upset, Captain. Most of them swore off liquor for two days after they heard about your accident."

"They damned well should. Ain't been able to stop them from shooting up any camp since we left Omaha."

Georgiana watched Drake. His movements were still somewhat strained yet she marvelled at his powerful masculinity. Still pale from the trauma of his wound, his eyes were clear and his voice strong, his shoulder muscles rippling as he adjusted and sat up straighter against the headboard.

"Hardy, keep the men working. I'll be back at work in a day or so."

"The doctor said a week, Mr. Lassiter," Georgiana interjected. "I promised him that I would care for you. I'll not go back on my word."

There, she'd told him. A few days indeed. Did he think he was an ancient warrior? Wounded, but rising to do battle the same day? He'd need at least a week to gather his strength. Didn't the man realize he had a hole in his shoulder? She was agitated at the thought of his injury and how he'd been shot. A stray bullet in the darkness had almost cost him his life, yet he shrugged it off as if it were nothing more than a beesting. She prowled the room, fidgeting with the curtains, refolding fresh linens, smoothing the spread on the foot of the bed.

"Princess. It's okay. You can stop pacing. We'll take it a day at a time," Drake told her, the lively twinkle in his eyes warning her of a battle of wits during his recuperation.

After four days and nights of nursing Drake, Georgiana felt restless. Each time Siobhan had offered to relieve her of her nursing duties, she'd refused, an unfamiliar need rising deep inside her to care for him. Illogical. Most assuredly. But it existed just the same. Constantly in her thoughts, he had become important to her. If asked the reason, she'd fail to understand the logic in her fascination for the frontiersman.

Compelled to look in on Drake, Georgiana rose from the sofa-lounge. During the few days of his recuperation, whenever she took his food to him, he would follow her every movement. His eye contact was almost as unnerving as the strangely suggestive words and kisses he had previously bestowed on her. Never one to spend an inordinate time on her toilette, she felt as if everything she wore was askew or she was missing a piece of clothing.

This time before entering his room, she patted her hair and smoothed the front of her walking suit and the tiny bows on the bodice of the jacket. Shoeless, she dug her toes into the luxurious carpet and hummed a tune.

She found her patient leaning against the panelled wall next to the bed. He had found his trousers and had attempted to pull on his shirt. "Oh, no, you don't!" Georgiana scolded. "You're not ready to leave." She felt ludicrous, a five-foot, six-inch woman with hands on her hips, dressing down a six-foot, three-inch giant of a man who outweighed her by more than four stone.

"The doctor left a few minutes ago. We both concur. I don't need bedrest anymore. I'm going back to work."

It wasn't so much the tone of his voice as the words. They stung. He was leaving her. She'd worried about him, taken care of him, wiped his heated brow, and now he thought he could just put on his trousers and walk out. Just like that.

Well. She wouldn't argue with him anymore. His strength had returned day by day. Every bit of food she had brought to him, he'd devoured. He'd only had one night of disruptive sleep. So why was she worried? Let him leave, she chastised herself. "Would you like to eat your lunch before you leave?" She dropped her eyes from his face to his naked chest and realized too late the mistake.

During the week she'd cared for him, she'd taken special care not to touch him unless absolutely necessary. She had been too affected by the sight of the hard muscles of his chest and arms. But what ploy could she use now? They were face-to-face.

"I need something else right now." He touched her chin, taking it in the palm of his large hand. Her heart hammered, her blood pounded, her face grew hot with humiliation. On each occasion when he'd touched her she had flushed like a silly schoolgirl. Transfixed, she could only stand and watch him lower his head toward her.

"Princess." His mouth brushed across her lips, touching gently, seeking entry. "Open up. Let me taste how sweet you are," he cajoled, his voice rough, deep and seductive.

Georgiana breathed deeply, and her lips parted slightly, just enough to allow his entry. Soon his tongue explored intimately the inner recesses of her mouth as he kissed her slowly, thoughtfully, his hands drawing her closer to the heat and strength of his body. He pressed harder, his kisses urgent and hungry. She leaned against him, wrapped her arms around his neck, and eagerly participated in the exchange of kisses. In an erotic fog, she almost failed to hear the sound of footsteps in the passageway.

Lifting her head, she listened with bewilderment as a familiar voice reached her. "That Irish woman told me you were busy. You can't be too busy to see me."

Georgiana jerked from Drake's hold and lost her balance. He grasped her around the waist and tugged her back, resting a hand on her waist. She shot him an icy stare and gave an irritable tug at her dressfront where two of the ties had been loosened.

"What is going on here?" her stepbrother demanded as he entered the room.

CHAPTER 3

Viscount Beeton's appearance was not appreciated by Drake. The interfering Englishman was becoming a nuisance, one that Drake could do without.

"Mr. Lassiter has been recuperating from a gunshot wound. I've been nursing him," Georgiana explained, a little breathless, her mouth puffy from Drake's bruising kiss.

That damn Englishman doesn't miss much, Drake thought. Beeton took in the scene, visually cataloging the small room, staring at the mussed bed, and the saddlebags on the floor, a once-over of Drake's naked chest and the shirt thrown across the back of the chair. "By the look of this cozy arrangement, I would think he loved every minute of your ministrations." He riveted his accusing gaze on Drake and Georgiana while he crossed his arms and leaned against the console table.

A muscle tightened in Drake's jaw. He watched Georgiana closely for her reaction to Beeton's improper words. She didn't waste time.

"Your intimations are in bad taste, Lawrence." She glared at her stepbrother with burning eyes. "You're not welcome if you plan to continue that way. Siobhan and I've cared for

Mr. Lassiter since the night he was shot. The doctor didn't want him moved."

The princess could push the truth a little too easily, Drake pondered. She'd breached the world of propriety by caring for an unmarried man alone because most of the time Siobhan Ryan had stayed out of sight. That had shocked, yet pleased him. What other surprises would she have in store for him if he made the effort to become better acquainted?

Slowly the viscount straightened, his hands pressed to his sides. "How close were you to dying?" The tone of Beeton's voice gave the impression he truly was disappointed that Drake hadn't died.

"Close enough," Drake replied with heavy irony.

"Too close," Georgiana whispered as she stared at his gun and holster where they lay on a chair. With his hand still at her waist he smoothed the crisp material of her dress, physically reminding her that he was very much alive.

"Somehow I'd thought I'd find a warmer welcome, Georgiana." Lawrence stared at the spot where Drake's fingers pressed against Georgiana's hip. "But you've disappointed me. I've traveled thousands of miles and instead discover you warming the arms of an American laborer."

Georgiana raised her hand to strike Lawrence, but Drake grabbed it. She didn't feel guilty at the need for violence for her stepbrother's bad manners, his familial devotion was a sham. It wasn't until four years ago during her Season and the announcement of her large dowry that Lawrence had even noticed she was alive. Before then she'd overheard him describe her as a "leggy little twit with a mop of pale hair." Why wouldn't he just go home to England?

"There was no need for you to follow me." She had been a fool to imagine an ocean and thousands of miles of land could serve as a buffer against the antagonism he seemed to delight in. "Please wait in the saloon, Lawrence. I'll join you shortly for tea. Mr. Lassiter has a few items to pack before he leaves. He may need some help."

"Fine. I want to discuss investing that additional money in

a consortium." He smoothed his hands down the front of his frock coat.

"The same organization backing de Lesseps?" she asked.

"No," he said gruffly. "That fool will only lose money."

"I think he has the possibility of greatness. The Suez Canal could yield me high returns if I invest in that project."

"You're a fool!" He snorted. "What does a woman know of money matters?"

"Father wasn't a fool. He taught me everything I know about the financial world."

He quieted instantly, glaring at her with an alarmingly bitter expression. Georgiana couldn't believe the effect her words had upon Lawrence at the mention of her father. It seemed the name John Radcliffe still had the power to keep her stepbrother in line.

Very quietly Lawrence left the room. Alone again with Drake, she was aware of his arm across the back of her waist. Needing some distance, she stepped away from him only to have his hand tighten on her hip, stopping her as he growled, "You're not going anywhere."

His words sounded too harsh, too chilling, unlike those intimate moments before Lawrence had marched in and interrupted their warm, passionate kisses.

"Are you here to take your money out of the Union Pacific Railroad?" His accusing gaze never wavered.

Who was he to question her business dealings? She hesitated before answering him as she blinked with bafflement. Why did it matter to him whether her money was in railroads or shipping? "I don't see that it's any of your concern," she said simply. Turning sharply, she started to move away from his disturbing closeness.

"Anything that could disrupt the laying of rails is definitely my business. Come on, lady." He pulled her around gruffly, grabbing her by the shoulders. "I asked you a question. I want an answer."

Georgiana blared at him, "You want! Lawrence *wants*!" With a strength that amazed her, she pushed at his wrists and dislodged his large hands. She paced the room, edging closer to the door with each pass around the end of the bed. "My father left me a fortune. The railroad stock is a large portion of that inheritance." She took a calming breath and stared at him. "I haven't decided yet if I am going to *increase* my share in the Union Pacific. That's why I'm in America."

"Are you going to allow that stepbrother of yours to influence your decision?" Drake pointed with his thumb to the doorway that Lawrence had so recently exited.

"Lawrence and I don't see eye to eye about how to handle my finances. But that doesn't matter. What *is* important is what my father taught me. I can hold my own any day with financial advisors."

He gazed at her with darkened eyes as if deep in thought before he spoke again. "About your investment in the Union Pacific . . ."

She marched around the bed until she stood facing him. "That again?"

Anger flared in her. She could see an answering response in his harsh glare and the twitch in his square jaw. Conversing with men about business matters had never been pleasant. They could never accept the fact that a woman's mind could formulate and execute commercial decisions. Because she had previously experienced men's disdain, she stood ready to do battle with Drake on this issue.

"If talking about the railroad makes you madder than a stampeding herd of buffalo, then we'd better move to a larger arena," he groused.

So he *did* want to argue. Well, she was ready. Through narrowed eyes she glared back at him.

"Whoa!" He raised his hands in supplication, whistled and then grinned, a lopsided smile, the harsh lines gone. "Could we start over again? I've been caged in this car too long." His sharp agitated movements around the small bedroom testified to his boredom. He picked up his shirt, grunted in pain and pulled it over his head. "I need to ride out to the end-of-track. Come with me. This isn't the place to discuss the building of a railroad. I want you to see how it's created from the ground up. You need to see its soul."

His invitation was intriguing, but . . .

"We can leave early tomorrow morning. I'll have the railroad cook pack a picnic lunch. We'll be gone most of the day."

Until he mentioned a picnic, she wasn't sure she wanted to go with the arrogant man. But a picnic! That was too much of a temptation to resist.

"Why don't I have Washington pack us a lunch? He's a very good cook and I can guarantee you won't starve." She smiled over her shoulder and stopped dead in her tracks when Drake started to push his shirt into his trousers.

"Whatever you plan is fine," he said.

His eyes darted from her face to his task, his fingers painstakingly loosening a button to allow more room for the bunched-up material. He lifted his head, his eyes deep, dark and smoky as he scrutinized her reaction. Wanting so much to stare coldly and keep him at a distance, Georgiana had to look away. Too much had happened. They'd shared too many kisses for her to be unaffected by his actions, she thought with a shudder.

Oh God! I've seen the man naked and stayed detached. I've tended his wounds and kept my head. Why does the simple act of him tucking his shirt into his pants tangle my nerves and make me want . . .

Before she made a fool of herself, Georgiana mumbled she'd be ready in the morning when he came for her and rushed from the room.

Drake chuckled. She may have run now but tomorrow would be another story. He got busy gathering up his few possessions. His freshly laundered shirt had been neatly mended, the hole left by the bullet almost invisible. His upper body was still stiff and his movements were slow. Minutes later he lifted the saddlebags over his good shoulder. Walking toward the doorway, he spied a piece of linen resting on the table next to the entrance. He touched the material with his finger and lifted one concealed section to discover colorful stitches in one area and unadorned pattern marks in another.

It took several seconds for him to make out the scene in the design. He recognized the camp where he and the princess had first met. Bonfires flashed around tents. Trees and bushes had been added for color.

But the most striking form in the piece was a man's face. The image's stubbled chin, the high forehead, the angular cheeks and jaw, suggested the owner had a stubborn streak. It all would fall into place nicely if the seamstress was very good at her art.

He considered the physical attributes depicted in the sampler and his mind wandered back to his childhood. Visitors had always commented on how his not-so-handsome features were different from his brother's perfect lines. Michael had a sensitive face, not a hard, startling one like Drake's.

Drake shifted the saddlebags on his shoulder and considered the number of tedious stitches that were woven through the sampler. Days—if not weeks—of work had been performed on this piece, yet he'd been her patient for only four days. Much thought and preparation had gone into the sketching of this pattern. That meant Georgiana had spent much time thinking of him and their meeting more than two years ago.

Why? he asked himself repeatedly as he exited the bedroom and left the railcar by the rear platform.

Gathering her wits after the episode with Drake, Georgiana found Lawrence standing at the window, his hand clasping the crimson damask curtains. When she looked over her stepbrother's shoulder, she easily picked Drake out of the crowd of railroad men who had waited for him to emerge from his sick bed. Shoulders that seemed as wide as the ties used on the rails, Drake eclipsed everyone in the

NIGHT TRAIN   45

group. He towered over them with his six-foot-three frame and the added height of his Stetson. He pushed his hat back, rubbed the back of his hand over his forehead and continued to hold a conversation with the men. Georgiana's heart warmed as she relived the similar ways she had touched him during his recuperation.

As her stepbrother turned toward her, Georgiana felt a distinct drop in temperature. She instinctively shivered at the coming confrontation.

Unable to cut off the fleeting contact she had with Drake, she stood a moment longer watching his interplay with his friends, then motioned for Lawrence to join her. "Let's get it over with, Lawrence." Staying away from the settee and keeping her distance from him, she decided to sit on a red velvet side chair. He'd have to take another chair and sit alone.

"You always look so severe when we talk, sister dear. Can't you smile more?"

"You haven't given me many reasons to be happy."

"But I came a long way to offer you my assistance."

"Don't try to flatter me, Lawrence. You've only ever wanted to help one person. Yourself."

He rose and moved closer to Georgiana's chair, dropping his hand casually on her shoulder. "But, sister dear, I love you. Mother and I want to look out for you. We're family."

She cringed under his touch, took a deep breath and adjusted her smile. "I've told you there is no reason for your concern. I have Siobhan, and I can make my own decisions as to the disposition of my wealth."

His hand on her shoulder tightened to the point of pain. "When you marry, your husband will control your money."

She glared up at him and shrugged away from his touch. "Exactly why I don't plan to marry."

"Frankly, my dear, I don't believe you. You're ripe for the picking." His disapproving gaze strayed to the window where they had stood looking at Drake.

"Men must think women wait to be plucked like a piece

of fruit. Most of the men with whom I am acquainted believe women do not know their own minds. My plans are different." She forced a demure smile. "If I ever discover a man who will allow me to think for myself then I may consider marriage. Until that time I'm happy with my life."

His expression grew serious. She thought he was angry at her words, but then one corner of his mouth twisted upward. "Very well. I can't force you to listen to me, but at least visit my ranch while you're here. I'd enjoy showing you the acreage. It's the least I can do for my sister."

"Thank you, Lawrence, but I'm waiting for Thomas Durant. We are to go over a prospectus for an additional investment in U.P.R.R. stock. But he has been delayed."

"Then I must stay and see to your safety."

"That's not necessary. I'm sure I'm well protected. If I have any problems I can call upon Mr. Lassiter for his help."

"And what protection can he offer you? The man was shot outside your railcar."

"He told me it was an accident. I know now to stay inside at night when the workers get a little wild."

"That's not good enough, Georgiana. I'll take you to my ranch where you'll be safe."

She raised her eyebrow at his audacity to give her orders. "Don't dictate to me, Lawrence."

His mouth took on an unpleasant twist. "You were always headstrong, Georgiana. Have it your way. If I can find decent accommodations in this filthy hellhole of a town, I'll be near if you should need me."

"Do as you wish, Lawrence."

"He always does, Georgie," Siobhan said from the doorway, where she turned sideways to enter while supporting a tea tray with her hands.

"It's nice to see you again, Miss Ryan," Lawrence muttered, sudden anger lighting his eyes. "I was merely explaining the dangers to Georgiana. We wouldn't want her to have a mishap and die here on the frontier."

"We all die, Lawrence. Many of us will go to heaven,

while others will go through eternity in Hades." She glared at him with a telling expression. "I promised John Radcliffe I'd watch over Georgiana. I mean to keep that promise. Until the Lord takes me from this world."

"What if it's sooner than you plan?" he asked in a harsh, raw voice.

"Oh, I think the Good Lord will give me enough time to fulfill Sir John's request." Siobhan placed the tea tray on the table and settled herself on the settee.

"What other requests did you handle before John died, Miss Ryan?"

Georgiana sensed a terrible tenseness in the room. What exactly did Lawrence mean by his question? Looking to Siobhan for an explanation, Georgiana found her friend's hand frozen on the teapot and her lips thinned with displeasure.

"Don't bother pouring tea for me. I'm leaving. I need something stronger," Lawrence said.

He managed to move quickly through the parlor and out the rear door of the railcar before Georgiana could ask him what he had meant.

"I've never seen Lawrence like this," Georgiana breathed in a low voice.

"Haven't you? I remember a similar outpouring of solicitous concern when the Honorable Ian Chamberlain sent his calling card."

"But Ian had been father's solicitor and a very good friend. I couldn't turn him away."

"Certainly not." Siobhan's voice rose an octave. "But Lawrence thought there was a romantic interest. And that's the same reason he dislikes Drake Lassiter."

Georgiana's breath quickened, her cheeks warmed. "There isn't any romantic involvement between me and Mr. Lassiter." She let out a long, audible breath, her words grating too harshly on her mind. Was she lying to Siobhan as well as herself? Freely she had enjoyed Drake's kisses. Was that romantic involvement?

Georgiana circled the parlor and stopped briefly to look out the window, hoping to see a certain American standing near the railcar. But he was gone and she berated herself for continuing to dwell on the too-handsome American. She had to keep her emotions in check. She had important decisions to make in the next few weeks.

She'd read about the Suez Canal and wanted to see for herself what the Frenchman de Lesseps was doing in the desert. Once she saw the railroad, and then the canal, she'd be able to make a sound decision regarding the placement of an additional investment.

A strange restlessness overcame her. As she peered out the window she had the distinct feeling that Drake was the cause of this unfamiliar chaos. Controlling her life and having the freedom to do with it as she wished had always been a part of her orderly existence.

Looking to the sky, she watched an eagle soar freely. No shackles, no ropes bound it. For a moment, she was overcome with jealousy for something the bird so cavalierly experienced. The men and women who inhabited this land were independent pioneers with a strong spirit of adventure. Drake was such a man. Knowing him had shaken the roots of her existence. Knowing him made her feel naked and helpless. Knowing him left her without a hope for that much-loved freedom she had worked so vigorously for all her life.

CHAPTER 4

Georgiana silently scolded herself for watching Drake and not the countryside as the buggy creaked and swayed along the dirt road, rutted by the hundreds of wagons that traveled back and forth to the end-of-track. She'd spent too much time lately observing the man and his movements. With a pang of guilt she sat quietly, her hands clasped in her lap. Looking down from their vantage point on a small hill overlooking the road, she marveled at the organized chaos of the construction camp.

Along the side of the newly laid track, men climbed poles like agile monkeys as they strung copper wire for the telegraph line. Dust, mixed with the hum of their labors, floated above the work crews like a great grayish-brown storm cloud.

Three diamond-stack, wood-burning locomotives pushed the work train with its various cars forward along the newly bolted and spiked rails. The crew of Irish rail-handlers threw seven-hundred-pound rails, and ties and spikes from the small cars that ran along behind the big train. The noise sounded like a bombardment, echoing through the land's gullies and hollows.

When Drake hollered for a lone horseman to join them,

Georgiana could barely hear his deep voice above the clang of iron.

Hardy Anderson doffed his hat to Georgiana. "Good day, ma'am."

"Good day, Mr. Anderson," she answered, smiling at Drake's friend.

"What's the progress, Hardy?" Drake tied the reins on the brake and stretched his cramped legs.

"Jack Casement may outdo his one-day record of six miles of rail. The track layers have nearly four miles down and the men think before the day is done they'll lay eight, maybe nine."

Satisfaction glowed on Drake's face and his smile broadened in approval. With a warm glow Georgiana gloried briefly in the shared moment. Overseeing the building of his railroad coast to coast charged Drake with the sureness and rightness of his dream. His dynamic vitality renewed her own sense and purpose.

Georgiana hadn't had the heart to tell him when he invited her to ride along that this was not the first time she'd visited an end-of-track. She'd seen similar activities on the Continent when visiting Thomas Brassey's camps. He'd built railroads the length of the Continent.

Watching Drake's joy at the lengthening ribbon of track secured her own convictions about traveling so far and personally watching the construction of the transcontinental railroad. Instantly she knew that coming to America had been one of the most important decisions of her life. The shock of that discovery overpowered her.

This was Drake's railroad—body, heart and soul. His blood must surge through his veins to the beat of the rail spikers. Amazed at the thrill it gave her, her own heartbeat accelerated.

Along the right-of-way, the crews laid rail at the rate of approximately two hundred and forty feet a minute while armed soldiers kept patrol.

"The military is along to keep everything quiet." Drake

began to explain the detail of army men. "During the war, the USMRR construction crews were unarmed and defenseless. Too many of my men lost their lives, victims of cavalry and guerrilla raids. It's been quiet for the last few months, unlike when we went through Nebraska."

Drake brought her attention to a man wearing a cossack cap and fur-trimmed coat, a bullwhip wrapped in his right hand like a snake. "That's General John S. Casement. He's in charge of the track layers. He and his brother have a contract with the railroad to handle the grading as well as the laying of track."

"How can the men work such long hours and still travel back and forth to town?" Georgiana looked out over the land, expecting to see a tented city for the men's comfort when the work was done. But everything within her range of vision was organized for labor.

Drake pulled his gloves off, dropped them on his lap and settled into a more comfortable position. "Casement designed the train with four large boarding cars to keep approximately two hundred and fifty men at the end-of-track while the other men return to town. That way he rotates the crews. The men sleep in two of the long Pennsylvania passenger coaches, eat in one and cook in the other."

He wrapped and unwrapped the reins. She'd noticed the same restless energy when he'd been confined after his accident. He was a virile man who drew his strength and vitality from the rustic environment of his work.

If she hadn't traveled with him, would he have stripped naked to the waist and joined his men, driving the spikes with the tremendous strength of his broadly muscled back and shoulders? Imagining all that power and force made Georgiana weak inside, her stomach lurching dangerously each time she even used the word "naked" in her musings.

Deep in thought, she didn't hear Hardy's good-bye. Drake drove a short distance, the noise of the work crews receding behind them. He brought the conveyance to a stop in a shady area, then he jumped to the ground and lifted their picnic basket from the buckboard.

"Something smells mighty fine." He picked up the lid and peaked inside. Before she could scold him, he pulled out a chicken leg and took a big bite of the crispy crust. "Mmm-mmm." He licked his fingers and stared wordlessly across at her.

How can the simple act of nibbling a piece of chicken affect me so? she thought as he stood there, boldly provocative. She swallowed with difficulty and found her voice. "Hungry?"

"Yeah. You could say that."

A devilish look came into his eyes. Drake's lips parted and his tongue slicked across them.

Nature responded around them, merging with the boom of men forging a road through a wilderness. Active horned larks, searching for food, investigated a dead branch of a cottonwood. A dragonfly buzzed a slow-moving stream. Could Drake hear the tumultuous beating of her heart? Yes, he must, for a satisfied light filled his eyes.

"Are you ready?" he asked.

Blood pounded in her brain, leapt from her heart and made her hands tremble as she clasped them tightly in her lap. A deep breath helped to calm her raging emotions before she said, "Ready?"

"To eat." He held his hand out for her.

Needing to calm herself, Georgiana closed her eyes for a moment before accepting his hand.

"You won't find scenery like this anyplace in the world. This area of the Wyoming Territory is protected by mountain ranges on the western slope of the Continental Divide. This winter has been relatively mild and spring is already putting in its appearance. Though we may still be hit with a good storm."

It seemed he wanted to coax her into a better mood when he picked up the picnic basket and gathered a blanket from the buckboard. "Take a good look."

Taking her to a grassy area, Drake set the basket down.

Newly hatched butterflies weaved from patch to patch of wildflowers. Staring at the landscape, she recognized only a few of the wildflowers that blanketed the valley. Sand lilies and bluebells mingled with the green grass creating a colorful sampler. Was there an end to the splendor of this wide-open country?

She gave the area another look before gazing up at his face. His smile melted her heart.

Doffing his dove-gray Stetson, he wiped his sweaty forehead with his arm and peered off into the distance. Fine white lines fanned out around his eyes for he squinted without benefit of the shade from his wide brim.

His hair dropped unevenly across his forehead. Instead of following his finger to some distant site, she kept her eyes on the side of his face. His profile spoke of power and ageless strength. The set of his chin suggested a stubborn streak to which she'd attest. Shot only five days ago, Drake had refused to stay in bed.

"So what do you think of our countryside?" he asked.

"It leaves me quite breathless." *Both the man and the land,* she finished to herself. Her mind still whirled from thoughts of him in the buff and from the kisses they'd shared in the last few days. Breathing normally in his presence had become a burden and utterly hopeless.

"How would you know? You haven't really looked at the view," he teased as he pivoted his head in her direction.

His dark eyes probed hers sharply as if he knew the reason for her disinterest in the scenery. She took a quick sharp breath. He mumbled, "Damn," under his breath before he moved his free hand recklessly to her neck, sending sparks along her spine. His lips brushed hers then turned more persuasive, tugging at her self-control. His powerful kisses forced the firm ground to vanish under her feet as she struggled for coherency while he created a wispy cloud of mystery. Why can't I resist him and be decisive like I am in my business dealings? she thought.

Drake's lips parted in a soul-reaching message, his tongue dipping into the deep recesses of her mouth. Warm and inviting, his breath caused her emotions to whirl. She grasped the front of his leather vest, her knuckles white, waiting for cool sanity to flood back through her body. Her hands opened, palms flat against his hard, muscled chest.

"Drake . . . stop." She murmured breathlessly.

"Honey, I'll never stop kissing you if you say my name like that." His lips rested a breath away from hers, his one hand wrapped in the curls gathered at her neck while he still held his hat with the other.

"I . . . thought you wanted to eat?"

"Yeah." He blinked once, then again, as if he had to remember something important while he cleared his vision. "We'll get back to this later," he mumbled, his last kiss a warm caress—a reminder and an invitation.

Drake lifted the top of the picnic basket and surveyed the contents leisurely. "Your porter has packed a picnic fit for a princess," he exclaimed, leaning comfortably back on one hand while lounging on the blanket.

"Washington's work is impeccable. He's packed the most elegant china for our lunch." She held the other side of the lid.

He pulled out two pieces of chicken, uncovering a section of fragile porcelain in the bottom of the basket. His mind was playing tricks on him. It had to be. They were a thousand miles removed from civilization and polite society, yet the pattern of birds and landscape on the gold-enriched Sèvres was the very same pattern used the evening of his pre-wedding party at the Van Dyke's.

His gut twisted. Eyes clouding, his mind reeled under the onslaught of painful memories. Memories better left alone . . . of the night before he left New York eight years ago.

Martha and Peter Van Dyke, members of the Knicker-bockers, New York's social leaders, had attempted to sway their daughter from marrying "that Lassiter boy, one of those nouveaux riches." They wanted her to marry an upstanding young banker or lawyer, not an engineer, but Amelia Van Dyke had accepted his proposal over her parents' objections that he did not fit into their way of life. That night, to stop their daughter's marriage, they revealed a devastating secret. Drake was a bastard.

Drake's mother had tried to explain, but his bitterness ate deep inside his soul. He refused to listen to the tale of his conception. He walked out, never learning the name of his natural father.

Could his mother have ever loved him? She'd betrayed him every moment of his life by keeping the truth from him that Clinton Lassiter wasn't his father. In his mind, he kept hearing the sound as he'd yanked the tablecloth from the Van Dyke's table. The shattering china had been a symbol of his shattered dreams.

"Drake." Georgiana's sweet voice broke into his unpleasant thoughts through the cobwebs of his nightmare. "Is there something wrong?"

Wrong? Maybe just my whole life. "No," he said with quiet emphasis. The memory of that meal at the Van Dykes' was an intrusion upon his picnic with Georgiana. Hesitantly he accepted a plate with biscuits, slices of apples, and chicken.

The cut-glass crystal and fine linen napkins were additional reminders of Drake's past. He thought he'd left that life behind, yet here on a patch of green in the southwest corner of the Wyoming Territory he was partaking of a fancy picnic lunch with a beautiful society woman.

They ate silently, Georgiana evidently sensing his turmoil.

Minutes later she gathered the remnants of their lunch, wrapped everything but the apple cores in a napkin and stuck it in a corner of the basket.

"You forgot to put this in the basket," he scolded, pointing to the half-eaten fruit.

"No I haven't."

She jumped to her feet, smoothed her skirt, bent over, picked up the fruit and walked toward a stand of cottonwoods where the buckboard stood. Before Drake could admonish her about not getting too close to the two fillies, she offered each horse a snack.

Drake watched in astonishment as his unpredictable princess talked to the horses with tenderness as they devoured the treats she offered them. Whether she was serving a picnic lunch with china and crystal or feeding animals out of her hand, she inexplicably stripped him of the armor he had learned to wear whenever he was with a woman with social standing.

Replete, Drake stretched his legs the length of the blanket, rested one elbow on the grass and savored the moment. Her scent lingered softly, drifting on the breeze. He folded his hands under his head and closed his eyes.

He hadn't thought of New York so intensely in a long time. Usually he worked long hours. It was easier that way. But Georgiana had changed all that. Here he was basking in the noonday sun, enjoying a picnic with a beautiful woman, a woman who had the capability to shake his world. He had to fight the arousal that ambushed him every time he and the princess were together.

"Are you dreaming?" she called to him from the distance.

"Sort of," he replied.

He opened his eyes and stared at her as her skirts shifted with a light gust of air. Looking for more food, the pinto muzzled the palm of her hand, licking the lingering apple nectar.

She gently rubbed one horse's forehead as the other nudged her skirt. Hot desire rushed through him. He had to force himself to take the next breath. He'd love to nuzzle a few of her very intimate places.

What exactly was Georgiana Radcliffe, a stunning woman, doing in the middle of nowhere enjoying a picnic with a rough railroad worker? He was afraid to ask.

As she strolled through the early spring grass with her head thrown back as she looked at the sky, she twirled, her arms held out in a wide circle.

When she stopped she turned and stared over at him. "Can I help, Drake?"

Go to bed with me for a week. Maybe then I can strip you from my thoughts, tear you out of my soul, burn you out of my gut. He'd wanted her from the very first moment she'd stepped into his life in that bathhouse on the prairie. But remembering the Van Dykes and their disdain only fueled his resolve not to get involved any further with a socially prominent woman.

"I'll be all right." He shrugged off her request. When he sat up, he dropped his gaze to the grass under her feet. To his surprise he saw a pair of women's shoes a few feet away. He grinned, chuckled. The princess had taken her shoes off. How unusual for a lady!

He lifted his head and watched as her cheeks tinted a rosy red. Her blue eyes sparkled with interest and intelligence before she regarded him with a speculative glance. "A picnic isn't complete without walking in the grass without shoes and stockings," she thoughtfully explained. The fringe of her lashes cast shadows on her cheeks when he didn't speak. Did she expect him to chastise her behavior?

He exchanged a smile with her, then shook his head when he stood and grabbed the picnic basket. As he drew closer to one of the cottonwood trees he easily spotted a nest on the leafless branches. It was composed of sticks and twigs and lined with grasses, rushes and similar material. A blue heron's nest. Were there any eggs? he wondered. Closing in on the area, a mother bird flew to the nest, settling on two eggs.

The princess watched quietly, her eyes growing wide at the beauty of nature. Yes, he'd been correct about the shaded color but he'd forgotten the luster, the fire buried deep in her eyes.

He told her to put her shoes back on and strolled to the buckboard, giving her privacy to complete that task.

"What am I going to do with you, Princess?" he mumbled. He'd thought he had discovered that answer minutes ago but that was before he had found a princess with naked toes.

Retracing their journey from Bear River City, Drake pulled off the road so they could stretch their legs after the long buckboard ride. He stopped at a dry patch of ground, hunkered down and traced his finger in the dirt.

"No one knows exactly where the two roads of track will join. The experts says somewhere in Utah. So, we're laying as much rail as we can until Congress finally decides the official meeting place. Look here. Maybe this will explain it." Drake picked up an arm-length branch and scratched in the dirt. "Imagine this is Promontory Range."

Inclined toward creating her own images in her samplers, Georgiana cast a critical eye at his dry painting. Pressing her hand against his left shoulder, she leaned close and inevitably noticed the scents that clung to his body. Leather, horses, the fresh frontier wind and a uniquely male aroma meshed into a mixture no man's cologne in polite society could evoke—totally devastating to her senses.

As Drake's lines grew in length, twisting around a pile of large rocks that he'd gathered to display the height and breadth of the Promontory Range as it jutted into the Great Salt Lake, Georgiana pressed closer to see the area near the tips of his boots. When she touched the crook in his elbow, he flexed his arm, shifted his body and lifted his head.

"Don't stop now," she said, her palm on his muscles in a silent plea to continue.

Looking at her, his eyes darkened. For a heartbeat, his breath caught in his throat and then whistled out between clenched teeth. "Are you sure you want me to continue?"

His question was rhetorical. More than the desirous gaze, the tone of his voice, deep and provocative, startled her. He had twisted her words and his meaning was too clear. New sensations flooded her. She blinked and lowered her eyelashes, her chin pointing down.

"You're the sweetest thing I've ever seen." Drake swiveled around on his boot heels and tilted her head up with the edge of his index finger. "You flush like a newborn baby." His fingertip slid down her throat to the collar of her blue riding outfit. "Are you the same shade of pink all over, sweetheart?" Never taking his eyes from hers, he flicked the top button open. When he opened the next button, her knees failed to hold her. She slumped against his strength, tilted her chin, and scanned his face as she sought a clue to the complex man holding her.

He chuckled. "Don't faint now. I haven't found those pampered places yet."

"You must stop kissing me," Georgiana declared, trying to gain control of the situation.

"Why?" Drake peered at her through hooded eyes while he stroked the indentation above her collarbone.

"Because it's not right." She pursed her lips in a prim pose.

"Honey, you're wrong. This is so right."

He tightened his arms around her and showed her exactly what he meant by reclaiming her lips. His tongue traced the soft fullness of her mouth, then became more demanding. This must stop, she scolded herself as she succumbed to kisses that left her weak and confused.

I will not allow him to control me. She wanted to be as free as the eagles that flew across the prairie sky. She wanted to keep her life as uncomplicated as possible. This attachment to Drake must *stop*!

She pushed against him, allowing a few inches to divide them. "Drake. I can't think when you kiss me. You make me feel—"

"Like you've been punched in the gut and you can't take another breath."

She jerked her head to look directly into his eyes. "How did you know?"

"Because that's how I feel, honey. That and other things." He studied her face unhurriedly, feature by feature. She felt warmed by that enigmatic gaze, dark and powerful one moment, bright and playful the next. "But if I tell you everything I'm thinking," he added, "I'd scare you."

Scare me? she thought. No, Drake it's not you who scares me. I frighten myself because I am fascinated by you. You've inveigled yourself into my every thought, my every action. Your influence is everywhere. For God's sake, you've even invaded my cross-stitching.

"I think we should talk about something else." She pushed gently at his chest. "Why don't you explain to me why the Union Pacific and the Central Pacific are laying parallel roadbeds. That should keep your mind busy on other things besides frightening me."

A frown etched into his rugged features and deepened into wry laughter. "Honey, if I'm not real careful you'll make me dance a tune I never thought I'd recognize again."

"And what would that be?"

"Love and sunshine."

"Have you forgotten how to love?"

Drake's expression darkened. "There isn't a woman alive who could show me."

"Surely you don't believe in this big country . . ." She panned the horizon and spread her arms wide to encompass the largeness of the area. ". . . there isn't a woman who could love you? Everyone has at least one redeeming trait."

"Thanks for the lefthanded compliment." His eyes lightened. He lifted his hand, smoothed a few wind-tossed tendrils from her mouth, and brushed his fingertips along her jaw.

"You're welcome." She whisked her hand across her flushed cheeks waylaying his continued attention. "Now tell me how you can be so sure you're unlovable?"

"Oh, believe me, I've tested that theory. And I've lived to

tell the story." Drake shifted positions and returned to his picture in the dirt.

But you haven't forgotten the hurt. Have you, Drake? she reflected while she watched him continue his etchings. What kind of women could cut you with such expertise, and so deeply? How do you live with that wound day in and day out? Georgiana guessed that Drake spent very little time expressing his inner emotions. If she wanted to know more about this man she would need to nurture the trust he had placed in her hands.

Later on the trail, Georgiana asked Drake to stop the buggy near a patch of wildflowers, their spikes of orange blooms bright against a background of gray vegetation. A quartzite boulder sat in the middle of the field. It rose high above them and cast a shadow when Georgiana strolled around its base.

"Do you suppose it fell from the sky?" She glanced at him over her shoulder as he followed her and she started to climb up the side, her blue eyes lit with mischief.

Her boot slipped once and his heart skipped a beat. "Be careful. Don't fall off." Drake took her hand, helping her balance until she found a large indentation and sat down.

"Come up. Join me. It's warmer here than on the ground." When she lay back against the boulder, threw her hands out and offered herself to the sun, he could only stare, wishing she would offer herself to him as innocently. "I can feel the heat from the rock radiating through my blouse." Her breasts pushed against the white cotton material, taunting him with their fullness.

If his temperature rose any higher he'd have heatstroke. Drake tipped his Stetson back off his forehead. He'd begun to believe every pair of pants he owned had shrunk. Either that or the princess had the power to make him too big for his britches. "I'll stay here." On good, solid ground he finished silently.

He turned his head a fraction of an inch. That was enough

for him to remember why they were out in the open on the windswept prairie and why he had driven her here. The railroad.

Pulling his hat down over his eyes, he pointed to the horizon. "Off there, ninety miles away, is Promontory."

Georgiana followed his gaze. She saw what was and what would be. Rails in the distance, ribbons of gleaming iron that ran over bits of wood with the Herculean strength to join a nation from coast to coast. The thought of how much her father loved this land brought a lump to her throat. "My father planned to return to America and see the joining of rails. He kept a map and made notations after receiving correspondence from Thomas Durant on the railroad's progress."

Drake studied her thoughtfully. "Then do you want to explain to me why you haven't invested the additional capital in the railroad? Bankers and lawyers could have taken care of the transaction for you. Could there be another reason for your trip to the frontier?"

CHAPTER 5

Why? Georgiana had asked herself that very same question many times during the journey from England. Siobhan had questioned her also. It wasn't until a few hours ago, when she had watched Drake's expression as he talked with her about the railroad, that she finally had an answer. She'd come because of an attraction for Drake but she soon learned that he loved hard iron more than he could ever love a woman. And if she didn't watch herself he'd use the attraction between them to control her and her fortune.

"Proving I can make sound financial decisions is very important to me. My father taught me well and left my inheritance in my hands to do with as I will."

"I'm aware of that. But can't you put your stubborn streak aside for a moment and listen to your senses? Look through your eyes, listen with your heart, smell the land around you?"

She did just that. Her gaze wandered over the landscape, capturing the vastness of the land. She tasted the early spring air on her lips, mingled with Drake's kisses. Quietly she listened to the sounds of rustling wind as it dipped low to the soil and jutted high to the clouds, rustling everything in its path. "Is your job truly so important to you?" she asked.

He slid onto the ground below where she sat perched on the boulder. "During the War I was an engineer with the United States Military Railroad. We built roads of destruction for four years in and out of the South. I'm tired of tearing up track. I want to build a railroad that will last for generations." He slapped his hat against his thigh.

Interesting, she mused. A man with a dream and the determination to see its completion.

She shifted her gaze downward. The few silver streaks in his dark hair softened his devilish appearance, making him seem human and much more vulnerable. "You have the sort of determination that made Thomas Brassey successful in building railroads. Have you heard of him?"

He looked up at her. "What engineer hasn't? He's the self-made multimillionaire who built railroads all over the world. How do you know so much about Brassey?"

"He was my father's childhood friend. Later, they built railroads together on the Continent. He visited our home in Yorkshire many times. On one occasion Father allowed me to join them in the library while they discussed the supply railway Mr. Brassey built to relieve the British soldiers who were dying from cholera and starvation at Sebastopol during the Crimean War."

"The generals swore he couldn't do it. But his engineers completed the job and Brassey was a hero," Drake added.

"He always seems to build roads that no one else would even imagine could exist. One of his first projects collapsed but he rebuilt it because he said he had contracted to construct and maintain the road. He said nothing would prevent him from being as good as his word."

Drake replaced his hat, shading his eyes from the bright light. "I've seen sketches of his work. I admire the arches he uses in his designs."

She thought hard about her next words. Drake loved the railroad. To her, it was an investment, one of many her father had bequeathed to her. But more than the money, there were lives to consider. Was he aware of the safety hazards she had seen in her trip West? "Your railroad designers could take a lesson from Mr. Brassey. I've been across your new trestles, and I very much question their safety. With the guylines improperly placed, there is a lack of stability. That's one of the reasons I am thinking of investing in a safer venture."

She shifted, uncomfortable with the discussion. She knew Drake resented her words; it was inevitable. Men never allowed her to expound any of her ideas.

Drake's expression was one of disbelief. "You can sure try a man's patience, Princess." He shifted his gaze to her face, a stern expression darkening his features. "What the hell do you know about engineering? Our procedure is entirely proper for a railroad building into a new territory." He clamped his mouth shut as he pulled his hat down on his forehead.

Evidently no other person, especially a woman, had ever questioned his professional competence. She offered a silent prayer of thanks to her father for educating her beyond the required literature, music, language and flower arrangement.

"Drake, during a long retreat to my father's estates, Mr. Brassey infused me with his love of railroads. He taught me how to read topography maps and encouraged my father to allow me to accompany them on a survey for the Vienna to Trieste line. When we returned to Yorkshire I helped him compile the costs of construction, maintenance and operation. So, I understand about your profession. Even with the problems on your railroad, this venture is a great achievement for your country. I think you're a good engineer with the determination to see this project completed."

He jumped to his feet, jamming his Stetson on his head. "Thanks," he said, his voice rife with mockery. "But how in the hell did you come to that conclusion?"

"The morning after you were shot, Hardy told me about

working with you during the War. He said you swore that after the conflict you would build railroads across the nation. Here you are in the middle of the frontier. That's admirable."

"Then you should know that the railroad is my life. Don't go interfering with that dream." He grabbed her, lifted her down from the boulder and for one brief moment, when their faces were so close, his eyes darkened with a curious emotion. She thought he might kiss her again.

His hands dropped away. He went to go sit on the buckboard, his face as hard as the stone boulder she'd lain against.

She had wanted that kiss. She hesitated, torn by conflicting emotions. *He is without a doubt the most irritating man I know, and easily the most stubborn.* She brushed her skirt and repositioned her hat before she joined him.

Sitting on the seat inches away from him, she was relieved when he kept his eyes on the road, snapped the reins and set the horses on their way. She sat straighter on the seat, distancing herself from the man and his magnetic dominance over her thoughts.

"How was your picnic?" Siobhan settled on the red velvet side chair, picked up her cup of tea and looked over its rim.

"It was very enjoyable." Georgiana took her shoes off. Wiggling her toes, she lifted her legs and tucked her feet under her dress on the lounge.

"I see you had the opportunity to run in the grass with your shoes off."

"How—"

"The green stains on the bottom of your feet."

The woman knows me so well, I can't lie to her, Georgiana thought. "Yes, I did walk in the grass."

"And what did your Mr. Lassiter think of an English lady taking her shoes off in front of a stranger?"

"He's not *my* Mr. Lassiter! And he's surely not a stranger."

"Well, he's not your husband or your intended. What were you thinking?"

That I was safe with Drake. That he allowed me the freedom to do as I please. Searching for a plausible explanation that Siobhan would understand, she said, "He understands how it feels to be free."

"And how free have you allowed the American to be with you?"

Georgiana swallowed hard, trying to manage an answer. With Siobhan's intuitive nature it was near impossible to keep anything from her. And considering she was the closest friend she had, why would she want to? Confiding in Siobhan might help ease the tension of the conflicting emotions she was experiencing.

"He's kissed me. Several times."

The expected reprimand never came. Instead Siobhan set her cup down and sat back in her chair, a grin of amusement touching her mouth. "I won't sit in judgment, if that's what you're expecting. But since I'm older and I have a bit more knowledge of the ways of men, I'll give you a little advice. They'll all want you for your fortune and beauty. The man who loves you will acknowledge you have a brain."

"No man I've met has been able to overlook my fortune," Georgiana sighed. "And precious few even care if I possess a brain." *However, unlike other men, Drake conversed with me about business.*

"I know. But wait for the man strong enough to allow you freedom to make up your own mind." Exchanging a smile with Georgiana, Siobhan asked, "Are you considering an extended stay in this country?"

"I had not planned on leaving until Thomas Durant arrives. I would think you wouldn't be anxious to begin another trip."

Siobhan rolled her eyes and shook her head. "I have a feeling my condition will improve on the trip to the Suez." As an afterthought, she added, "But I'm not so sure yours will."

Contemplating her friend's question and remark set Georgiana's mind into a whirlwind. A few days ago, she had thought a short visit to the United States would accomplish her goal of looking at the progress of the rails West. Then from there she would travel to the Suez project.

But now there was Drake.

Drawn to the enigmatic American, she had learned that not all frontiersmen were a violent breed. Yet though she felt safe when they were together, that very fact scared her. Her independence was too important to give up because of certain feelings she experienced when she was held securely in Drake Lassiter's strong arms.

She thought about Siobhan's observations about love. Lawrence shunned her intelligence. He'd proven more than once how important her money was to him. But Drake, now that was a different matter. They'd actually had a business conversation, partaking equally. He'd shown a growing respect for her knowledge of railroads, once he'd listened to her talk of Brassey and her father. He continued to confuse her. Astound her. Bedevil her.

What was she to do with him?

"Get enough gear together for a seven-day trip." Drake sat behind the desk in his tent while Hardy paced back and forth, glancing over in his direction.

"A week? What in tarnation are we going to do on the road for that length of time?"

"We're going to check out the temporary bridge at Devil's Gate. The report"—Drake held it in the air for emphasis—"is not good. The river is swollen with melting snow and Eicholtz is having trouble with the vertical support pilings."

"Leonard should learn how to build rails on flat ground before he builds bridges."

"It's not his fault the canyon walls constrict the river and there's a strain on the bents."

"You're the boss, Captain. I'm ready to ride now." Hardy

grabbed his hat from the wall peg, dropped it on his sandy blond head of hair and moved to the door, his spurs ringing in the small room.

"Take your time, Hardy. I have some unfinished business. We'll leave tomorrow at first light."

Drake followed Hardy to the entry, watching him mount and ride off toward the supply yard. When he raised his arm to close the door, he could feel the lingering effects from his gunshot wound. It itched like hell.

That made two wounds he'd like scratched. If he reopened his shoulder, he'd be on the sidelines for another week. If he reopened his heart to a woman, he'd suffer for a lifetime.

Instead he had to settle for a gentle massage on his shoulder and a cold plunge in the river every night he walked past the princess's railcar.

He returned to his desk to continue his notes on the rockcliff gorge. The construction crews were strung out as far as the dangerously sharp curves at the edge of the turbulent river in Weber Canyon. A few minutes later the telegraph key on his desk started clicking. Holding his pen, Drake touched the metal piece and tapped the proper code for the sender to continue the communication. Drake wrote swiftly, then sent back his acknowledgment and ended his transmission. The message was brief.

Thomas Durant, Vice-President of the Union Pacific, would arrive in Bear River City in one week. Until that time Drake was to entertain Miss Georgiana Radcliffe, a visitor from England. At the end of the telegram, Durant cautioned Drake to act in a gentlemanly manner and to look after Georgiana's welfare.

"I'm always a gentleman, Thomas," Drake mused, his lips twisted wryly. He crumpled the paper into a ball. In one swift toss it landed in the open door of the potbellied stove, kindling for this evening's fire. "It's the women who need to be reminded that they should act like ladies."

His thoughts settled on one particular female. One who

melted and shivered warmly under the assault of his kisses. One who allowed his tongue to play tag in the moist recesses of her sweet mouth. One who trembled as he stroked her perfect skin while soft sounds purred at the back of her throat.

She was unlike any other woman he'd ever met. He'd discovered a princess who walked barefoot through the green grass of Wyoming. That was the difference. Shifting his back against the hard chair, Drake rested his elbows on the desk and bridged his fingers across his upper lip.

So now what, Lassiter? The lady is not for you, he admonished. You knew that two and a half years ago when you first touched her silky hair. But she came back to America and now you can't stay away. Can you?

If only he could halt the kaleidoscope rushing through his mind. The creamy skin of her neck. Her silky blonde hair. Her brilliant blue eyes. Her naked toes. He pictured those cute toes dug in against his buttocks, her thighs spread wide as he rode her, driving deeper, taking her to a fantastic world of desire and passion, pleasuring her in ways she'd never have thought possible. That's what taunted him by day and haunted him by night. He had to have her.

Once they came together, he'd finally stop picturing her face on every woman he met. Once he took her to bed he'd forget the sweet scent of wildflowers that clung to the hem of her skirt. When he finally kissed her too many times to count, he'd forget the heavenly taste of springtime that clung to her lips.

Simple to come by, sex followed the campsites, found in every town along the right-of-way. But logic reminded him passion and love weren't as simple. Society placed restrictions on such activities. And a lady would not flaunt the restraints for any man, especially a man without knowledge of his bloodline.

All the excuses seemed inconsequential. After all, he was a man; she was a woman. Her responses to his kisses were anything but innocent. Her reactions to his caresses only sparked his burning need to discover the wanton who lived in his dreams. He wanted his princess and she clearly wanted him.

Knowing he'd go mad if he stayed in his office thinking about her sweet attributes, he decided to take a short ride to one of the work camps. Now would be an opportune time to ride out, work side by side with the men and test his shoulder's strength.

Drake left his desk and in three strides reached the door. He pulled his hat from the peg on the wall. Molding the crown and brim with his fingers, he slipped the hat on and stomped out of the office. Hard work was good for what ailed him. Sweaty, back breaking labor would overpower his desire and take care of his problem.

"That's a dollar for the Red Jacket, gent." The burly bartender stuck his hand out, palm up to collect his money for the drink. Lawrence pulled out a five-dollar gold piece, placed it on the scarred wooden bar and leaned closer. The noise from the full band playing on the raised platform was deafening.

"Before I pay for the drink, I want some information." Lawrence slammed his palm over the coin.

"I ain't no bookstore. They just opened one three buildings down." The bartender thumbed to his right side and jerked his head in the same direction.

Lawrence held his temper. "Barbaric imbeciles," he said under his breath. "I can't find the people I'm looking for in a bookstore."

"Make up your mind! Do you want information or am I running a lost and found?"

"Both. For helping me, the coin is yours." Lawrence lifted his hand so the other man could have a good view of what he offered.

The man looked down at the coin. "Not enough."

"Listen, you bloody fool, that gold piece is more than a railroad worker earns in a day."

Showing a glistening gold tooth in the front of his mouth, the saloon keeper chuckled. "Ain't that the truth. Excepting if you ain't noticed gent, I ain't building the railroad. Yancy sees to its waterin'." He grabbed Lawrence's hand, plucked the five-dollar gold piece off the bar, lifted it to his mouth and bit down on the coin with his side teeth. "Just testing."

"Well?"

"Another one of them shiny coins and you'll think I'm the local librarian."

Lawrence pulled another gold piece out and handed it over. Then in a low, rough voice he said, "I need a couple of men to do a job for me with no questions asked." It might be noisy, but it wouldn't do for anyone standing nearby to hear his conversation with the bartender.

"I think I can find you the right men." Unconcerned with Lawrence's need for information, Yancy turned around. He picked up a few shot glasses and wiped them dry with the towel that hung from his waist. He restacked them next to a variety of cigars, cut-glass goblets and pitchers lined up under the gilt-edged mirror behind the bar. Then he faced Lawrence again. "What exactly do you want done? I know two men who ain't too particular about the kind of job they do. If you get my meaning. They're pulling their pay today and leaving town on the next train East. A little extra cash would help until they find work."

Perfect! A few rough railroad workers would know the best way to eliminate Drake Lassiter. Then they would be on their way to new jobs, leaving a dead man and no clues.

He enjoyed the idea of getting the better of the arrogant American. After finding a flushed Georgiana in Lassiter's arms, Lawrence decided the man had gotten in his way once too often. He couldn't allow Georgiana to become involved with another man. He had plans of his own for her and her fortune.

He checked out the saloon's clientele. The mob—railroad men, soldiers, merchants and mule-whackers—played poker, dice, keno and faro. Sprinkled among the men was a small quota of saloon women.

Lawrence rounded on the bartender. "I need men who can keep their mouths shut. They'll need to leave town as soon as the job is completed."

Yancy scratched his dark winged eyebrows and looked around his establishment before leaning over the bar, nearer to Lawrence. "Either of the men I mentioned will be the spawn of the devil himself if you give him enough money."

"Perfect!" Lawrence tempered his enthusiasm. He told Yancy to have the men contact him at a small boardinghouse on the other side of town. After he dropped another gold piece on the bar, he strode out smiling, confident he would see an end to the interfering American within the next few days.

Drake watched the monumental windmill spin slowly in the distance, bringing its neverending supply of water to the dry surface of the Wyoming plains. The view toward the east was one of vast grassland interrupted by a ribbon of steel rails, canvas shanties, large tents and hundreds of people going about the business of supplying the line. To the west, the best organized, best equipped and best disciplined track force of one thousand men hammered away at the earth, laying the foundation for the transcontinental railroad.

For the last four years he'd often gone without food, sleep or dry clothes. He'd ridden when he'd been bone weary, the numbness so unbearable that it sent him to his knees once he dismounted. All because he was resolved to allow nothing to interfere with the attainment of his goal to join the nation with rails from coast to coast.

Durant's private car, temporary home to the princess and Siobhan Ryan, sat on the lone siding on the outskirts of town.

"Mr. Lassiter. I wasn't aware that you were waiting."

It wasn't only the underlying sensuality of her voice that Drake found so captivating but also the enticing rustling of her multiple petticoats. Listening to the sounds associated with females was once again a new experience for him and his heartbeat pounded as loud as a mountain waterfall. Not for the first time since they'd met, he discovered an invisible web growing between them. He couldn't wrench himself away from his ridiculous preoccupation with the princess.

He turned slowly, faced her and tipped his hat in greeting. "Morning. I couldn't help admiring the view."

She closed the door and stepped back under the overhang away from the direct rays of the sun. Eyes wide and clear, chin high, spine straight and touching the hard wood door, she held court. "You must see such scenery every day."

"Sure. But the landscape changes constantly. And each time you admire it you're in awe of the beauty all over again."

Like now, he thought. He tipped the brim of his hat back on his forehead, whistled under his breath and impudently stared at the most interesting scenery he'd seen all day. A rush of pink staining her cheeks, she was lovely in her gold-colored foulard dress, trimmed with black velvet and buttons. He couldn't resist a lingering look at the linen sailor collar framing the creamy naked skin above the low-necked dress. A knot rose in his throat. He shifted his gaze downward to the hem of her skirt and laughed out loud.

"Now, that's a damned interesting view. You don't like shoes very much, do you?"

She drew her breath in, closed her eyes and adjusted the skirt to cover her toes. "I enjoy the freedom of going barefoot." Her chin lifted another notch when she focused her deep blue gaze on him. "I wasn't expecting visitors."

"This isn't exactly a social call. So don't worry about your toes showing." He pushed the material back out of the way and stared down at the hem. "Cute."

Georgiana slapped his hand away and smoothed down her skirts. "Really! You're the most exasperating man I have ever met."

His smile turned to a chuckle. "Probably the most interesting one you'll ever know."

Georgiana had to agree but wouldn't tell him that. His strong hands behind his back, he grasped the waist-high rail. Boots, trousers, cambric shirt, a rawhide vest, all well worn and clean, covered a well-formed body. He was by far the most stimulating man she'd ever had the misfortune to meet. Unlike the dandified Englishmen of home, this man exuded compelling power. Yet she experienced no fear at his continued nearness.

"How much longer before the rails are joined?" she asked, crossing the platform to join him. As she stood next to him, she kept her eyes straight ahead and focused on the clouds on the horizon. If she stared at him she'd make a fool of herself, for each time they were together her emotions whirled and skidded. Each time she looked at the handsome American, her flesh prickled with shivers of delight. Each time her mind told her to resist, her body refused.

"Congress hasn't made the decision on the site yet. But I expect it will happen sometime in early May. The crews have closed in on each other and in some places they are running parallel."

Georgiana turned her head and met Drake's gaze. If she wasn't careful she knew he would break down her barriers effortlessly. After her father's death, Ian Chamberlain, his solicitor, had tried to woo her. Her stepmother, Edythe, welcomed Ian's attentions, telling Georgiana that the marriage would be a good match. Ian was a dear friend, but certainly not a possible suitor. He didn't love the countryside as she did. Her father had kept a fine stable and she'd learned to ride when she was eight. A groom or her father accompanied her on her daily excursions across the rolling hills of her home. Her mother on occasion would join them until she was taken ill and confined to an invalid's chair. After that tragic occurrence, Georgiana spent a great deal of time caring for her mother and less time in a saddle. Her mother had tried to coax her out for rides but Georgiana refused. Her mother's care was more important than her need to ride.

But during one of Ian's visits, Caroline Radcliffe had asked him to take Georgiana riding. He declined. Then Georgiana learned why a man of the town was rarely in attendance at his estate near her home in Yorkshire. He didn't ride.

She'd seen Drake ride through Bear River City. He sat a horse as if born to it with skill and an easy hand. She'd watched him smooth his fingers across the horse's forehead, bend down low and whisper in the animal's ear. The horse's reaction, its chest blowing in and out, was immediate and very much like her own when Drake touched her. Right now her heart was thumping erratically.

"I always get side-tracked around you," Drake broke into her improper thoughts. "Thomas Durant wired me about his delay. He instructed me to see to your comfort. Now, I'd like to personally make you comfortable, but I'm going off on a field trip for a few days. I'll have a guard posted outside your car. I'm not taking any chances with your safety." He frowned. "Make my life easier. Go back to England. Extend your investment in the railroad stock. After we join the rails you'll make a fortune from the freight and passenger train revenue."

Drake waited for the princess to lift her chin, stare him directly in the eye and tell him to go to blazes. But when their gazes met, her eyes were shadowed with pain. Shivering, she rubbed her palms along the length of her arms. Moving away, she opened the door to the railcar, angled her head and looked back at him, her eyes wide, her voice a whisper.

"This railroad. That's all you care about. There has to be something else you can believe in, Drake."

She left him with those words hanging over him while he walked back to his office. Yes, he'd once believed in the sweetness of a woman's love. But then Amelia Van Dyke had looked at him with dark eyes of disdain and called him "Bastard!"

He'd lived for eight years with that accusation hanging over him like the Sword of Damocles. What would the princess think of his kisses, once she learned that he was a bastard? Would she flinch as Amelia had on that cold November night so many years ago? Being a blue blood, Miss Radcliffe would casually flick him out of her life like a piece of dirt on the hem of her dress.

But maybe he was wrong. Since her arrival, he'd discovered a warm, intelligent woman with rich kisses powerful enough to almost drop him to his knees.

Did he really want her to leave before they had the opportunity to explore the growing passion that seethed between them? That question followed him the next morning when he rode out with Hardy.

The bridge at Devil's Gate rose from the Weber River. Swollen by an early spring thawing, the turbulent water put a serious strain on the vertical support pilings. Drake remembered the conversation he'd had with the princess about the safety of the railroad bridges. Damn! The woman was right. If he hadn't seen for himself how badly the lines were run for Devil's Gate, he'd still be angry at the woman for her audacity at telling him how to run his railroad.

After walking across the trestle and observing the river's flow for thirty minutes, Drake conferred with the bridge engineer, Leonard Eicholtz, and suggested extra timbers be bolted in place and guylines strung to each bank. Eicholtz agreed and gave the order for the additional work to be done at first light.

Drake and Hardy slipped inside a tent to catch some sleep before heading back to Bear River City the next morning.

"If only all my problems could be handled as easily," Drake muttered. He took his holster and gun and settled them on the floor under his cot.

"Aside from itchin' after a beautiful woman, what other

problems have you got?" Hardy moved around the small tent and placed his revolver in the same manner as Drake.

Drake stripped down to his trousers, folded his clothes and neatly stacked them on top of his gun. He pulled back the wool blanket and sprawled on his back, cradling his head in his palms. Hardy stood, towering over him. "You looking for an answer?" Drake asked.

"You bet!" Hardy smirked and chuckled, his hazel eyes sparkling as he waited.

"You saved my life once. And you think that gives you the right to know all there is to know about me," Drake said indulgently and turned over on his side. "You've been riding on that for seven years. Let it be, Hardy."

"Hell! There ain't no entertainment this far from town. I need somethin' to take my mind off how bored I am."

Drake snorted, rubbing his hand over his face as he lay back on the cot. "What do you want to hear about first? The Central Pacific is beating us in laying track. We need more troops to secure the right-of-way and keep our workmen safe. Indian hostilities have been renewed with disregard for the treaty at Fort Laramie. Not to mention the financial backers are not pleased with their near-to-nothing quarterly earnings." Drake stretched. His feet hung over the edge of the short cot. "Add to that one princess—a pampered, privileged, society female."

Hardy whistled. "All true, Captain. But that doesn't change the fact that she's intelligent, beautiful and has a good head. She hasn't caused you one bit of trouble since she arrived."

Not true old pal, Drake wanted to throw back at Hardy. Trouble! The lady's presence wreaked havoc with his peace of mind. Until she left Bear River City his life would continue to be in turmoil.

"Go to sleep, Hardy," Drake mumbled as he settled against the stiff cot, hoping for a quiet, decent night's sleep. He finally dropped off.

* * *

NIGHT TRAIN

Drake knelt between Georgiana's creamy white thighs and plunged into her silken heat. He placed her long legs across his shoulders, caressing her long shapely calves with his palms. Her moans of pleasure rose and fell in cadence to his motion until their perfect rhythm shattered as they were both flung into a whirlwind of release.

"That was nice," she murmured moments later as she snuggled against his shoulder, her arm crossing his chest. With her slim fingers, she traced his shoulder muscles.

Drake settled among the pile of pillows. "All you can say is 'that was nice,'" he teased. He kissed her forehead, pushing her hair away from her eyes.

"What do you expect after two years of marriage?"

"A little more than *nice* from my wife would do. Maybe I've been working too hard on the new railroad project. Clinton tells me I need a vacation. Now, I'm not so sure we shouldn't get away from New York's heat for a few weeks. The mountains are cooler."

"Hmmm," Georgiana breathed into his ear. "That sounds nice."

"Nice! You're an educated woman, m' love. Could you come up with another word to describe our activities together?"

Georgiana lifted her head from his shoulder. An amused expression curled briefly around her mouth before she looked at him, her eyes darkening to indigo. She'd moved her hand while he'd spoken. It now cupped him. His breath caught. Her palm caressed his soft skin lovingly.

"Husband," she whispered. "Could you be nice to me again?"

Her smile lit up the ebony room. As the pulse of their passion escalated, Drake groaned deeply, holding back his climax. He needed to hear her tell him again in her husky, after-lovemaking voice how nice he was. Soon, sweetheart, he crooned. Soon.

Something soft hit him on the side of the head and a man's gruff voice shattered the sensuous sounds. The bed disappeared like wispy smoke through his fingertips. A dream with the princess as his wife?

"For God's sake! Have some mercy, Drake. Stop moanin' and movin' like you got a woman in bed with you. A man needs his sleep," Hardy trailed off, mumbling under his breath.

Stunned, Drake took some time to recognize Hardy's voice. He opened his eyes and stared at the top of the tent. Large shadows roamed across the ceiling, moving like creatures of the night. A few feet away, the canvas cot stretched under his friend's movements as he tossed and turned, settling on one side with the blanket pulled high over his head. Minutes later all was quiet except for an occasional snore from the other bed.

Drake's heartbeat calmed and the fire that burned in his blood cooled. With sharpened senses, he lay stiffly on his hard cot. Closing his eyes, he sought the alluring dream once more, but it was gone. Lost.

He feared it would elude him the rest of his life.

His continuing attraction puzzled him. The dream that Hardy had interrupted had felt so real. He licked his lips and still tasted her sweet kisses. When he breathed, he inhaled the fresh scent of wildflowers. And the feel of her rounded curves still warmed his palms.

But she wasn't the woman for him. Though they were attracted to each other, she'd never settle for a future with him. There were too many differences. An Englishwoman of her standing would never be attracted to an American railroad worker. He had to remind himself that he was a bastard, a man with tainted blood, too lowly for the likes of the princess, once she knew the truth.

Night settled around the railroad camp. The rumble of the rushing river stirred his thoughts. She'd asked him if he'd ever believe in something other than his railroad. What he hadn't told her—or even admitted to himself—was how deeply he wanted to believe that his princess could one day believe in him.

CHAPTER 6

Midnight.
Restless, Georgiana brewed a cup of tea and carried it onto the rear platform. Darkness flooded the Wyoming Territory; a few bright stars lit the sky. She sipped the warm liquid, allowing it to soothe her as she listened to the muted sound of the railroad workers' wild gunfire continuing off in the distance. It was safer inside the private car but since her arrival at Bear River City she'd been unable to control the overwhelming curiosity she had for this land.

Yet the memory of another night such as this, the night Drake had been shot, chilled her. She set cup and saucer on the rail and pulled the shawl higher on her shoulders. If Drake were here with her, she wouldn't be cold. The thought of his smoky gray eyes brought a warmth deep inside her unlike anything she felt for the eligible English bachelors of her acquaintance. Wrapped in the rugged American's powerful arms, she felt safe within a warm cocoon.

Standing against the rail, she tilted her head back, losing herself in stargazing at the twinkling signposts of fantasies and dreams. Her father had instilled in her a love of the beauty and majesty of nature. Since his death she had found little comfort in the sky and its constellations, but she now discovered a renewed fondness for the world around her.

All because of Drake Lassiter.

When he had taken her to the construction camp and declared no woman could love him, his words had unsettled her. They haunted her still. What little she had discovered about Drake led her to believe that a woman had destroyed something in him. Georgiana knew the key to understanding him lay with the discovery of who and why.

A breeze caressed her neck, reminding her of Drake's provocative kisses. She drew a deep breath and forbade herself to tremble. The startling thoughts made her draw the woolen Kashmir shawl closer.

"You're too beautiful to be standing alone out in the cold wishing on stars."

Startled at the sound of the dreamy voice, she gasped, "Drake!"

Before she could turn and face him, his arms eased around her. He crossed his hands over hers and rested them high on her waist, just below her breasts, pulling her back against his sturdy yet comfortable chest.

"I wanted you to know I was back," he whispered against the soft skin behind her ear, a tender kiss his greeting.

Her breath caught. Her emotions whirled. He had the power to catch her unaware. Her mind became a spinning top when Drake kissed her.

Physically she continued to struggle against his magnetism as she stared at the sky. "You could have waited until morning."

"I was going to wait. But then I saw you standing here. How could I resist?"

"Indeed," she remarked, defiance saturating every tightly wound nerve ending. She straightened her shoulders and cleared her throat. "Was there a special reason you needed to see me?"

"Maybe." His voice was husky, intimate and arousing.

"You'd better tell me." She needed to hear his reply but

was afraid the answer would lead them down a wayward path.

Suddenly she found herself spun around. She leaned lightly into him, tilting her face upward. He bowed his head and murmured, "All I can think about is how beautiful you are." His lips pressed against hers, then gently covered her mouth.

Delicious sensations overcame her as he kissed her. The dreamy intimacy of his caress, being held against his powerful body with such tenderness, surprised her. "Oh, Drake," she whispered against his mouth. He showered kisses around her lips, along her jaw, across the soft curve of her throat. She raised her hands, touching his trail-roughened beard. Her fingertips rose higher as she traced his brows, ready to dig deep into the thick hair at his forehead.

Her palm slid across a thick bandage wrapped around his head. As he groaned, she pulled away from his mesmerizing kiss. "What . . . what happened to you?" Her gaze followed the halting movement of her fingers over the area and then dropped to the bruise that discolored the side of his face. Her eyes widened in dismay.

"A little accident on the way back from Devil's gate, he answered with a wry smile. "I got too close to the Sharp and Young blasters. Livingston, the foreman, assured me the combination of glycerine and powder was safe. I was talking to a teamster. He evidently heard the 'let it rip' signal and didn't tell me. He left in a hurry."

"Oh, Drake," she gasped, appalled at the extent of his new injuries.

"If it hadn't been for Hardy jumping on me and rolling us down an embankment, I'd be buried under a pile of boulders of limestone rock." He paused, the strain of telling her about the accident evident in his voice. "Unfortunately, one man died, three were terribly burnt, and Hardy and I were injured by flying rock."

How could she show disinterest in the man if he continued to appear on her doorstep injured? She threw her arms around his neck and settled her head against his chest. A strange protective surge rose in her as she listened to the heavy cadence of his heart.

She swallowed with difficulty and inspected his shadowed features for additional damage. "You need to be more careful."

"I've always been able to take care of myself. But if you would like the job . . ." His lips brushed against hers. "I'll listen to any offer." Raising his mouth from hers, he gazed into her eyes.

Disturbed by Drake's kisses, Georgiana eased from his grasp. She needed distance, for she found herself losing control at just the sound of his voice. When he held her and kissed her, propriety evaporated like the prairie's morning dew under the sun's heated rays.

What am I doing? she chastised herself. I've become so engrossed with this frontiersman that I have forgotten how our lives are so different. Until meeting Drake, she'd never experienced the magnitude of passion he inspired by his kisses. During her London Season eight gentlemen had courted her. But not one elicited the perplexing emotions that seemed to follow his trail like an errant wind.

"Princess? What are you thinking?"

"That you are entirely too familiar with me," she said with an entirely too impersonal tone.

Drake shuttered his eyes briefly. "When I'm with you I forget everything I've been taught about how to treat a lady. My mother would give me a good dressing down if she knew about our private moments." He gave her a cool, appraising look. What was the woman about? One moment she was clinging to him, her body soft and warm. The next moment she was like freezing water, chilling everything in its path. Gone was the heat buried deep in her soul that he'd grown to expect whenever he held her in his arms.

"I have no desire for frostbite," he said. He opened the door to the private car, stiffly stepping to the side for her to pass him.

She halted, lifting her gaze to him. For a moment, he looked into her shadowed eyes. Despite her distant expression, he wanted to snatch her back into his arms, drag her to a spot where they could be alone. He'd pleasure her for hours, building a fire that would engulf them both and heat the cold recesses of their souls.

A passionate challenge, the lady was hard to resist. Her vacillating response to him had his gut tied in knots. How could he let himself forget that she embodied everything he had left behind in New York: money, social standing, family and love? Lost to him forever.

But God, he still wanted her!

When the silence between them became unbearable, she disappeared quickly into the darkened interior of the railway car, her icy façade an extra shawl upon her shoulders. He walked away, thinking to himself that though the princess might look like warm spring sunshine, when a man got too close he discovered it was only the glare of the winter sun off newly driven snow.

The scent of last night's watch fires mingled with the swirling dust and morning winds off the prairie. His strides were quick and long as Drake hurried along the main street of Bear River City. Home to more than two thousand people, the town was dotted with shacks, log cabins and canvas and board shanties. A few of the larger buildings had signs over the doors: FRENCHY'S, a restaurant, lodging house and club room; WOODS AND KENYON, hardware; ADDOMS AND GLOVER, DRUGGISTS, purveyors of drugs, perfume and fancy articles.

Occasionally the ground shook from the early-morning blasting miles away. Many of the teamsters, blacksmiths, carpenters and masons staggered along the streets still wearing pieces of uniforms in which they had fought The War Between the States, as supply wagons rumbled past, headed for end-of-track.

A woman, dressed only in a fancy red-lace nightgown,

talked through the window of her tent next to the livery with off-duty track-layers and graders who stood around smoking and laughing. Drake shook his head. The contrast of the nighttime shootings and carousing and the peaceful daytime scene he passed was alarming. No wonder the papers back East called Bear River City "Hell on Wheels," the wildest base town yet.

He tipped the brim of his Stetson just low enough to touch the lump on his forehead. He'd torn the bandage off after leaving the princess last night. Angered at the turn of events, he hoped he could tear her from his mind as easily. Not likely! Not when he could still savor her kisses on his lips, sense the movement of her supple body in his arms or smell the wispy scent that clung to her flesh.

Thoughts of her muddled his brain and dried his mouth so much he hankered for a couple of shots of good old Kentucky. That would clear everything just fine.

Drake entered the saloon and sauntered along the unevenly matched planks. It was unusually quiet. The band members milled around drinking and sporting. At the end of the bar he pushed his hat high off his eyes and stood watching the bartender, Yancy, and the Englishman Beeton, converse. Each time he saw the viscount he became irritable, irrational and downright provoked enough to knock out a few of his front teeth.

"Yancy."

The bartender stopped his conversation and gave Drake the eye. "You want a drink, Lassiter?"

"Yeah," Drake let out a long, audible breath and leaned on the bar.

Yancy tramped toward him, bent down and pulled out a bottle. He opened it and poured Drake two fingers deep.

"To the top," Drake growled.

He tipped the now-filled glass to his lips and took a swallow. Tasting it on his tongue, he sucked in his gut and spit the whiskey all over Yancy's fancy red waistcoat. While the man reeled from the unexpected shower, Drake drew his gun, cocked it and pushed the end of the barrel against the bartender's jowl. For emphasis, Drake pushed a little harder on the gun. It made a deep indentation in the bartender's chin. "You still selling this swill to the men? I told you to order better or I'd close you down." With his other hand, Drake pushed the brim of his hat far back on his head, knowing that if Yancy saw his eyes then he'd understand the seriousness of the situation.

"Settle down, Lassiter. I did reorder." He gave the bottle a distasteful glance. "This is a mistake." He recorked the inferior liquor and found another bottle. "Try this."

Drake replaced his gun, his hand hovering over the handle of his weapon. Looking back over his shoulder, he watched as a few railroad workers stumbled in through the doorway. When he returned his gaze to the bar, a full glass of Kentucky's finest shimmered in the early-morning light. He retrieved a coin from his pocket to pay for his liquor.

"Yancy, I'll pay for Mr. Lassiter's drink."

Holding out the money to the bartender, Drake halted briefly, the distinctive British accent causing him to pivot his head. When the Englishman stepped closer, Drake's other hand automatically settled tighter on his holster. He looked at the man through narrowed eyes. He didn't trust him. They shared unfriendly stares across a sudden ringing silence.

"I pay for my own," Drake commented while Yancy took the offered coin.

"Been in a fight, Lassiter?" The viscount dropped the offer to pay for the drink but his expression grew tense, displaying an uncanny awareness as he studied the bruises on Drake's face.

"Yeah. A fight with some flying rocks." He sipped leisurely at his whiskey.

"Well. The frontier is very unhealthy."

"All in a day's work, Beeton. Tenderfoots like yourself should be on guard all the time." His voice was heavy with sarcasm.

"I'll remember your warning. But Georgiana and I won't be staying in camp long enough to worry about our safety."

"That so?" Drake drawled, wondering how long it would be before he and the viscount rolled around in the dirt. He was like a burr under his saddle just itching to be pulled out and trampled underneath his boot heel.

"We're waiting for Thomas Durant. Once Georgiana completes her business with the man I'll be taking her to my ranch for a visit before we return to England."

If that didn't beat all! So the princess and the viscount were a cozy twosome? Had she been lying to him all along about her money and her disinterest in her stepbrother?

"Won't be too soon for my peace of mind. An end-of-track camp ain't no place for a lady." Drake tossed his drink down, took one last look at the Englishman and walked out of the saloon.

"The man is ruining us free-enterprising saloonkeepers," Yancy grumbled. "He'd better watch himself. The next time he finds himself face to face with some lead it might not be an accident." He stomped away, pulling at his wet vest. "Mister, help yourself. I'll be right back."

"Take your time." Lawrence touched the rim of the heavy glass. He'd tasted the whiskey before. Rotgut. On one thing the American and he agreed. He pushed the tumbler aside, turned around and leaned back against the bar with his elbows.

"Well, Mr. Lassiter, who's going to get you first?" Lawrence threw back his head and let out a great peal of maniacal laughter. "My men or the local free-enterprising establishment?"

In the distance, the late-afternoon sun faded behind the western mountains. Drake lit the kerosene lamp on his desk. The boredom of handling the necessary paperwork for submission to S. B. Reed, superintendent of construction, wore at his sanity. He'd rather be out on the trail settling a construction problem than shuffling reports.

NIGHT TRAIN

"Damned too many of them," he noted, the numerous logs of his line foremen blurring his vision.

The cost of each mile of track had skyrocketed. His job was to procure provisions and keep the men working steadily, but immense amounts of money were squandered uselessly by higher authorities. Lack of Eastern supplies and the Indian raids had nearly brought the laying of rail to a standstill.

Spurs spiked the boardwalk in front of his tent, signaling Hardy's arrival. His friend entered, strolled across the room and flipped his hat down on Drake's desk, leveling himself on its edge.

"I heard you had a run-in with Yancy."

"I gave him fair warning. If the men grumble one more time about the Red Jacket he serves, he'll be on the next train going East."

"I'll be busy keeping my ear to the ground."

"Do that." Drake shifted the stack of papers, then met Hardy's gaze. "What else?" They'd been together too long. Drake knew when Hardy left something unsaid. He'd always grind his back teeth. Just like now.

"You being shot at the track and almost being buried alive at the blastin' area are a pretty coincidence." Hardy never was very good at keeping silent once Drake prodded him and he now spoke freely. "Now, I don't rightly mind savin' your hide"—he leaned forward and lowered his voice—"but it's becoming a habit. One I could live without."

"Hell! I thought you were sticking by my side because you liked the excitement of building this railroad," Drake barked.

"Yeah. That's got a lot to do with it. But hell, Captain! After General Haupt praised you for leadin' the men in unheard-of feats, I told myself I'd stick with you. During the War, you knew what the hell you were doin' when everyone around you was crazy with worryin' how we was goin' to lay track and tear it up again. I packed my few belongin's and went West with you because I always had a hankerin' to see the wide-open frontier." Hardy's hazel eyes were bright with merriment one minute and then in a flash pierced the distance between them. "I don't want to bury you out here, Captain."

Drake jerked to his feet and stood motionless in the middle of the tent. "It's not one of my fondest wishes either, Hardy. You're right about one thing. This coincidence doesn't settle in my gut too easily."

"Then I know what I got to do." He grabbed his hat from the desk, ran his right hand along the brim and started toward the door. "Some of the crews wouldn't take too kindly to you snoopin' around, but they'll not fuss if I ask some questions."

Drake took his chair again behind the desk, his paperwork piled as high as the crown of his Stetson. Rubbing the back of his neck, he warned Hardy, "We've made a few enemies in the last hundred miles of track. Don't forget that when you're out there. Just watch your back. Good bodyguards are hard to find."

CHAPTER 7

"Durant's train is expected in three hours," Siobhan announced as she entered Georgiana's bedroom. "He's invited you to a dinner dance tonight. One of Lassiter's dispatchers just dropped off the telegraph. He also mentioned Drake is out again near the border."

At the mention of Drake's name, a brief shiver rippled through Georgiana. She stopped brushing her hair and dropped her arm to her side. Stop it! she charged the flushed image in the glass. This foolish reaction to his name has caused enough turmoil in your life.

Georgiana turned from the mirror, her loosened hair swimming around her hips. Having completed her toilette and dressed in her camisole, pantalettes and stockings, she'd have enough time to rest before Thomas Durant's party.

"Shall I arrange your coiffure before attaching the crinoline bustle?" Siobhan asked, dressed in a suit of rich bronze poplin with a deep scalloped flounce. She stopped next to Georgiana and tidied the colored enamel-threaded bottles and jars that covered the dressing table.

"That's fine," Georgiana said absently while she pushed aside the items that had just been rearranged.

"Georgie, are you looking for this?" Siobhan held her

hand out, displaying a piece of jewelry as she tapped the toe of her bronze boot on the carpet.

"Where did you find it?" Georgiana picked the brooch up gently and held it in her hand.

She studied the back of the ruby and diamond heart-shaped brooch, its two large stones symbolizing entwined hearts. It had been her father's last gift to her before his death. As she clutched the piece to her bosom, she bowed her head, wishing the tears away before she made a fool of herself in front of Siobhan. She ached to see his face and hear his strong, deep voice again.

Papa, why did you die and leave me alone?

"Are you listening, Georgie? I found it on the rear platform."

Georgiana's mind froze on the last time she'd stood on the balcony. Blushing, she remembered she'd been in Drake's arms, shamelessly enjoying an intimate embrace. "The catch is broken. It must have dropped off last night. I mustn't lose it," she said, her voice thick with emotion. "Until I have it repaired, I won't wear it again." She opened the lid of her cross-stitching box and tucked the brooch against the silk and velvet lining.

Awkwardly, she cleared her throat but before she could speak Siobhan cut her off. "I helped John pick out that brooch for your birthday. He was happy that day. And so proud of you." Tears shimmered in her eyes. "I miss him too, Georgie."

Georgiana stared at the older woman, the silence looming between them like a heavy mist. But suddenly the fog cleared. Blind until now, her eyes opened to an astonishing fact. Siobhan had loved John Radcliffe.

Moving to the edge of the seat, Georgiana held the woman's hands and eased her down next to her. "You loved Papa, didn't you?" Georgiana asked gently.

Siobhan turned, throwing a hand over her mouth as a sob escaped her lips, her eyes growing large and liquid. Georgiana held her hand tightly.

"Don't go," she whispered before she reached out and hugged Siobhan, waiting for the ache of the inner pain to pass. Then, pulling two handkerchiefs from the drawer in the dressing table, she handed one to her friend. "Here. You're always without a handkerchief." She used the other to wipe her own tears. "Talk to me. Please."

Siobhan's mouth, as pale as her cheeks, quivered for a moment before she finally rose and moved away. Standing beside the crown-glass window, her hand was pale against the cherry and walnut panels of the wall. The early-morning light cast a firelike silhouette around her. With shoulders stiffened and head lifted, she looked like a queen ready to accept the members of her court. She turned to face Georgiana, her eyes now clear and shining with a special glow.

"I loved him very much. And he loved me, too," she said in a voice that seemed to come from a long way off.

"I didn't know," Georgiana blurted, scarcely aware of her own voice.

"I've wanted to tell you so many times. But a mistress is scorned in polite society. Your friendship means too much to me."

Uncomfortable moments ago, now Georgiana's heart leapt with joy. Her father had been so miserable on their American trip. On the night of the grand party on the prairie, he'd cursed Siobhan's mother for becoming so grievously ill and needing her daughter in Ireland. She recalled his concern over a pair of misplaced cufflinks and his complaint that Siobhan would find them quicker than his own valet. He had depended upon her helping him with everything.

Just as she now depended upon Siobhan's friendship and companionship.

"You'll always be my friend, Siobhan. You cared for Papa when Edythe wouldn't. She thought she would contract some disease from him."

When they had returned to London, her father's health improved after spending many hours recuperating in the gardens with Siobhan in attendance.

"If I had been a better nurse John would be alive now," Siobhan cried, a thread of hysteria in her voice.

Georgiana went to her friend, cradling her until the anguish passed. When Siobhan lifted her eyes, they were clear and bright, no shadow of the secret she had carried since John Radcliffe's death.

"Shhh. Don't torment yourself so. It's not your fault."

Siobhan lifted her head, staring blankly over Georgiana's shoulder. "He was getting better. Then he died"—she broke off in mid-sentence—"so suddenly. He told me he was going to divorce Edythe. He asked me to marry him, and move to America as his wife. Then Edythe returned unexpectedly from her tour of the Continent with Lawrence in tow." She blinked, then focused her gaze. "He wanted money from your father. Two days later John was dead."

"Don't do this to yourself. Papa loved us both too much to ask us to grieve so."

Siobhan's crying slowed, and she wiped at her eyes with the hankie. "Yes. He knew we were both strong and that we could go on. But, Georgie, I miss him terribly."

Georgiana could only nod her head, her own sorrow threatening to swamp her control. "I know. I know," she whispered.

Holding each other, they stood for a few moments. Then Siobhan took a last wipe at her cheeks, tucked the handkerchief in the sleeve of her dress, smoothed back her hair and dragged Georgiana back to the dressing table. "Come. Enough time for mourning. We must ready you for Durant's visit."

Still feeling the loss of her father, Georgiana hid the heartache behind the veil of hair that covered her face as Siobhan continued preparing her coiffure. How had her friend suppressed her feelings day in and day out after the loss of the man she loved? She marvelled at the woman's resilience and prayed to never know the desolation of loving a man so, only to lose him.

An icy chill spread through her. Maybe her prayers were

too late. Did the sensations she experienced when she thought of Drake Lassiter have anything to do with love? *Oh God! How could I allow myself to get into this predicament?*

Siobhan's agile hands conveyed comfort and friendship as she worked on Georgiana's hair, parting it in the middle of the forehead from the neck up to the middle of the head and then from ear to ear. Minutes later she had crimped the two portions of the front and twisted the strands together, fastening them loosely until she could braid the remainder of the front sections.

"You'll be the belle of the ball," Siobhan sighed, securing the three-strand braid together with the ends of the front hair with hairpins and weaving ropes of pearl, forming a bandeau around the head. "Maybe Drake will return tonight and dance with you."

"No," Georgiana snapped, amazed at the intensity of her response. "I mean, of course there is always the chance that he could return to camp. But he's a very busy man and may not want to attend the party."

Please, please, she added in a silent prayerlike whisper. Delay his return tonight. Nerves raw from recent emotional stirring begged to be soothed. If he attended the affair and asked her for a dance, how would she keep from throwing herself into his strong arms?

Skittish during the last few hours since they had returned to camp, Drake grasped his stallion's reins when a pygmy rabbit with a very short tail scampered across the trail in front of him. "Just a little piece of fluff, Jake old boy," he scolded, rubbing the horse's forehead and neck. He watched the nocturnal animal dig in the ground cover, pop a little morsel into his mouth and take off, his stomach filled with his evening's meal.

Up ahead, Drake joined Hardy. At their observation point on the rise overlooking Bear River City, they looked down on an oasis of settlement in the western wilderness. Visible uphill were grades cut through the rocky spine on the far side of the ravine. Rails surrounded by empty land stretched in both directions as far as the eye could see, the single unifying project for a nation so recently torn by rebellion.

"Looks like Thomas ordered additional cavalry regiments." Hardy pointed to the long rows of army tents stiffly standing at attention around the western reaches of the town. The narrow steel ribbon of the Union Pacific wound through the middle of town. A train fully loaded with two wood-burning locomotives, flatcars, two passenger cars, and a private car with American flags flapping in the late-afternoon breeze sat on the siding with Georgiana's private car.

"Thomas must be in camp. Just arrived, too. The wire screen over the stack is still red hot from the sparks." He lifted himself off the saddle, his palms pressed on the pommel. "Smells like something fancier than rabbit and buffalo for dinner tonight." His nostrils twitched. "Yep. Roasted antelope, tenderloin of venison and some catfish fillets." A wonderful aroma drifted along the plains and up the slopes of the hills.

Remembering the rabbit of a few minutes ago, a hunger of his own gnawed at Drake's gut. In spite of his distress, or maybe because of it, he chuckled. Damned if another "little piece of fluff" hadn't kept him ornery and out of sorts. He'd always looked forward to returning from the trail. He enjoyed the simple pleasures of life. Hot food, good whiskey, and a compliant female. In the past, he'd savored all three after a demanding reconnaissance trip.

That is, until the night he'd been shot and rescued by the princess. Amazing how one good woman could destroy all the fun in life. But he felt her enchantment out here on the trail and hadn't the power to stem his desire to be near her. He eased his stallion into a canter. Camp wasn't too far over the hill.

Georgiana smiled at the young cavalry lieutenant, resplendent in full-dress uniform. Blazing lights from a score of kerosene lamps lit up the large army tent that had been set up for the party. A handful of couples joined Georgiana and her dancing partner, their lengthening shadows dark against the canvas sides and ceiling. Tightening his hold on her waist, the man twirled Georgiana faster and faster around the wooden dance floor. Her heartbeats mimicked the rhythm of the tune. She'd missed the excitement of dancing.

Thomas Durant had certainly made every effort to make this night a success. Tables were dramatically covered with freshly laundered tablecloths, gleaming silverware, and spotless china. Fine, rich food: buffalo steaks, wild turkey, tenderloin of venison plus an endless assortment of sauces, pastries and candies complemented the surroundings. The damp scent of wildflowers, fresh with dew, coursed through the open canvas flaps and mingled with the smell of leather, wool and ladies' perfume.

When the music stopped, Georgiana thanked her partner, lifted her apricot faille skirts and made her way toward the table set with a punch bowl. Parched after dancing with officers and railroad executives, she wanted a moment alone and a cool drink.

Delighted to see Washington handling the liquid refreshments, she gladly accepted a lead crystal wineglass. Sipping from the long-stemmed goblet engraved with a locomotive, she was reminded of the strength of the land and the courage of its men to participate in the building of a transcontinental railroad.

"Quite a party, Miss Radcliffe." Washington poured more punch and then handed her a china plate with finger sandwiches made from assorted breads and filled with fancy creams and spreads. Careful not to drip the punch on her white silk puffed sleeves, Georgiana held her arms stiffly in front of her dress.

"I'm having a wonderful time." She balanced the glass and plate in her hands as she positioned herself to look for Siobhan. "Have you seen Miss Ryan?"

"She was dancing with Mr. Anderson the last I looked, ma'am."

Hardy here? Her breath caught for an instant and then rushed out. Could Drake be far away? That thought caused her to spin around, her body tense. The music started up once more. She watched the dancers, hoping to see Siobhan, but when she turned to her right, she bumped into another person.

"I'm sorry. Excuse—"

"Anything, sweetheart."

Tall and handsome in black evening attire, Drake could have passed as an English gentleman. His white necktie accentuated his darkly tanned skin. His ebony pants fit his long, muscled thighs like a layer of his own skin. She drank in the sight of him as she had the punch only a moment ago. A satisfied light came into his eyes.

"Drake," she whispered, too throatily.

"Every time you say my name I'm reminded of satin sheets, champagne and soft firelight."

The warmth of the night as well as the man's forwardness flooded her neck and cheeks with color. Yet for some reason she couldn't imagine him acting any differently. When she returned to her home the memories of his boldness would haunt her through the long, lonely years ahead. She stared into his eyes. Could he read the misery that was like a steel weight on her soul?

The musicians continued to play and dancers spun around the room. Drake touched Georgiana's wrist. She bit her lip until it throbbed like a pulse when he took the plate and wineglass from her hands and set them on the edge of the table.

"This is our dance."

Objections never entered her mind as he escorted her to the center of the tent. He placed one hand on her waist, the other in her right hand. In step with the lilting refrain of the waltz, the small flutters in her stomach threatened to turn into tremors when he slid his large palm across her spine.

Her eyes caught and held his. Did he know what his touch did to her?

"Smile. You'll have every officer here wanting to skin me alive for making you miserable."

"I'm not miserable." She smiled tentatively as they twirled around the dance floor, a kaleidoscope of scenes flying past them, creating a dreamlike atmosphere.

"How about one of those sunny smiles that light up your eyes? Show me, sweetheart, the face of a woman in love." His heated palm caressed the small of her back, warming her body, his smile as intimate as his kisses.

If she could show him the face of a woman in love would he then in turn show her the face of a man in love? Most likely not. He wanted her to smile graciously for his ego and for the crowd and for no other reasons. Hadn't he told her that there wasn't a woman who could love him?

He was an earthy frontiersman, a roughneck by the standards that were so prevalent in her society. Yet with all the edges that he possessed he was most assuredly a man who would fit in any drawing room in England. She managed a small smile as sadness pierced her heart. Wanting to remember this wonderful night, she gave herself over to the music, to the man. He will never know I love him unless . . .

Fool! Drake scolded himself. That's what you've become, Lassiter. Are you willing to risk a game of hearts with your heart so cynical you don't have a chance of winning? Can she give you something to believe in again? Or will she turn her back on you when she finds out what you really are? The questions were as complicated as the woman in his arms. It was a long time since he had allowed himself to care for a woman. Mentally, he still had reservations about his driving need for this woman. Nevertheless, he drank in the comfort of her nearness.

He couldn't take his eyes from her white silk bodice with its square neck trimmed in lace that matched the color of her eyes. The luminance of her soft skin dueled with the glow of the pearls in her hair. He'd discovered recently how warm her flesh was, tantalizingly so. Unable to rein in his rising desire, Drake whispered close to her ear, "You're lovely tonight, princess."

"Thank you, Drake." A twinkle of lamplight caught her eyes as she studied his face unhurriedly, feature by feature. "You're very handsome in your evening attire," she complimented him, her voice deep and sensual. Sizzling need rippled through his body. When she lifted her fingertips to his cheek and forehead and stroked him, saying, "Your bruises have faded. I'm glad," Drake grabbed her hand, squeezing it. He had to put an end to her torturous touch.

"The body mends quickly," he said, commanding calmness and steadiness in his voice and gaze.

"Does the heart heal as fast?" she asked.

His hoarse whisper broke the silence that enveloped them. "Sooner or later the heart mends, too."

As Georgiana caught her breath, weighing the import of his words, Thomas Durant, a tall, lean man with a drooping mustache and straggly goatee, said, "May I interrupt?"

Drake whispered, "Princess," and stepped away, allowing Durant to partner her.

The musicians changed the tempo of the music and Georgiana tempered the harsh uneven rhythm of her breathing as she spun across the floor in another man's arms. She stared past the Vice-President of the Union Pacific Railroad. As Drake nudged his way through the dancing couples, her glance strayed to follow his path, but Durant's flashing, penetrating eyes caught hers. He saw more than she wanted him to know.

"I'm sure you'll see my chief engineer later," he said with a laugh.

Georgiana wanted to run to Drake and chase away that warning cloud that had settled on his features. He needed a woman to mend his broken heart, to give him what small amount of strength and love she could offer. She could be that woman.

"I don't need to ask if you've enjoyed your stay on the

frontier," Durant teased. "Drake has pluck and energy and resources. He's easy to look at and listen to."

"I've had a wonderful experience. Drake has taken time from his busy schedule to show me the construction camps."

"Good. Then you must be ready to take the train tomorrow morning to Omaha. The prospectus on a new stock issue is almost ready. I had to leave before all the details were worked out. But I know you're a discriminating investor and this will allow you a greater share of the profits. We're a few months away from connecting with the Central Pacific," he said in his suave and persuasive manner. "The Union Pacific needs your additional investment."

At the end of the dance, Georgiana asked Thomas to escort her outside for air. The ever-burning watch fires crackled in the night breeze. Georgiana knew Thomas wanted her to join him in Omaha within a few days, but the more she thought about her decision the less she wanted to leave Bear River City. The overriding reason for her journey to America no longer seemed important. Investments could be made and liquidated at whim. But emotions were stronger and needed nurturing.

Then how do you tell your heart to stop beating to the tempo of the anvil chorus that built the rails? How do you tell your eyes to cease staring at the beauty of the panorama that surrounds you every day? How do you stop the prairie wind from whispering of your love for a man whose first, last and only desire is to build a railroad? How? Her heart had questions that only one man could answer. Drake.

Knowing she couldn't leave tonight, she turned in the moonlight to her host. "If you can spare your private car for a little while longer, I'd like to stay in Bear River City. I need time to consider the matter of investing more here."

For a moment surprise settled into his brown eyes. Then with a knowing nod, he said, "Of course, my dear. Washington and the car are at your disposal for as long as you stay in America. If there is anything else I can do to make your visit more pleasant, don't hesitate to contact me."

"I appreciate your kindness, Thomas. I don't know what Siobhan and I would have done without Washington." *Especially the night Drake was shot.*

"I'm aware of that each day he is not with me."

"I should send him back to you. But he is such a jewel."

He agreed with her, but as they spoke his voice had concern in it. "Forget my sales tactics for a minute. I'd like to talk to you as a father would. John was my friend. I'm sure he would want you to be happy, but this is no place for a lady. I don't think a longer stay here is prudent," he commented.

"But it is my decision to make." She patted his forearm. "I'll be fine."

Resignation darkened his face. "Do you mind if I smoke, my dear?" Thomas pulled a large Havana cigar from his waistcoat.

"Not at all. I enjoy the smell of good tobacco." She closed her eyes, lost in smoke-shrouded memories of days spent in the library with her father and Thomas Brassey, listening to their tales of railroads built across mountain passes where goats could not tread. They had been pioneers in Europe just as Drake was in America.

While smoking, Thomas paced the small area in front of the dance tent with the music ringing out into the night. "I'm sorry I can't stay with you longer, but President Grant has requested a meeting of the Government Directors and I must be in Washington in three days. My train leaves in a few minutes for Omaha. Then after my meeting it's on to New York for a week. There is a pleasant weekend planned on my schooner, *Idler*. We'll cruise up and down the Hudson River. I've invited Clinton Lassiter, Drake's father, and prospective investors, politicians and judges."

The heavy lashes that shadowed Georgiana's eyes flew up and she spun around at the mention of Drake's name. "Drake's from New York?"

"Yes, and a member of a very well-to-do family."

Thomas puffed on his cigar, blowing smoke into the starry night.

Her heart pounding, Georgiana stepped closer, seeking information regarding Drake, about his family, about his past. "Why is he here, on the frontier, building the railroad?"

"You'll have to ask Drake."

"Ask me what?"

Drake emerged from out of the shadows; his shoulders were a yard wide, straining against the fabric of his clothes. His movements were swift, full of grace and virility. His gray eyes clung to hers, flat, as unreadable as stone. She could not stop herself from wondering why he'd never volunteered information regarding his family or his background.

"Thomas mentioned that your father was joining him on a cruise up the Hudson River. He must be very proud of your work with the railroad."

"I wouldn't know," he said uncomfortably.

She detected the odd note in his voice. Her mind wandered to previous conversations she'd had with Drake. A fleeting phrase came to mind when they'd been out to the construction camp. *No one would love him.* That certainly sounded like a woman had had a hand in making him an outcast to society and his family.

"Sorry, Drake. I seem to have sung like my caged canaries in my office in New York," Thomas interjected.

Puffing deeply on his cigarette, Drake shook off Durant's apology. In the silence that engulfed them, Georgiana's mind worked with terrific speed. But before she could cast out questions to either of the men, Thomas's valet walked out of the tent searching for his employer. Stepping off to the side, Thomas had a brief conversation and then sent the man off to do an errand for him.

"I'm afraid my time schedule calls for my return to my train. Enjoy the party. It will continue all evening. Some of my guests will take a later train. I'll say goodnight, Georgiana. See you in a few weeks in Omaha." Leaning over,

Durant kissed her on the cheek. Drake lifted a dark eyebrow at Thomas's last words.

"Drake." He shook Drake's hand. "Only a few more months. You're doing a great job. Keep the rails moving." He chuckled sharply before moving away from the tent. He stopped and looked back. "What do you know about Crocker's boast that his men can lay ten miles of rail in a single day?"

"I know Jack Casement has been pushing our crews. We've laid seven and one third miles and the men want to break that record."

"I've wagered $10,000 that it can't be done. Crocker himself covered the bet."

"I'll let General Casement know."

After a few words with Drake, Thomas followed his valet's route and disappeared into the darkness behind the canvas tent.

Alone with Drake now, Georgiana weighed the evening's events. He had his back turned to her, but as usual when in his presence her heartbeat quickened. Cool only moments ago, her skin heated. When he turned and didn't move toward her, the prolonged anticipation was almost unbearable.

"Must you always look so enchanting?" he asked in a raspy voice.

He grabbed her wrist and dragged her into the darkness, her long trail of apricot silk snagging on the ground vegetation. "Drake! Where are you taking me?"

"Not far enough, Princess. Not far enough."

When they were a distance from the party, he halted and reeled on her, the ground uneven and hard under her satin slippers. Her momentum carried her the short distance and she smashed against his chest, the air in her lungs whooshing out. He stared down at her, gray eyes penetrating her soul. Her heart leapt, making her knees tremble, the physical exertion playing havoc with the low neckline of her dress. Her nipples, swollen and throbbing, pushed against the lace trim. Leaning down, Drake explored first one and then the other swell of her breast with his tongue, tracing sensuous paths of ecstasy and tantalizing possessiveness across her chest.

"Thank God you're not leaving with Durant."

His deep, sensual voice sent ripples of excitement swelling through her. His hand slid across her silk-covered belly setting off fire sparks in the secret recesses between her thighs. She met his eyes, glazed with a sheen of purpose. Georgiana leaned into the hard wall of his chest.

"I couldn't leave tonight," she said.

"Why couldn't you?" He cupped his hand under her chin and lifted her face.

She shook her head and lowered her lashes, realizing she'd been unwise to confess her need. The strange surge of passion frightened her. Feeling she was quickly losing control, she pushed back from Drake's hold, calling up her old ice princess reserve. "You don't need to hold me any longer. I'm on flat ground now." If only that were true. Every time he was near she was off-balance.

"Having you in my arms has become an uncontrollable habit," he said.

His words forced her to open her eyes and stare at him closely. "I shudder to think what your other habits might be."

"Honey, a warm woman, good Kentucky whiskey, and a fine cigar suit me just fine. I usually—"

"Drake!" Georgiana stopped him before he elaborated. "I don't want to hear anything more about your American frontier practices."

"Men are men all over the world. Tradition has a lot to do with a man's hankering." A subtle shadow crossed his face before Drake slid his hands along her sleeves to her wrists. For a moment she thought he would move away. But she was wrong. So very wrong. He dragged her hands up the front of his shirt and circled them around his neck, lowering his mouth to her lips.

"Come with me into the night. I know a place where we can look at the moonlight and stars."

"Does this have anything to do with a man's hankering?"

He laughed. "It can. I want to show you a view of the valley from a very special place."

"Is that an excuse?" she asked too calmly.

His gray eyes widened in astonishment. "You don't pull any punches, do you, Princess?"

"I don't want to waste time."

Drake rested his hands casually on her shoulders, causing her flesh to tingle. "I've never had a woman complain about wasting time with me."

His words and his touch elicited involuntary tremors from her body.

"All women find you interesting?" She continued to probe his reasons for tonight.

He cocked one eyebrow and smiled. Amusement flared in his eyes. "I'm not concerned about other women. Only you."

He was asking what she thought of him. It was difficult to answer while his thumbs drew circles on her neck. Lawrence and too many of her suitors had left her chilled to the bone. Drake was the first man to touch her so intimately, so warmly. Too late she found that she was responding to those sensations.

When she looked up at him with her vivid blue eyes, Drake saw a mountain lake in summertime—warm and clear, a place to submerge and forget the aggravating circumstances of the everyday world. He couldn't remember a time he'd been at peace long enough to enjoy the finer points of a woman's body or her mind. "For once I want you to be Georgiana, not the Princess. Make a decision with your emotions and not your business sense. Come with me."

CHAPTER 8

Confused thoughts and feelings assailed Georgiana. Drake's palm was warm against her skin, his gaze a searing glow. A part of her reveled in his open admiration, yet she thought about her actions. As disarming as Drake could be when he wanted his way, she knew he would abide by any decision she would make.

But beyond everything else was the erratic beat of her heart, the tingle in her fingertips and the heat that flooded her skin. Aware she was susceptible to a man's charms for the first time in her life, she was nevertheless rocked by the need to enjoy this enchanting night alone with Drake.

She lifted the hem of her skirt. "I must change into my riding clothes," she blurted out, smiling when his face broke into a wide grin.

Taking her hand, he swiftly led her back to the light coming from the tent and then down the path to her private car. At the steps, he held her for a moment, his lips brushing against hers as he spoke. "Be ready in an hour," he commanded.

He didn't wait for an answer.

She stared wordlessly at his back as he bolted across the tracks toward town. The temperature had dropped and the cool night air bit at her exposed flesh. She was riding out into the star-filled night with Drake. A new and unexpected warmth surged through her.

"We missed you at the dance."

Georgiana jumped at the sound of Siobhan's voice. Her friend was poised on the bottom of the iron stairs. Hardy, dressed in a dark suit, stood nearby. His eyes were trained on the path Drake had just taken.

"Georgie, are you coming back to the party?" Siobhan asked.

"No. It's such a nice night, Drake is taking me for a ride. He said there is a vantage point from where we can see the entire valley. I was on my way to change my dress."

"I'll help you," Siobhan offered, showing no sign of shock at Georgiana's decision. Siobhan ascended the stairs. Over her shoulder, she murmured to Hardy, "Thank you for the dances, Mr. Anderson. I had a lovely time."

He tipped his hat. "My pleasure, ma'am."

Georgiana tugged at her full skirts, entering the car at a frantic pace. Siobhan was right behind her as she rushed down the corridor to her room. Emotionally exhausted, Georgiana dropped to the edge of the bed, kicking off her silk slippers. Tearing at the hooks on the back of her skirt, she heard the silk rip.

"Be careful." Siobhan chided. "You'll destroy your lovely dress. I'll do that."

In short order Siobhan plucked the dress over Georgiana's head. Off went her crinolines and bustle and then Georgiana removed her long gray coutil corset.

"Georgiana Mary Radcliffe. You can't go out without a corset."

"I can't ride if I wear this long thing." She held the stiff material up as evidence for Siobhan to see. She dropped it on the bed and took another from the dresser drawer. "I'm going to wear this one."

Siobhan raised a brow at the black corset with its red silk thread. "Scandalous," she said.

"It may be, but at least it's shorter and softer than the gray one I've been wearing all night."

Donning the more comfortable corset, Georgiana breathed easier. Adding pantalettes and stockings, she stepped into her split riding skirt. Thank you, Papa, for teaching me to ride astride, she thought. She tugged on a white linen shirt, over which she added a warm, full-sleeve jacket. Looking into the mirror, she shrieked, "My hair!" Pearls dripped onto her forehead, strands of hair falling into her eyes.

"Here. Sit at the dressing table. I'll take care of it."

Deftly removing the adornments, Siobhan rearranged the coiffure into a long three-strand braid that followed the full length of Georgiana's spine to the small of her back. She added a black velvet bow at the end to keep it neat.

After hooking her boots, Georgiana added a pair of unadorned black Marseilles kid gloves to protect her hands when riding. "I'm ready," she declared with a smile.

"Do you know what you're doing?" Siobhan stood behind her, holding her by the shoulders, the tenderness in her expression shimmering in the looking glass.

"Going for a ride in the moonlight."

"Very well. You're not a child anymore." Siobhan increased the pressure on Georgiana's shoulders. "But may I say something as a friend?"

Impatient to be off, Georgiana could only nod in assent for she knew that Siobhan was going to scold her about being a lady and acting like one. But what about acting like a woman? she silently lamented. Would that be so bad?

"This is very serious, Georgiana. You have always questioned any gentleman's regard for you. What about Drake? Think with your head and not your heart."

Georgiana stood there, blank, amazed, and very shaken, refusing her mind the freedom to wander down the trail that she was taking with Drake tonight. But that hadn't stopped Siobhan from reminding her. Siobhan had always been able to read her face and thoughts so well. Going alone with a man into the night was against propriety and all socially acceptable customs. Her reputation might be in shambles when they returned.

She inhaled briskly and her heart reminded her what was important. Drake wanted to ride with her in the moonlight. Tucking the esteem of good people in her skirt's pocket, she was glad she hadn't refused Drake's request.

"Good Lord, Siobhan. We're going for a ride."

"All right, but remember what I said," her companion admonished.

Siobhan's words played around in her head as Georgiana rode across Wyoming's rich grasslands, following Drake across a canyon stream bordered with red birch and a variety of willows. After an hour and a half in the saddle, the rich fertile prairie gave way to a rocky hillside covered with a dense thicket of maple, chokecherry and mountain mahogany trees. The pungent, aromatic smell of sagebrush suffused the landscape. The air around them grew chilly, their breath puffed steam in the night.

Drake halted on the ridge and waited for her to come alongside his horse. He then drew her attention to the high peak far to the north. "That's the Bear River Divide. It's covered with trees, but unfortunately, it's blue spruce which is brittle and splinters too easily. Undesirable as timber."

"Is that why you bring timber to the rail site by river?"

"Yes. But as we advance farther west, the price, dammit, keeps rising."

Why is he talking about money tonight? Was Siobhan right? Men always thought of her holdings when they were attracted to her.

"Drake. Must we talk of business or the railroad on such a beautiful evening?"

"You're right. Ask me about the magnificent landscape. Ask me about the vastness of the plains, and the solidness of the walls of granite. Ask about the wonderful time I have planned." His voice deepened when he spoke those last words. His gaze raked boldly over her.

Happiness filled her as she talked. "Tell me about that area. There." She lifted her hand and pointed to the distance.

"That's our destination." Drake swiveled in his saddle and followed her gaze to a hill separated from the main range by a grassy plain. Limestone and slate shales protected the entrance to small caves. Rocks jutted at high angles into the night sky, long shadow fingers in the moonlight.

"We're going to look at stars from a cave?"

"Among other things."

He edged closer to her horse, reached for the braid that ran down her back and tugged on it firmly until she tilted her face up to look at him. She smiled nervously when the beginning of a grin tipped the corners of his mouth.

"I've ordered only the brightest stars in the heavens for you tonight," he told her, his voice low and so near her ear that she shivered at the intense heat from his mouth.

Slowly he slid his tongue down to the base of her neck, nipped her chilled skin, and kissed away the twinge of pleasurable pain. Reeling from the sensations and from the unexpected movement of her horse, she grabbed for Drake, not realizing he already had her safely wrapped against his side. The altitude is affecting me, she thought, feeling faint for the first time in her life.

"Let's go." He eased back onto his saddle, the mystery in his eyes beckoning her irresistibly.

Without the intimacy of his heated caress, her head cleared. Drake spurred his horse along the moonlit trail, looking back once to ask if she could make the descent safely. She motioned that she was fine and drew a deep breath, forbidding herself to tremble as she plunged on down the western base of the promontory.

Small springs burst from the foot of the mountain feeding a large stream that flowed through rock and sandstone into the broad sand and mud flats.

On the bottom of the green valley, Drake pointed his horse toward the entrance to one of the caves they had spotted from up high. He pulled to a stop near a copse of cottonwoods and a small trickle of a stream. Dismounting, he tied his horse's reins and then helped Georgiana, his hands moving gently down the length of her back. Her body melted against his and her world was filled with only him.

"Be careful where you step. The ground is uneven here," Drake warned.

His fingers meshed with hers; she followed him along the rocky approach to the cave. Low-lying bushes scratched against the slabs of granite. On the ground tiny creatures scurried for cover. As she neared the darkened cave, she thought she heard the sound of bubbling water.

She halted, pulling on Drake's arm. "What is in there?"

"Trust me, sweetheart."

He didn't give her the opportunity to think. Suddenly he was lifting her into the cradle of his arms. Lowering his head, he whispered a command for her to do the same, and they disappeared into the recessed entrance.

Seconds later her eyes adjusted to the shadowy interior and she gasped at the sight that welcomed them. Bright moonbeams streamed down through a gap in the overhead rock lighting the entire chamber. A waterfall plummeted six feet into a pool of crystal-clear water. A few feet away another pool bubbled up frothy with steam.

"A hot spring!" As excited as a child with a new toy, Georgiana kissed Drake's cheek. A warm glow flowed through her.

He stared in complete surprise. As their eyes met he tightened his hold on her and said, "I hope that's the first of many kisses, sweetheart."

She gave him a questioning look, her face inches from his.

"Kisses," he whispered again, caressing her with his eyes. "Stay here," he commanded in a voice huskier than before and set her on her feet. "Indians would have a hard time dragging me away, but I must take care of the horses."

Watching him walk back the length of the cave, she pressed her hand over her mouth. Oh, my. Such behavior. She'd actually kissed him first. Until now he'd usually established all of the rules during their intimate encounters, leaving her dizzy with astonishment, sending her pulse beating as fast and noisily as a pile driver. A delicious shudder ran through her body. It continued to pulse after Drake left. She had kissed him!

Georgiana wandered around the grotto, touching the ancient rock and listening to the music of tinkling water. At the edge of the pool she stared at the image of the moon caught in the water's depths. Kneeling down she tentatively touched the water, ripples waving across the smooth surface. The moon disappeared.

"Don't you know you can't catch the moon?" Drake's dynamic voice resounded through the chamber and through her heart.

"I did for a moment," she exclaimed excitedly. "Watch." The small wave she had made with her hand stilled and the bright moon reappeared.

When he joined her near the pool she gloried briefly in the shared moment. His eyes were so dark she could see the reflection of the moon in their smoldering depths. If only she could capture that light as well.

He held her chin in the palm of his hand and asked, "Would you like to take a bath?"

"Here?" she asked, her voice high and reedy.

"What better place? It's private. The water's very warm."

"But—"

"Go ahead. I brought along a bar of soap and some towels. I'll wait outside." He set their saddlebags on a rock and walked back toward the entrance to the cave.

Could she strip naked and bathe with Drake nearby? Durant's private car was equipped with plumbing and a small tub, but not an unlimited amount of hot water. Her inclination to soak indefinitely was enticing. And Drake had acted like a gentleman by leaving her alone in the grotto. But the words he had spoken to her during his convalescence haunted her now.

"I'm no gentleman."

I'm safe, she thought. Drake would never do anything to hurt me. I know that. I feel it in my heart and soul.

There was a large rock between the two pools of water high enough to serve as a table. Soon her clothes were neatly piled on the top, next to the supplies Drake had brought along.

Georgiana waded into the pool and swam farther out into the center. Closing her eyes, she lay back in the warm water, a lassitude skimming over her flesh. She felt decadent. Free. And more gloriously alive than any time in her life.

The breach in the overhead rock over the hot spring pool was a window to the sky above. She lost herself in the mesmerizing scene above—the black velvet heaven and its diamond-bright stars. She scrubbed the soap across a piece of rough material and when she rubbed her skin the scent of flowers wafted up as layer after layer of bubbles burst in the air. Relaxed, her arms and legs floating like feathers, she yearned for a soft, warm bed and comforter. Maybe one of Washington's stupendous meals served in bed with a superb glass of wine as a complement to the food.

Immediately Drake appeared in her dream, his body pressed to hers on the bed as they shared the meal. He sipped some wine from his goblet and then offered it to her. Their fingers entwined around the fragile stem. When she lifted her eyes to his, she held her breath. They were warm, smoky and hungry for more than food or wine. His mouth descended to hers, his murmurs of how she had bewitched him spilling from his lips.

Over the gurgling sound of the spring she heard a muted fluttering, accompanied by screeching sounds coming from the back of the cave.

Unnerved with the continued noises, Georgiana

screamed. Drake came at a run. He tossed his cigarette against the grotto wall and pulled his revolver out, ready to do battle. His gaze ricocheted around the chamber, straying back to her as she floated in the middle of the hot spring.

"Are you all right?" he asked, relief shining in his eyes when he saw she was unharmed.

"I think something's back there. I heard some scratching sounds."

Going where she pointed, he disappeared into the corner that led deeper into the side of the mountain. She anxiously waited, not breathing easily until he returned and reholstered his gun.

"Only some bats," he told her. "They won't bother us. They have a private entrance on the other side."

She shivered, but not at the thought of the nocturnal creatures sharing their cave. His steady gaze only intensified the tingling along her spine. He beamed his approval at her evident enjoyment in the pool. "I'm going to start a fire so you'll be warm when you're finished."

The sounds Drake created while he worked: the whistling tune, the crackle of the campfire, the shuffling of his boots in the sand, enhanced her feeling of privacy. It became a private place for the two of them to stay warm, protected from the elements.

"Do you need your back washed?"

Her vision disintegrated like the popping bubbles that surrounded her with Drake kneeling on the sand at the pool's edge, holding out his arm, a towel draped over it.

"Drake, this isn't a good idea." Her nipples hardened. *Can he see the way my body is responding to his words?* Crossing her arms over her unusually sensitive breasts, her body floated unimpeded toward shore pulled by his mesmerizing influence.

"My intentions right now are all good," he said, the deep timbre of his voice tugging her closer.

A flutter of passion embraced her—a hungry spirit spiraling through her being. Drake Lassiter had been the only man in her chaotic thoughts for more than two and a half years. No other man had ever made her feel like a woman—a beautiful lady of his dreams.

She thought of Siobhan's reminder to give her body only if she could give her heart. In Drake's embrace she had always felt totally alive, wonderfully safe and immensely free. Wanting him had taken over her mind and spirit. Loving him would encompass her life and give her heart a reason to beat every second of every day.

Instinctively her body arched toward his. Gently he wrapped her in the soft material, lifted her into his arms, and pressed her head against his shoulder. Her senses spun with the power of his masculine scent. Her entire body trembled in his embrace as she recognized her womanly needs for the first time. She met his passionate gaze.

"Let me love you," he whispered.

Georgiana lifted her arms and wrapped them around Drake's neck and told him, "Show me the stars."

His mouth covered hers hungrily, hard and warm. She'd responded before to his kisses, but never like this, never so wantonly, never with a fire that needed fuel. "Yes. Yes," she murmured.

She lost herself in the frenzy of their mutual passion. Minutes later, his breath warm and moist against her face, they parted, her heart racing, her back resting upon a soft wool blanket. He knelt before her, his gaze warming her entire body. He fondled her collarbone, the crests of her breasts, her thighs, long calloused fingers accurately discovering her points of passion.

When his hand grasped the edge of the towel, her entire body tightened, filled with wonder and excitement. He tugged sharply at the cloth. She lay naked to his gaze; her eyes widened in anticipation of strange new feelings. With painstaking care he cupped her breasts with his large hands, then stroked his palms downward, skimming each side of her body to her thighs.

"Whenever we've been together, I've been half mad with

the thought of what was hidden under your many petticoats. Dear God, now I know." He moistened his lips, staring at her with luminous eyes. "I don't want to hurt you."

Go slow, Drake, he admonished himself. Settling back on his heels, he drew in a deep breath, closed his eyes and gripped his thighs. *You're out of control. Keep your mind clear of the sexual pleasure that awaits. You might hurt her.* He was the first man to make love to her and he wanted it to be a sweet, very sweet encounter for her. So sweet she'd come back for more.

"Drake." She slid her palm into his, meshed their fingers and lifted the entwined hands to her lips, the stroke of her tongue firing the pulse of blood in his loins. "Love me."

He didn't know where this night would lead. The future had been bleak until he'd found Georgiana. Now he had a slice of sunshine whenever they were together. Since that first time when she had walked into his life dressed in a ball gown, hundreds of miles deep into the Nebraska prairie, he hadn't thought of another woman.

He kissed her hand and laid it on her stomach. Standing, he stepped back, never taking his eyes from the lovely vision that lay before him. He shrugged his vest off and tore his shirt over his head quickly, dropping them haphazardly on the edge of the blanket, ignoring years of keeping his possessions neat.

Down to only his trousers he hesitated, for across Georgiana's pale and beautiful face a bright flush raced like a fever. Her eyes, wide, and deep indigo with wonder and alarm, clung to his. Not wanting to frighten her, he washed away his expression of hungry lust and exchanged a tentative smile with her, then shook his head as he knelt down on the blanket next to her.

"Relax, m'love. I don't want to frighten you. I want you to want this. As much as I want you." He gently explored the soft lines of her waist, the shape of her hips, the length of her curvaceous legs.

"Let it happen, Drake," she murmured, reaching out for him before he could change his mind or disappear.

Wanting him so desperately, Georgiana dragged his hands to her breasts, her nipples firming instantly under his touch. He moved and covered her body, his eager lips a torturous instrument sweetly lingering on her mouth, near the underside of her breast, down to the inside of her thigh. Her body trembled at each loving caress.

Fingertips wrapped in velvet and dipped in fire stroked her at the apex of her thighs. He took time to explore, arouse, to give her pleasure. Becoming his pupil was the greatest delight of her life. When he stood to remove his trousers, she whimpered. Cool air rushed across her skin. She needed his strength, his warmth, his love.

He dragged his trousers down his muscled legs, exposing his hardened flesh to her eyes. Of all the conversations with Siobhan, why hadn't she offered Georgiana more details of what went on between men and women behind closed doors? She couldn't tear her gaze from the elemental male beauty so evident in his body.

"I'll be gentle," he promised, his hands tenderly spreading her legs. He smoothed his palms along the sensitive inside skin above her knees and knelt for a moment before her.

"I know. Don't worry. I want you." Her voice was entrancing. Her eyes pulled at him, imploring him to love her.

"Oh, God, Georgiana," he whispered, his voice low and rough as he heeded her plea.

Covering her completely, chest to chest, thigh to thigh, legs entwined, he held her head, his palms spread wide at her temples. She was soft. Oh, God, so soft. He moved his hips in closer to her heat. When the tip of his manhood reached its goal, he wanted to bury himself deep, without thought to ever leaving her. But he held back, driving slowly, deliberately, into her softness, hesitating when he felt her virginal veil. The hot, exhilarating rush of blood through his veins intensified as he gazed into Georgiana's glistening eyes. Holding tight rein on his desire, he studied her face for signs of pain. When she closed her eyes against his delicate intrusions, he soothed her with words of comfort and pulled her close, breathing soft encouragements into her ear when he made a long full thrust into her wet, hot sheath. A startled moan escaped her and tore through his gut.

He shifted his hips, partially withdrawing. Her body needed to adjust to his heavy invasion. Before he could ease from her, she tightened her hands on his buttocks and drew him back into her feminine valley.

"Don't leave me." She moistened her lips and breathed deeper, her eyes wide with glistening desire.

Her plea spurred him to answer her escalating passion. He buried himself deep. No other woman had taken him so sweetly, so surely, as his princess. She'd only made one demand on him—that he not leave her. He'd never had a sweeter command in his life.

He pressed his hands tighter against her temples, primal instincts rising in him. She was his mate. She was his forever.

Georgiana steadied her gaze and stared into Drake's smoky eyes. His lips twitched in an attempted smile, but passion kept a hard control on his features. She had the insane desire to touch his mouth and she lifted her hand to his face to stroke his lower lip. Teasing her, he ran his tongue across her fingertip and then playfully bit it.

She shivered and lifted her hips.

He stroked harder, deeper.

She threw her head back, her neck slim, white and inviting to the trace of his fiery tongue along her skin.

She gasped at the building sensations. Drake covered her mouth with his, silencing her sounds of pleasure, allowing them to echo sweetly through his soul.

He seized her tightly against his chest. He nipped the soft flesh below her earlobe. Finding her enjoyably sweet and feeling her quivering, he grew bolder in the motion of his hips and the demands on her body. Easing his hold, he hovered over tender pieces of silky skin with lips heated with the fire from his soul. He fondled her high firm breasts, her long slim torso, her smooth flat stomach. She came alive under his caresses.

"I've a fever that won't quit," he moaned. "I need you. I need you . . ." Like a tumbleweed in a windstorm, his control ran away from him.

Georgiana settled into Drake's embrace as he repeated the words over and over. He wrapped his arms around her waist, sank into her wet heat again and again, and embarked on an ancient rhythm that her body instinctively recognized. They traveled to the edge of the heavens, tossed about like feathers among the moon and the stars.

When Drake lifted his head, his gaze rested on her face, then moved over her body slowly. "How do you feel?"

Licking her lips and letting out a deep sigh, she smiled. "Wonderful."

"Are you sure?" He eased out of her, laid down, and pulled her against his side, resting her head on his shoulder. He gently placed a kiss on her temple while stroking her hair.

"It's not often a girl goes to the moon."

He chuckled and wrapped his arms around her, cuddling her close. "Is this better?"

"Hold me forever and I'll be happy." She moved her fingers to his shoulder, her arm pale against the deeply tanned skin and mat of dark hair that covered his chest.

"Could you really be happy in such a place? I wonder. What about your plans to travel? What about your wealth and its inherent responsibilities?" he growled almost bitterly.

He'd beset her with questions. Could she stay in America; never to see England again? Could she share her wealth with her husband once she married? She halted, her palm pressed against his shoulder, her gaze searching his face for additional answers. Was this Drake's way of asking her to stay and marry him?

"I can't help remembering Durant's words. You've been waiting for him to arrive for weeks. Why didn't you leave with him tonight?" Drake asked.

Because I was falling in love with you. She could no longer hide the knowledge from herself. In a short time she'd come so far in her relationship with Drake. Much too far some would say. She wanted to savor every moment they had together.

Forgetting the outside world, she laughed in sheer joy. "Look at the display the moon and stars are putting on for us."

"What do you mean?"

"Well, stop looking at me for a minute. Lie on your back. You'll see a spectacular sky filled with the moon and millions of bright stars."

"But I love looking at you, Georgiana."

"Thank you."

"For what?"

"Until tonight, you've always called me Princess."

He cleared his throat. "Tonight was special." In an attempt to glaze over his admission, he said, "I have an idea. I want to see the sky and you at the same time."

Wide-eyed and a ready pupil, Georgiana's gaze was bold. He'd never met such a puzzling female. She was beautiful, vivacious, an astute businesswoman. She could be childlike when she dispensed with her shoes and fed apple cores to horses. She could impassion him to heights he'd never dreamed of such as she had done only minutes before.

She was a woman with social standing, he a man society had turned its back on. Soon she would leave the frontier. Leave him. As he lifted her to sit astride him, his palms caressing her buttocks, tugging her down so a slight shift of his hips could allow him entrance to her, he was startled by the thought that flashed through his mind. He'd awakened her passionate nature and he'd be damned if he'd allow another man to ever have her. Seizing her hips, Drake drove upward, staking an eternal claim to her . . . but not knowing if they had a future past this night.

CHAPTER 9

A cold wind blowing across Drake's naked back woke him from his cozy dreams, dreams that for once were not fantasies. He hadn't fantasized a night of passion with Georgiana, making love on the sand and in the hot spring. Nor making love with the moon and stars shining in her eyes. Nor making love until he watched a faint line of pain groove her forehead, proving that he'd gone too far their first night together.

Her warm body was pressed against his chest, his hand on her hip, his fingers entwined with hers above her head. She was real. She was a miracle. She was beautiful, the most enticing woman he'd ever known.

He gently laid her down on the blanket and watched her. Her breath sighed lightly between parted lips. When she opened her eyes, sleep-filled but responsive to the sight of him, his heart leapt in his chest.

"I can't see the moon or stars anymore," she murmured, stretching like a lazy cat, her hands in fists above her head.

"Sleepyhead," he challenged. He kissed her taut nipples, feeling them harden into tight pebbles against the tip of his tongue.

"Mmmmm. How long have you been awake?" Her lashes flashed over her diamond blue eyes.

Lifting his head a fraction of an inch, he stared at her breathtaking face. "Long enough to want you again."

She wound her arms around his neck and snuggled closer to his heat. "Warm me up. It's a bit cold in here."

"Yeah it is." A cloud of steam rose from the hot spring as its warmth blended with the cool air of the cave. "Sweetheart, don't move. I'll get some wood to replenish the fire." He dropped a short kiss on her mouth before she could object. "I'll be back in a minute." After pulling the blanket over her, he tugged on his trousers and disappeared through the low hanging entrance to the cave.

Minutes later, he returned with their horses in tow, a few logs in one arm, snowflakes scattered in his hair and across his shoulders, and a frown on his face.

"It's snowing." He stopped a few feet from her, dumped the wood on the sand, and shook his head.

"Snow?" Shivering, she pulled the blanket tighter around her shoulders.

"Damn! We're smack-dab in the middle of a vicious blizzard. I should have recognized the wind shift direction from west to east." He looked across the cave to the gap in the rock over the hot spring. Snowflakes danced in the mist floating up from the hot spring. The sky was black, but the moon and stars were now hidden by dark gray snow-laden clouds. "I was a little preoccupied," he stated wryly and turned his gaze to her again.

"What are we going to do?" she asked in an unbearably calm voice.

"Keep warm." He picked up his shirt and pulled it over his head. "And stay out of the weather."

"How long do you think we'll be here?"

"I don't know. A few days. The snow is still coming down hard. But we have food, water and a warm place to sleep."

"Will anyone look for us?"

"Not in this storm. Don't worry, sweetheart. I can get us back to town once the weather breaks. Hardy will probably be on the trail before the sun shines again."

"He'll be concerned about your delay. Won't he?"

"Yeah. He's my guardian angel."

She leaned forward, the blanket gaping over her breasts. Her voice was low. "He thinks you're a god. I've seen the respect he has for you in his eyes."

He cleared his throat as he joined her on the ground. "I don't know why."

"I do. You're wonderful," she said.

"'You're wonderful'" he repeated in a husky tone. "Come here," he commanded, his voice low and purposefully seductive when he knelt down before her. She threw herself into his outstretched arms. "Aren't you afraid people will talk about this?"

"Since I am an heiress, I've been able to bend society's rules. Men and women tend to accept my business manners because I have money."

"But this?" he persisted.

"I can't help what people say or think. You know the way it is. Thomas mentioned that your family is from New York."

She watched his face intently, looking for a change in his expression. Why wouldn't he tell her about his family or his background? She wanted to know about his life before the railroad, but his hard features remained, never wavering.

"We're a long way from New Yorkers and their dictates. A late winter snowstorm can catch anyone unawares. And there shouldn't be any repercussions because of that. Everyone should be damn glad we lived through it." That was his way of glossing over his former life in New York. And to further befuddle her and keep her from asking any more questions, he planted kisses on her shoulders, the side of her neck, and her pouting lips. "If not, they'll answer to me."

"Ever the cavalier, my love," she chided him.

Drake never blinked at her intimate endearment. She had

deep feelings for him, but he clearly had no idea how deep they ran. No doubt he dealt with the need for female companionship by using the simple barter system of the camp followers. That way nothing of value was invested. Though she cringed at the idea of him with another woman, how could she judge him for those actions? Last night had showed her he was a man with unquenchable sexual needs.

She'd seen dark shadows in his eyes too many times when she'd inquired about his past. *But he must feel something for me!* Even though their relationship was tenuous, she trusted him and the way he made her feel. That would have to be enough for now.

"After we have some breakfast, I know a way we can stay warm." His eyes glittered with an alluring mischief.

Her own grew misty with thoughts of this being their only day alone together. She dropped her eyelids to hide her distress, hoping he would accept it as only a show of desire. Moments later, she knew she had fooled him, for he lifted her in his arms and strolled to the edge of the hot spring, her body on fire for his love.

"I thought you said *after* breakfast."

"I'm hungry now."

The thought of sharing the explosive sensations again with him stirred her private places. Her aching breasts swelled and sought the succor of his heated touch; her dry lips craved the hard, moist touch of his mouth. Plundering the long hair at his neck, her fingertips weaved through the thick strands, needing to be filled with something tangible, something to hold on to that was real.

"What are you hungry for?" she asked, her arms tightening around his shoulders as she whispered in his ear. She stroked the soft skin along his nape with her tongue, then nipped gently with her teeth as she tasted his musky male-scented skin.

"You," he told her in a raspy voice.

As he turned her around in his arms and lifted her legs around his hips, entering her in one deep long stroke, she knew he'd trained her well in this night of loving. He'd become the master of her body, her heart, her very soul. But now, as the apprentice, she wanted to teach him three words to succor her starving soul, to blaze across the dark heavens, to shelter her heart for eternity. She gazed at him, her expectations burning bright, saying with her eyes what she dared not say with her lips. *I love you.*

"How about something to eat?" Secure on the blanket laid out on the cave's sandy floor and still wet from frolicking in the pool, Drake rested on his elbows, lifting his heavy weight a fraction from Georgiana's replete body.

"Having exhausted me, now you'd better feed me before I die from hunger or overexertion," she stated, a delightful shiver running through her, for they were joined below the waist and she could feel every breath leaving his body.

"Princess, your wish is my command."

When he eased away from her and rolled onto his side, she grabbed his hands. "Don't," she stammered. "Please, don't call me Princess."

After so much intimacy, she frowned at the nickname he'd called her so often. She couldn't accept the implications of her inadequacy as a woman any longer.

She'd learned to take on the world from her father's knee. He'd taught her to accept each man or woman for their own worth not based on family connections or bloodlines or on their fortunes. And she would not allow anyone, especially Drake, to think that she was just a pampered female.

"Sweetheart, I'm sorry," he said, stroking her jaw with his thumb. "It's just habit. I haven't thought of you that way since we rode away from town."

She threw her arms around his neck and hugged him tightly, resting her head against his shoulder. Breathing in his unique scent, she felt safe and secure within his strong hold. She kissed the hollow where his pulse, his lifeline, beat strongly.

"Are you going to lie around all day? It's time to eat."

Drake scrambled from the blankets and began to dress. "Can you cook?" He threw the question over his shoulder when he pulled his shirt on, tucking it into his opened trousers.

A question you should be asking your future wife, she shot back silently. A frontier wife would need to know how to cook. Where were her thoughts leading? She would never be a frontier wife. "A little. Nothing elaborate. Siobhan taught me. We take turns preparing meals on the cook's day off."

"That's something. I'm going to scout the area for a supply of firewood. You can unpack the supplies in the saddlebags and start preparations for the meal. By the time we return to town you might be sorry you didn't leave with Thomas last night."

"Is that what you think? That last night meant that little to me that I would wish it away?" She stared at him. He stopped in his tracks and she wished he would turn and look at her.

"Drake." She swallowed with difficulty before she continued. "Don't lie to me. Tell me the truth."

He moved restlessly, his knuckles turning white as he clenched and unclenched his hands, then he finally turned to tower over her.

"Last night and this morning were very special, but I don't know about anything beyond these granite rocks." There was a thin smile on his lips, his eyes had lackluster shadows that hid their sharp gray color.

She sat on the blanket, her fingers hidden but wrapped tensely in her lap, uncomfortable with the spoken truth. What had she expected? Platitudes of undying love? To her making love had been total commitment of her heart, body and soul. *What will I do now?* Tears threatened to spill over her cheeks. She drew a deep breath, rocked back gracefully on her heels, and recalled a childish fantasy. It was of a very special someone kissing her. She'd found that one remarkable man, but dark clouds threatened their happiness. Until he trusted her with his fragile past there was no future for them.

"Yes, it was very special," she said. "Can we make a pact?"

He stared. "Yes," he said, without so much as a query as to what she was about.

"Let's not talk about the future until we are free from the snowstorm. For a little time can we live in our own little world? Soon enough we'll have to remember who we are and what we must do."

A gleam of interest in his gray eyes and a simple nod acknowledged her request. He went about his chores, leaving her to dress and rearrange their supplies.

After breakfast they gave the horses some oats and fresh water. Hands entwined, she followed Drake through the opening in the rocks. The temperature was cold but not frigid. The snow blew across the open plains, swirling and hampering their vision. If they attempted to ride back to Bear River City they would travel blind.

Shivering from the new sights and experiences, Georgiana snuggled against Drake's chest, his arms warm and reassuring. They stood safely under an overhang of rock, watching the snow quickly coat everything in a white mantle.

"What's that moving in the snow?" Georgiana straightened, pointing to a clump of feathers that fluttered in the wind.

"That's a flock of prairie chicken." Drake tugged her back into his arms. "They burrow into the snow during blizzards."

She sighed, Drake's arms gently trapping her as he rocked from side to side. "The poor things. Don't they freeze to death?"

"Oh, some may. But their feeding and roosting grounds are covered in snow. They dig in until the snow melts and they can prance around in the mating ritual."

She tilted her head and stared into his eyes, a blush touching her cold cheeks. "You're teasing."

He laughed and hugged her closer. "I'm not. The courtship drama is amazing to behold. The sound is like blowing across the open neck of a bottle." His evocative voice and his warm breath blowing in her ear radiated a shimmer of heat along her spine. "A male selects his spot on the booming ground. He runs forward, stops, then pats the ground with his feet. To get the attention of a female, he inflates his orange air sacs, lifts his orange eyebrows, spreads his tail and begins to boom. Then he fights the other cocks to keep them from mating."

Will you fight such a battle for me, Drake? Can't I belong only to you? "It sounds much like men fighting over a woman." Her cheek grazed his, his lips inches from her mouth.

"Most males of the species recognize territorial rights. But the human kind sometimes needs a little prodding with a Colt to keep to those boundaries."

"Just like with Lawrence?" As close as they were, she could feel the anger flare, flooding throughout his entire body at the mere mention of her stepbrother's name.

"Yeah," he replied sharply. "From the moment I saw you in that bathhouse, I knew there was something between us. You were never far from my thoughts after that night."

His words warmed her heart. Now she knew he had experienced something special just as she had during those few minutes when she had sought asylum from Lawrence's drunken advances in the railroad bathhouse.

The night of isolation they had just spent away from the outside world heightened her desire for a future with Drake beyond the granite walls that bound them. But that might be days away. And right now she didn't have the stomach for a confrontation with him regarding the future.

He tugged her closer. "Did I thank you for breakfast? It was mighty fine." He rested his arms on her shoulders, his breath coming out in tiny puffs and disappearing into the chilled air. He traced the long column of her neck with his thumbs.

"I never thought I'd enjoy a meal of beans, hard biscuits and fried meat. Thank you for your help."

"A campfire is no place for fancy vitals. Does your finger still hurt?"

"Not much." She bent down briefly to pick up a handful of snow. Balling it around the finger she'd burned when the coffeepot slipped in her hand, she settled back against Drake's warmth. "This helps. It doesn't hurt now."

"I don't want you to singe any more fingers. I'll cook the evening meal."

"You will not." She twirled in his arms. Melting snow dripped from her hands onto his wool jacket. "It is a woman's job to take care of her man." She gasped, her loose tongue always got her in trouble. "I mean . . ."

She stammered while his luminous eyes widened in astonishment.

"I know what you mean. Now let me show you how a man treats his woman," he murmured huskily, his agile fingers working on the closures of her jacket before lifting her shirt and rubbing his cold palms over her warm flesh, the conflicting temperatures raising gooseflesh.

Fully aware of the hardness of his thigh brushing against hers, heat rippled under her skin as she recognized the fascinating flush of sexual desire that flowed only when she was with Drake. Cool air swept across her breasts until his palms pressed against her, the heat from his hands intoxicating. Her eager response matched his. Before she could catch a chill he swept her into his arms, returning to the warm haven they'd created.

The late winter snowstorm raged for twenty-four hours. Cozy and warm within their cave, Georgiana learned the finer points of Drake's tutelage in giving and receiving pleasure. Meanwhile, she taught him how an aspiring student is always ready to please her favorite teacher. They rose to a higher plane of loving: on blankets, on the sand, in the hot spring, in the cold pool, under the waterfall, even outside in the snow. They'd discovered an insatiable appetite. There was no worldly food that could appease their needs. They slept only when exhausted.

Georgiana awoke the morning of the following day to see golden rays of sunshine streaming in through the canopy of rocks and dancing on the waters. She rested on Drake's shoulder, feeling an intense need to remember forever this morning, this past night and day that would be a prelude to the rest of her life.

In repose he looked like a loveable little boy, sleeping deeply without a care in the world. But she knew when he awoke he'd be ready to return to the world and take on anyone to secure the expansion of the railroad.

How can I not invest the additional money to see his dream fulfilled? she pondered, restlessly shifting against his side.

"Uh," he murmured, and without opening his eyes tightened his hold around her waist. "Let me gather some strength, sweetheart." He moistened his lips. "Then I'll take you back into the hot spring."

"You have more strength than I'll ever need," she purred in his ear as she touched his hardening manhood.

Settling deeper into the blanket that covered the ground, he turned onto his back and dragged her over on top of his chest. She swung her head in a slow, lazy circle, her unbound hair swishing around her shoulders and dropping across her breasts. Her nipples played hide-and-seek as she moved above him. She pressed against his hard stomach muscles with her elbows, watching him through lowered eyelids.

He grabbed a handful of her hair and held it up, studying it in the light. "I've never been smothered by hair so velvety before."

Her eyes widened. "A first for you, Mr. Lassiter?" Then she batted her eyelids.

"You're unbelievable!" She feigned disinterest in him, closing her eyes and lifting her chin. Her tongue slid across her lips, making them wet in the way that she knew drove Drake mad. He laughed, a chuckle rumbling deep in his chest. "I've created a wanton."

"How so?"

"I'll show you."

Spinning over, he bound her under him, his eyes deep with desire, his hands tracing patterns of flames across her awakened flesh. With his tongue and lips he played a game of fire and ice. Then he stopped abruptly, his even white teeth hovering over her nipple, his fingertips stroking her flesh. "It stopped snowing." He raised his head from her breast and looked up at the top of the cave. "The sun's out."

Breathless from his delectable assault, she babbled, "I know. Yes," while she attempted to pull him back to complete his ravishing of her more-than-willing body.

Her fingers met empty space, for before she could draw another breath, Drake had jumped to his feet, tugged his trousers on and strode out of the cave.

He returned less than a minute later, too soon for her to have gathered her skittering nerves. She'd lain quietly in the prone position, her eyes closed as she waited for him to return to her. When she looked at him, he stood tall and handsome, his chest bare, his feet naked and his hair tousled from their frantic lovemaking last night. Desire had shaded his eyes for too many hours but she recognized the compulsive work-a-day expression that now covered his face. Their idyllic time was now at an end.

"I've spotted some men on the promontory. I'd better add wood to the fire. If it's Hardy he'll smell the smoke and come on into the caves."

"I'll get dressed." She scrambled to her knees, pulling the blanket around her. "Then I'll pack our supplies."

"Georgiana." He sighed heavily, his voice filled with anguish.

"Please. Not now." She closed her eyes, feeling utterly

miserable. The outside world was closing in on them too fast.

"Georgiana." This time his voice deepened when he spoke her name. He lifted her up against his chest, looked into her eyes and kissed her with more passion than he'd unleashed on her until now. But soon his mouth softened with tenderness, his hands cupping her cheeks and his lips slowly caressing hers, whispers of her name dripping from them until he noticed the tears streaming down her cheeks.

Using his thumb, he wiped the streaks away. "Sweetheart, it's all right. You'll see. I told you if anyone makes crude remarks about you they'd answer to me."

She had to swallow a sob in her throat. Her cavalier. His expression was grim as he watched her. He's worried about my reputation, she thought, while I fear this may be the real end of us.

"Thank you, Sir Drake." She blinked, then focused her gaze and cast an approving half smile to waylay his concern. She lifted her mouth and offered him a kiss, the touch of his lips sending a shock through her entire body.

For one heart-stopping moment when his gray eyes probed to her very soul, she thought he would say to hell with the rescuers and take her deeper into the frontier where no man would find them. But then his gaze roved over the cave, their home for the past thirty-six hours. "Some castle, Princess," he said, holding her hands up to his lips and kissing her fingers. "I know you'll be glad to return to town."

No! No! she wanted to scream, but knew the words would change nothing between them. He had a railroad to build, a dream to complete. And for the first time in her life she was unsure of her own future and where her travels would take her.

Drake added logs to the fire, the flames and smoke shooting up through the gap in the rock. She hurried about her business, brushing away the tears that refused to dry. She dressed, arranged her hair, packed the remaining supplies and joined Drake, who had taken the horses outside the chamber.

The day was bright, clear. The sky with its wispy clouds was the bluest she'd seen since arriving in America. The crisp cool air took her breath away, but not as much as the man who stood holding the reins of their horses. Drake's hard jaw, covered with a couple days' growth of beard, lifted at an obstinate angle, easily recognizable. It was the very same as when he had refused to stay in bed with his injuries from the gunshot.

She heard shouts in the distance while he secured the supplies to their saddles. Only very few minutes remained before the intruders arrived. She lifted her hand, stroked his bristled cheek and kissed him gently on the lips. "Don't ever think that I am ashamed of what happened here. I'll never forget. Never."

For a moment, a wistfulness stole into his expression. "Neither will I." Then he kissed her one last time.

They stood, each holding their respective horse's reins while Hardy and a handful of railroad workers rode across the rocky incline that led to the cave.

Hardy took his hat off and whooped and hollered before he stopped a short distance away from them.

"Damn, Captain." He dropped his Stetson back on his head. "Miss Radcliffe." He nodded to Georgiana. "We been huntin' for you since the snow stopped. Mighty good to see you both in one piece, but I should have known the captain here would find a warm place to hibernate in."

Drake helped Georgiana up on her horse. "Yes. We did," he said absently, his gaze seeking hers. Then he shook his head and dipped his hat down further on his forehead.

Drake sat in his saddle, tugged on his gloves and pulled on the reins, turning the horse in the direction of home. "Miss Radcliffe decided to return to Omaha in a few days and I thought she'd like one last look at the breathtaking scenery and sky that we order only for special guests."

At Drake's request Hardy stayed while the others rode

off, leaving the two men to escort Georgiana back to Bear River City. She breathed deeply of the clear air as they crossed the grasslands and retraced their journey. Had it only been a day and a half ago?

The pristine snow reflected the sun's rays, occasionally blinding them. The fallen snow, so cold and pure, melted under the onslaught of the rays of the bright sun much like she had melted under Drake's heated embraces.

He'd once called her an ice princess. Had he been correct to give her that name? Maybe. At one time she would have taken offense to the term. When they had made love she felt warm and alive. But now she wasn't so sure. For as she traveled through the frozen wonderland away from the warm haven she and Drake had etched out of rock and snow, an icy cloak surrounded her heart.

CHAPTER 10

Georgiana awoke slowly and blinked her eyes. Turning over on her back, she pressed a pillow to her bosom, then stared absently at the morning glory design in the hammered gold ceiling. In the week that had passed since she'd been with Drake at the cave, her mind and body had been anchored to the dreams that visited her each night. Those dreams refused to disappear with the sun's rising, and were so vivid she'd open her eyes in the morning's light only to quickly close them again, seeking passage back into Drake's arms. But no amount of fantasy would bring the flesh and blood man into her bedroom.

He was gone again on a reconnaissance trip, but Siobhan had learned at the railroad office that Drake was due back in town sometime today.

Siobhan constantly asked questions about their journey to Suez, but how many days could she stall if her dreamed-filled nights were any indication of how much she missed him? Her friend would soon see through the thin veil of excuses.

"Are you planning to stay in bed all day?" Siobhan entered her bedroom, pulling the velvet draperies aside to allow in some light. She opened the corner wardrobe to choose a day dress and shoes.

"This should do. There's a bit of a spring in the air. The snow's almost all melted."

Georgiana knelt on the bed and peeked out through the thin lace curtains. The sky was blue, the bog alongside the track was dry, and a black-and-white mapgie, its feathers shining like gunmetal, flew back and forth from a tree outside her window to the overhang of the car. It chirped occasionally as it built a nest for its young from an intricately woven mass of sticks and thorny twigs. "It's a beautiful day." *I wish Drake were here to share it with me.*

They could go riding. To the end-of-track again, to watch the wondrous creation of the road. Be honest, she scolded, you want to be alone with Drake.

Georgiana's private car was parked away from the main street of the town, and she doubted she'd be able to see when Drake returned from his trip. In the past, he'd come to her. A wicked idea overcame her—this time, she'd go looking for him.

She climbed out of bed and paced the short length of the bedroom. Siobhan fluffed out a suit, one that Georgiana especially liked with a lilac silk walking skirt, violet silk tunic, and pompadour basque waist. A linen collar was formed by three overlapping revers. "Put that back," Georgiana directed. "After breakfast, I'm going riding."

Siobhan ceased fussing with the material and looked askance at Georgiana. "You know Drake wouldn't like that idea. It's unsafe."

"I won't have him playing nursemaid. He's been gone for days and I want to get out. Sitting and cross-stitching in a stuffy railcar is not my idea of seeing the American frontier."

"We'll talk about this after we eat." Siobhan smiled benignly as if caring for a temperamental child and closed the wardrobe door, the dress still in her hands.

"Siobhan! I want my riding habit." Georgiana plopped

down on the edge of the bed and tossed her heavy braid over her shoulder. "Please," she implored, "today is too glorious a day to argue."

"Very well." Siobhan opened the door and grabbed a black riding habit from inside. "I agree. The day is a-wasting."

After they breakfasted on cornbread, potatoes and broiled chicken in a cream sauce served on toast, Georgiana addressed the porter while he cleared the dishes from the table. "Thank you, Washington. You perform miracles with what little provisions you have stocked."

"Mr. Durant told me to buy whatever I need to keep you and Miss Ryan comfortable. Mr. Anderson has been helpful in locating what I need each day."

"Hardy?"

"Yes, ma'am. I wouldn't be surprised if after the war that man could have found Jeff Davis for the Federals who were looking for him."

Washington disappeared moments later, his tray laden with the remnants of the meal. Georgiana and Siobhan lingered in the small dining area. Standing at the satinwood sideboard, with stores of delicate china and polished pots, pans and porcelain, Georgiana poured coffee, added sugar and rejoined Siobhan at the table.

"How can you drink that barbaric brew?" Siobhan frowned.

Until a week ago she'd enjoyed her tea and on occasion cafe au lait, but now after spending two days snowbound with Drake, she enjoyed the strong black drink and relished the adventure of having helped Drake cook their meals. She savored her thoughts of their time together.

Her image in the bevel-edged French pier glass that hung on the wall startled her. The light from the chandelier sparkled, dancing fireflies on the cherrywood paneling. Her eyes were dark as a clear winter sky, her cheeks flushed pink with the memory of a moonlight swim. Drake had twirled her around in the pool under the waterfall, the cascading water and moonbeams sprinkling their moist skin. She'd shrieked when the chilled water splashed on her back. And then he had laughed and whispered she would not be cold for long.

The recollection of that exuberant sound and then how he had loved her later that night raced like a fever through her body. Georgiana brushed her warm cheeks and fought the urge to laugh much like Drake had done that all-too-long-ago evening, but she lost the battle as a small chuckle escaped her lips.

"Praise the Lord! I haven't heard you laugh in such a long time." Siobhan's lilting voice caught her unaware.

Georgiana stared across the room at her friend, a soft smile on her lips. For a moment she had been back in the cave with Drake in the moonlight. "I was remembering a very nice moment in my life."

"Could it have anything to do with the two days you were stranded with Drake in the snowstorm?" Siobhan asked, staring at her with that glance that Georgiana knew so well.

"I love you dearly, but when you're able to read my mind I fear you're a witch."

Siobhan set her cup on the saucer and came over to Georgiana and hugged her. "And I love you, too. You're like a sister to me. Don't ever worry about that special sight I have. It has never brought ill to a person." She stepped back, her eyes deep pools of wisdom. "But I do see heartache ahead for you and Drake. Also I see a great joy." Siobhan held her hand up to silence Georgiana when she opened her mouth to question her declaration. "I'm not certain if the two are connected."

"That's the problem with your talent. It's so unreliable."

A sadness stole into Siobhan's face and she spoke in a harsh, raw voice. "Yes . . . it is. I always believed your father would live."

Georgiana let her mind wander to thoughts of what life would be like if her father had lived. They would have returned together to America and had such a wonderful time as they watched the growth of the iron rails through this country. Without a doubt he would have liked Drake. She could not help but smile as she remembered how alike her father and Drake were. An ocean separated the continents of their birth, but their love of the land melded their souls.

"I'm going riding," Georgiana said, affirming her earlier pronouncement.

"Not alone, you're not." Lawrence stood leaning casually against the door to the observation deck. "Knowing the unruly sort that inhabits this pest-riddled town, I cannot in good conscious allow you to go unescorted. Although I must say your constitution has not been affected by your terrible experience in the blizzard. I couldn't help notice when I entered the dining room how your cheeks were stained pink." He entered the car, closed the door behind him, but stayed on his side of the room. "Where is your protector?"

"I could ask the same of you, Lawrence, dear brother," Georgiana countered. "If you are so concerned about my welfare, where have you been?" She riveted her accusing gaze on him.

His mouth was set in annoyance as he picked up a brass clock from the table and then jammed it back on the marble top. "I found accommodations. Bored with the lack of activities in this frontier town, I hired two men to show me the countryside."

She found herself inexplicably dissatisfied with his explanation. The man was devious and she didn't believe for one minute he had wanted to take in the scenery. After a long pause, she responded sharply, abandoning all pretense of civility with him.

She placed her hands belligerently on her hips. "Then you have no cause to complain about whatever attention I receive from Drake Lassiter."

His expression grew hard and resentful. "Shouldn't he be taking you riding? Or has he tired of you so quickly?"

Taking a deep, unsteady breath, she stepped back, the thought freezing in her brain. Is Drake tired of me? Was she just another of his conquests? she asked herself, wanting to put all the pieces together. She wouldn't believe that he felt nothing for her.

Lawrence's mocking tone was no doubt meant to taunt her, but she noted a strain of anger in his words, almost a spark of jealousy. "Remember your position in Society, Georgiana. You're a very wealthy woman, and men will take advantage of you."

"Brotherly concern? Or is it interest for my fortune?" Georgiana charged back at him, wanting to rebel against his concern. The citizens of this frontier town were far removed from civilization and she hadn't heard any gossip about the two nights she had spent with Drake.

"Not only your money, Georgiana. I told you once before that you were not safe in this barbaric area. If you insist on riding, I'll join you."

"That's not necessary."

"But I insist." He stood solidly at the entrance to the railway car, barring her exit.

Normally she would disregard Lawrence's interest in her well-being, but she reminded herself that Drake, a man at home in this environment, had been shot and almost blasted to kingdom come. What would be the harm of riding out with Lawrence?

Georgiana continually asked herself that question as they rode down the congested thoroughfares of Bear River City or she recently learned, Beartown. Dressed in her black riding habit, a blue grosgrain cravat at the neck that matched her eyes, she looked as they passed massive tents that housed saloons and gambling dens. Men and women moved from the log cabins and shanties in a continual stream. She'd heard that the "fallen women" and unscrupulous men working in these establishments were but pawns of liquor wholesalers and gambling syndicates operating out of cities in the Midwest and East.

Farther down the road were tar-paper shacks, false-front

stores, and dance halls. An occasional boardinghouse and a meager bookstore gave the town a veneer of respectability. The dust from passing supply wagons blended with the arid wind, men's curses, women's bawdy laughter, and an occasional sharp crack of gunfire. Although she was never one to run from fear, Georgiana felt somewhat relieved that Lawrence was along for the ride.

"This is a good opportunity to speak with you about your stock in the railroad." Lawrence shifted the reins in his hands, his gaze roving over the milling townspeople. "This road is being built into an uninhabited region, much of which is desert. It's so primitive no one can forecast the potential revenues from the line. Yet you continue to hold to your father's decision. This will be folly."

Hastening along the road to the outskirts of town, Georgiana held onto her temper as tightly as she held onto the reins. "You see it as such. I see its potential to help develop a great nation." *I see its soul.*

"You must have read about the other roads built into the fertile Mississippi Valley. They became insolvent and the stockholders lost all their money. There's a good chance that your U.P.R.R. stock will be valueless."

When Lawrence joined her and they rode side by side, she turned her gaze. She lifted her chin, determined to stay calm under his superior male attitude. "How many times must I tell you? Lawrence, it's *my* gamble."

Weary of the turn in conversation, she allowed the horse its freedom. She held on to her black beaver hat, its blue gauze veil streaming behind the chignon at the nape of her neck as the horse found its own rhythm and left Lawrence with his mouth open, breathing a dust cloud.

He caught up with her a short distance later near a small meadow. A stream of pure fresh water meandered through it. A few willows danced in the breeze, fanning clumps of wild roses, artemisia and rushes. The ride had invigorated her. Surrounded by the wide open spaces, her earlier restlessness left her.

"It's time to return, Georgiana. There are riders coming." He pointed toward the western horizon where the noon sun would soon begin is descent.

Distinguishable now as they closed the distance separating them, the swift riders proved to be Drake and Hardy. Drake rode tall in the saddle, his broad shoulders so wide that she had been unable to wrap her arms around them when they had made love. Just the thought of those hours of touching his broad chest and muscular arms sent shivers through her stomach and into very private places.

Drake recognized Georgiana immediately—her hair, the lift of her chin and her curvy body were a red flag. His senses were keen, the unreasonable need to be with her after so many days on the road devoured the last ounce of his control.

Dammit! How could she retain her loveliness in this country, away from the trappings of polite society? Each time he saw her again, he felt that familiar joy of when he was a child of eight and Clinton gave him a toy train for Christmas. For months after that he wouldn't allow it out of his sight.

He was bewitched, surely, for he couldn't stop gazing at Georgiana when he finally pulled his horse to a stop. Jake lifted his head, his nostrils flaring, a scent of something unpleasant nearby.

Beeton!

Drake rubbed the horse's neck, calming its instinctual dislike for the viscount. Damn smart horse!

"Georgiana." He nodded and lifted his hat. Dropping it back on his head he jerked a greeting toward Beeton. Recovering from his initial captivation with seeing her again, he spoke severely to her. "You shouldn't be this far out of town."

Sitting stiffly in her saddle, Georgiana acknowledged Hardy, introduced Lawrence, and smiled coolly at Drake. "Thomas told me I had the freedom of the line. I didn't think I'd need your permission also."

So that's it. Back to acting like an ice princess.

"Thomas put your safety in my hands. I'm responsible for you as long as you're on Union Pacific land. You can ride back with us."

"I'm not ready to return."

She stated her words quite simply, but he knew her to be a complicated and strong-minded woman. "We'll see about—" Drake stopped abruptly and clenched his teeth. He didn't want to explode. Experience had taught him—at least when it came to dealing with Georgiana and her need for freedom—that he needed to practice a great deal of restraint. She was one female who detested taking orders from a male.

He rubbed the trail dust and sweat off his forehead with his forearm, twisting his head to check the surrounding area for any immediate danger. They were not far from a crew that was replacing some split ties, and they could call upon them if the need arose. His gaze was steady, and instead of telling her to get her cute little bottom back to town, he tipped the brim of his hat in his best gentlemanly manner learned in his younger days and said in a calm voice, "Have a nice day, Miss Radcliffe." He and Hardy Anderson swung their horses east and rode away.

" 'Have a nice day, Miss Radcliffe!' " Georgiana spat out the words contemptuously and a little too loud. She twisted in her saddle, following Drake with a furious glare until he was a small dot behind them.

"Why do you put up with his insufferable ways?" Lawrence berated her. "He's only a ruffian, a common laborer. Don't encourage his attention, Georgiana. He's only interested in your money and how it can help the railroad."

So intent on watching Drake, she'd forgotten Lawrence's presence. The stinging words he'd spoken ran around in her mind. Common laborer. A ruffian. Insufferable. Lawrence was insufferable. She'd learned to keep out of arguments with him by ignoring him, but this time she couldn't disregard his implications.

Where was the man who had shown her the moon and the stars? Where was the man who had taught her what it was to be a woman for the first time in her life? Where was the strong wonderful lover who had stolen her heart?

Her emotions were spiralling out of control. Clicking her tongue and pulling on the reins, she ordered her horse to turn, and then headed toward town. Her beautiful day had been ruined. This wasn't the meeting she had expected with Drake after his long trip.

The next morning Georgiana took Siobhan with her to a small frame building near the center of town that housed the *Frontier Index*, the weekly newspaper that rode with the rails. They leisurely strolled the short distance hoping to find some reading material. She especially wanted to discover if there were any older copies of the paper with news on the construction of the Suez Canal.

"I think it's on the other side of the street." Georgiana encouraged her friend to join her as she took a right turn at the corner tent. After passing a clothing store, a number of saloons and gambling houses, she saw a sign on the building at the end of the row proclaiming it as the paper's home. But as she marched past a small tent, she came to a standstill. A modest wooden sign that hung over the door read: DRAKE LASSITER, ENGINEER U.P.R.R. He'd only been footsteps away.

Upon her arrival in Bear River City, she'd obviously turned into an addle-brained woman. The two nights of lovemaking she'd shared with Drake at the hot spring evidently meant nothing to him. Since then, she'd seen him only once—yesterday on the trail where she'd gone with the express purpose of surprising him. Instead he'd scolded her like a schoolroom child, leaving her adrift without his strong familiar hands to guide her.

"Are you going in?" Siobhan touched the handle on the door ready to enter Drake's office.

"No!" Coward! she scolded herself.

Georgiana grabbed Siobhan's other hand and rushed headlong down the main street, evading the dangerous rolling supply wagons, horses with riders, and gangs of strolling men. Out of breath, she and Siobhan reached the boardwalk. She looked back at Drake's tent where he now stood, his eyes trained on her.

He called to her. Ignoring him, she moved along the boardwalk toward the newspaper office. She hadn't reached the next building before Drake clamped his hand on her wrist, stopping her in her tracks.

"Let go of me!" she demanded, pulling at his tight grip. "You're creating a scene." She gave a cursory glance in the direction of the citizens who walked by.

"I'm not letting go until we're in my office." Drake stepped down into the dirt and dragged her back across the street, eating up the distance with his long strides. Pulling at him, she almost missed the terrible noise that descended upon them from a great distance.

She chanced to look up. They were directly in the path of a runaway supply wagon with a large team of horses. Frantic to get out of the way, she screamed at Drake. At that instant he hauled her up against his chest. He dropped to the ground, clasping her in a death hold and safely rolling away from the sets of thundering hooves that missed them by the width of a piece of paper.

When the cloud of dust settled and the ground stopped moving, she opened her eyes. She was spread atop Drake, his arms tightly wrapped around her back, her hands wrapped around his neck. Her hair fell in streamers over her eyes, her white linen collar stained and ripped beyond repair, her black beaver hat in the dirt, its ribbons and gold-and-white feathers crushed.

"My God, Georgiana, are you all right?" He held her in his lap, holding her gently, his breath warm against her clammy cheek.

"I think so." She ran her hands along her arms, shifted the

front of her dress back into place and pushed her hair off her face before picking up her hat.

"Let's get off the street."

He helped her to stand. When she swayed, he lifted her into his arms and carried her to his office. "Miss Ryan, please open the door," he asked Siobhan, who had rushed to their side. Once inside the cool tent, Drake sat her on the edge of a cot. Placing a kiss on her forehead, he said, "Rest here," before he stood up.

She gasped, realizing a shiver of panic and grabbed for his hand, imploring, "Don't leave me." She stared at him, using her eyes to plead with him also.

His gaze was gentle, understanding as he nodded and sat on the cot. "Dear Lord, you could have been killed," she moaned, her lips pale.

"No, I could've lost you," he said, his words harsh, his voice deep from the strain and flying dust. When he lowered her head against his shoulder and held her tightly, his gray eyes were full of life, pain and warmth.

Her whole body felt like ice, for she still trembled from the ordeal. She heard Drake tell Siobhan to pour a drink from the bottle in his bottom drawer.

Drake had to lift her chin as he offered her a sip of whiskey. She shook her head, but he refused to adhere to her wish. "You're shivering. It will warm you. Drink," he coaxed, tipping the glass to her lips.

Georgiana sipped the strong alcohol, and then swallowed a mouthful. Instantly warmth spread from her mouth to her belly. Her eyes watered and she smothered a cough with her hand. Drake lifted the glass to his lips and snapped back his head, draining the liquor.

Gazing over at Siobhan who sat at Drake's desk, Georgiana watched her friend toss a drink down like it was a cool glass of lemonade on a hot Fourth of July, her coloring changing from a deathly parchment white to just slightly pale.

"More, Georgiana?" he asked, lifting the glass for Siobhan to refill.

"No . . . That was quite enough."

"How are you feeling now?" he asked, his tone having a degree of warmth and concern.

"Much better."

He smiled and kissed her quickly on the lips. "Good," he said before his face went grim. "You can't go back out on the street like this." He waved his hand in front of her damaged bodice.

"I'll go to the train and bring back a new blouse for you, Georgie," Siobhan offered. "It won't take me but a few minutes." She lifted her skirts and vanished from the tent.

Slowly, Drake rose from the cot, but Georgiana still held onto his arm. "I'm not going far. I want to get you a cloth so you can clean up."

He went to the far corner of the tent. There a table held a white pitcher and bowl. He poured water on a piece of material, returned to Georgiana, and handed it to her. "You have dirt on your face and neck."

Mechanically, she accepted the wet rag and began to wipe at the smudges on her face. There was a looking glass on the wall behind Drake's desk, but she didn't think she could walk the distance. She looked up at Drake as he stood towering over her and saw the corner of his mouth twist upward. "Here let me. You're only making mud," he said, sitting down beside her.

He took the cloth, rubbing softly at spots on her cheeks and forehead. When he moved down to her neck and bosom, the air in the tent grew warm, her body languorously leaning into his touch.

"When I saw those horses bearing down on us I thought . . ." she whispered, near tears as she studied the face of the man she loved, his brows drawn together in an agonized expression.

"Sweetheart." He halted his cleansing actions and pulled her to him, one hand holding the back of her head, while the other wrapped around her waist, gently pressing her tightly against him. "Shhh. Don't cry."

His hands comforted her, calming her until she could breathe easier and gather her frenzied thoughts. He refused to allow her to move when she tried to lean back. "Don't." He sighed heavily. "You feel too good in my arms. That's where you belong," he whispered.

He brushed a soft kiss across her lips, then gently covered her mouth. The delicious sensations exploded in her when he crushed her to him, his mouth now hard and hungry. She kissed him with greed, fed by the knowledge they both could have been killed today.

She felt the heady sensation of his lips against her cheek, along her neck, over the crest of her breast. What little cover the bodice afforded counted for nought, for he tugged it open and palmed her hardening nipples. When his mouth clamped over her already sensitive peak, gently biting then licking it with his tongue, she clenched her hands in his hair. She knew he was not unaffected by her caress, for his heart beat at breakneck speed not unlike her own.

He lay her down on his narrow cot, lifting her layers of petticoats and skirts and tugging her drawers open so he could smooth his hand back and forth on her belly. Demanding. Relentless. Unyielding. He moved his fingers down into the soft valley of curls and covered her intimately with his palm.

"God, I want you so much. Do you want me?" He planted little nipping kisses on her eyes, the edge of her lips and finally full on the mouth, his tongue straying deeply as his fingers slipped into her moist, hot center. The reaction to his intimate touch sizzled through her. "Do you, sweetheart?" Drake appealed.

He hovered over her, his desire entangling her in his erotic bedlam. She could no longer disguise her body's reaction to their brush with death. She gloried in their togetherness, in their passion. Her excitement mounted and insanity, hot and driving, drove her to jerk him down against her. She whispered her assent.

He tore at his trousers, setting himself free. In one swift drive into her, he went so deep that she stopped breathing, afraid that if she moved she would soar to an awesome, shuddering ecstasy too soon without him. Yet she welcomed the involuntary tremors of arousal that began, tossing her into a maelstrom of overwhelming sensations.

"Yes, sweetheart. Come with me," he cajoled her, his voice husky as he held her head in his hands and pumped in a smooth steady rhythm.

She took a gulp of much-needed air to keep from fainting. But as he kept up the tempo, an explosion of satisfaction mushroomed, beginning in her extremities and erupting where they were joined, tossing her into a whirling world of light-headed climax.

Within moments Drake slumped over her, his own gratification complete. His deep breathing softened so she could hear the noise on the street, the voices of the crowds, the mild wind rushing through the canvas walls of the tent. Sanity marched in with the sounds.

Aware of her state of dishabille, she gently pushed at him. "Drake," she sighed for she still felt the firmness of him inside her. He lifted his head in answer to her call, a brief flare of desire racing across his face when she felt her muscles contracting and causing his member to pulse with renewed life. Would he take her again? Her mind was working now and she knew Siobhan would return any minute. "Please," she appealed to him to let her up. "Siobhan will be coming soon."

Like a stallion sniffing danger, he reared up and deftly rearranged his clothes. She attempted to fix her hair, but the effect was feeble and she became agitated. Drake suggested she use the looking glass on the wall. Once in front of the glass, she aptly started repinning the loosened braids.

He joined her, gathering her against his chest, whispering against the nape of her neck, his fingers warm and strong as he pushed hers away and took over the task of pinning her hair. She held his arms, settling back against him, basking in the peaceful strength of his touch.

"Georgiana, I . . ." He let out a long, audible breath and dropped his hands from her neck.

For a moment she was disoriented, but she steeled herself against the heartache she experienced every time Drake let her go. How would she survive the final break when she would leave the frontier?

Drake's desktop was covered with papers and dispatch pouches and, needing something to occupy her mind, she sat down and began to straighten the papers in a neat pile. As she lifted one stack, she noted a telegram addressed to her. It was from her solicitor, Ian Chamberlain. The words seemed urgent. He wanted her to contact him immediately regarding any further investments.

"When did this come in?" she asked as nonchalantly as possible, lifting the paper in her hand and looking at Drake.

"Early this morning."

"Why didn't you dispatch this to me immediately?" she gasped, her throat still dry from the dirt she had swallowed in the street.

"I was on my way to your private car with a copy." He pulled a piece of paper from his shirt pocket to affirm his words.

"But you still stalled bringing it to me. Why?"

He sighed. "We're so close to the completion of the railroad. Only weeks now." Drake's eyes filled with a different sort of desire, this time for wrought-iron rails.

"I see. What was this, one last fling with the princess?" She clasped the bodice of her dress, suddenly feeling naked.

"I'd thought we'd have more time," he said absently.

"What for? Lies! To tell ourselves that what we had shared together in the moonlight meant something? Evidently it meant nothing to you. I've asked you about your family and you refuse to talk about them." She laughed wryly, her eyes burning. "New York? Isn't that where your family lives?"

Had she gone too far? He glowered at her and turned away. When he turned back his nostrils flared with fury. "My past or future doesn't count for much. The most important thing in my life right now is to keep the railroad from dying."

"You bastard!" *I'm dying. Our love is dying.*

Drake jerked back at her explosive words. Amelia, on the night she had spurned him, had screamed the word, a blow to his emotions that had followed him for eight years. This word spoken on Georgiana's lips would follow him for all eternity.

After their two nights spent together in the cave he wasn't sure he could live without Georgiana and her love. Yet if he told her the truth, she'd only curse him just as Amelia had so long ago. His heart had died a little that day. But if Georgiana knew the truth and she looked at him with as much disdain as Amelia had, he knew his soul would shrivel up and blow away as easily as the prairie grass in a drought.

And this time he wasn't sure he'd live through it.

"Princess, you're right. You're exactly like the women I left behind in New York. Is that what you wanted to hear? My past belongs to me!"

His bitter words cut her deeply. She'd given him her virtue, her trust, her love. In return he had given her only heartbreak.

A knock at the door halted their conversation. Drake turned away and harshly said, "Come in." Georgiana eyed her hat on the edge of the cot and picked it up, her emotions trampled as surely as the ribbons on her bonnet.

Siobhan stood in the doorway. Bleakly Drake stared at Georgiana, his mouth in a grim line. Then he was through the door, a loud slam echoing through the hollow interior of the tent.

"Georgie. My God, what happened?" Siobhan's eyes clung to Georgiana's.

For the first time in her life, Georgiana experienced helplessness. What could she tell her friend? Her heart was breaking and there was nothing either of them could do to keep it in one piece.

She moved her shoulders in a shrug, close to weeping. When Siobhan handed her the new blouse, her hands shook, but she refused her friend's help, took a deep, unsteady breath, and stepped back against the far wall and changed her soiled clothes.

"Do you want to talk?" Siobhan hurried over to her, and caught Georgiana's elbow.

"Not now. Maybe never." Taking a deep, unsteady breath, she looked over at the canvas cot.

Tilting her head to one side, Siobhan stole a slanted look at Georgiana. Then she straightened her shoulders and cleared her throat. "Let's go home."

Struggling to keep coolheaded, Georgiana hurried from Drake's office, Siobhan's footsteps thundering behind her on the boardwalk.

CHAPTER 11

Drake watched Georgiana's flight from his office. Down past Topence's Butcher Shop and Nuckles's General Merchandise she strode, Siobhan by her side, walking fast toward the private railcar. Now that she thought he was a thoughtless bastard, he knew he could never tell her about himself. If he went to her she would assuredly turn her back on him. The thought of her condemning him for his actions and not for his bloodline hurt the most.

Damn! He'd thought he'd thrown his emotions and their confounded entanglements out the window the night he'd left New York. Now, eight years later, his heart had soared back into his chest on the wings of a golden-haired temptress. What a fine mess! He slapped his Stetson against his thigh.

"I hear you've been eating some dirt. I leave you for a couple of hours and you almost get yourself killed." Drake knew Hardy had returned before he heard his voice, his friend's spurs jingling against the wood boardwalk that fronted the canvas tent. The news of him rolling around in the dirt in broad daylight must have traveled fast. He'd sent Hardy to a work crew three miles outside of town to check on their schedule.

He'd swallowed dust along with the fear-inspired bile that had risen while saving Georgiana. It had blended with the rich tang of Kentucky whiskey and the taste of her tongue in his mouth. It might be worth dying just to have her again deep in his throat. He was as hard as a piece of granite and she hadn't been gone for more than fifteen minutes.

"Yeah, hell, some days it doesn't pay to get out of bed. But then, when someone is trying to kill you, there isn't much you can do. Dammit! They could have killed Georgiana. I want those no good bastards found."

"Someone might have seen who was driving the team," Hardy said. "I've got a few ideas of my own. But let me test the water before throwing it your way. Don't want anyone to get scalded unnecessarily."

Drake didn't push any further for information. He knew if Hardy dug deep enough, he'd ferret out the culprits. And then it would be his turn to throw a little fear their way. "Hey, buddy. Don't jump in over your head. Come to me when you get the goods. I want a piece of those guys, too."

Hardy's eyes lit up. "Captain, you know I'm not a fighter," he said in jest, "I'm a lover."

Drake halted and shot Hardy a penetrating look. "Still be careful. My gut tells me this is real. And whoever's behind the attempts won't take kindly to your snooping around."

Hardy's mouth dropped open as if he was about to say something, but he clamped it tight before heading down the road alone. Drake headed off, too. Maybe he'd stop by Yancy's place and learn what was being scuttled about.

The sun stood straight up in the sky. The weather looked good—no towering fortresses of cumulus clouds. If the weather held, they'd get some track laid in record time. Maybe Thomas would win his $10,000 bet. At least one problem would solve itself, Drake mumbled as he entered the saloon.

"We're leaving for Omaha in the morning," Georgiana stated distinctly, lifting a forkful of moist fish covered in a light cream sauce to her mouth. "I sent a note to Mr. Reed, the superintendent. He has an eastbound train leaving early tomorrow morning. He will make arrangements to have my car hooked on before first light."

"Are you sure, Georgie?"

Georgiana was puzzled and shaken by Siobhan's sudden change of attitude concerning their departure. She hoped the woman wasn't reading the thoughts swimming around in her head. "I thought you wanted to leave."

"Oh, I'm ready whenever you are. That's not the problem."

"Problem?" she asked sharply.

"You can lie to me, Georgie, but don't lie to yourself. I don't care if we stay here or go to Timbuktu. I'm worried about you."

Georgiana set her fork down on the edge of the Sèvres plate, the same china that she and Drake had used for their picnic. Briefly she had thought Drake had feelings for her, but now she knew he had only used her. His railroad was more important to him than she could ever be.

"I'm fine, Siobhan."

On the outside, perhaps, but on the inside, the devastation of Drake's charges that she was exactly like the society women of New York weighed heavy on her already shattered heart. Had she been correct in her observation about who had turned Drake into a bitter man? She closed her eyes, reliving the pain of that final scene. Leave the frontier, she scolded herself. Leave while you can still pick up the pieces and find a life for yourself.

"I've wired Thomas Durant that I am investing additional funds in the U.P.R.R."

"Any decision you make is fine with me. I'll take care of packing your things safely away for the journey. Are you going to tell Lawrence you're leaving?"

"Yes. I'm sure he'll tell me that I've finally come to my senses," she shot back, tossing her hair across her shoulders in a gesture of defiance.

It was before the light of day the next morning when Georgiana was awakened by the sound of voices outside her compartment's windows. As she listened to the conversation it became apparent that the men were hooking her private car to the train. She relaxed, waiting for the sound of the steam locomotive's piston rods. A blast of steam from the boiler escaped into the quiet morning. With a screech and a jostling of the car, the coupling was completed. The train was underway a few minutes later.

Depressed, she lay abed. If Drake had had a change in heart he would have made time last night to come to her on the observation deck as he had before. He had cleared her out of his life just as the railroad graders blasted rock from the area along the building of the line.

Not waiting for Siobhan to help her dress, Georgiana threw the covers aside and hurried with her morning toilette, dressing in a simple black velvet skirt and white linen blouse.

Stepping quickly down the quiet companionway, she stopped at the galley to find Washington already boiling water for tea. The fire glowed in the range and shone on the polished pots, pans, pudding and jelly molds hanging on hooks above the dresser. She'd have tea this morning. She would put the recently acquired taste for black coffee behind her just as expediently as the train would cover the miles from town to town, from virgin territory to civilization. Could she put the unquenchable hunger she had discovered for an American frontiersman behind her as easily?

"Good morning, ma'am. Was your rest comfortable? I've made tea and shortly I'll have a special breakfast for you. You'll need your strength today." The porter stared at her from behind his spectacles, his eyes wide and bright with what appeared to be an uncanny awareness of the turmoil inside her.

"Thank you, Washington. I'll be on the observation deck. Call me when breakfast is ready."

"Miss Radcliffe. Mr. Fowler . . . I mean Viscount Beeton is in the saloon."

That stopped her. "When did he arrive?"

"With the men who hooked us to the train."

"Very well. I'll join Viscount Beeton," she called over her shoulder and continued down the corridor to the back of the car.

"How are you this morning, my dear?" Lawrence rose from his chair and allowed her to sit before taking his chair again. "I thought I'd ride back with you to Omaha."

"This is a surprise." Her mouth was set in annoyance. "Nice of you to ask if you could travel with us."

"Family doesn't need an invitation."

At this moment she didn't care. She didn't have enough fight left in her to argue with Lawrence. If he wanted to travel in the public cars on the train, that would do. She mentioned travel arrangements and he offered no resistance. That was odd. Lawrence never acquiesced on anything.

"Aren't you going to your ranch?" she asked.

"I may still travel there. I wanted to see you safely back to Omaha. And this will give us an opportunity to talk—"

"Unless you want to walk to Omaha, don't dare mention railroad stock or money in the same breath."

"But Georgiana," he pleaded, jumping to his feet.

She would not be deterred. She'd made her decision and it was final. "This is not open to discussion, Lawrence."

"Very well. I'm going outside to smoke a cigar and I'll join you for breakfast when your incompetent porter has it ready."

"Washington's not incompetent. And I will not have you disturbing him while you're a guest on this train."

Lawrence's stomach clenched with rage at her audacious behavior. Telling him what he could do or not do with a servant! He would bide his time. When they returned to England he'd make her see what an excellent husband he would be. Then once they were married, her money would be his.

Drawing a cigar from his inside pocket, he twirled it around between his fingers. Soon, he'd make the silly twit dance to his tune until she was nothing better than an upstairsmaid, his lustful wishes her carnal commands.

"Miss Radcliffe's train left before dawn," Hardy announced, walking with Drake down the main street of town, the sun bright in the clear sky.

Did Hardy think he needed a reminder? Damn, he knew exactly to the minute when Georgiana's car was added to the eastbound train, because his heart had stopped dead at that moment. It was only by sheer grit that he had finally gotten it pumping again. But, oh God, the ache wouldn't leave!

His desk was piled high with work. His clothes were thrown haphazardly on the floor of his tent. His personally brewed coffee tasted bitter without the sweetness of Georgiana's kisses. How had his life come to this? For the first time since walking out on his family eight years ago, he felt the loneliness of his existence.

Since that night when he'd opened his eyes and seen Georgiana kneeling over him after he'd been shot, he'd felt brief snatches of warmth and sunshine in his life. Oh, she'd had a cool façade. But he had soon discovered a deep core of heat and had touched it, using it to his advantage, melting her frozen exterior into hot pools of desire.

That warmth was slowly draining from him the farther her train traveled the rails east to Omaha. What could he do about that? Dammit, was he really going to let her go?

"Do you think we could intercept the eastbound train at the Green River stop?" Drake asked without thought to the ramifications of his decision.

He wanted her back. No matter the cost.

"The train has a layover there to take on passengers and send telegrams. I'll bet you a new Stetson we can catch up with it before it pulls out again."

"You're on!" Drake thundered, his steps taking him across town to the corral as quick as lightning.

Saddle weary, dirty, smelly and thirsty, Drake and Hardy were waiting at the railroad office when the eastbound train pulled into the Green River station at three o'clock, two hours behind schedule. They'd followed the old pony express route and changed horses three times. A division point on the Union Pacific, the city of Green River was built on the north bank of the Green River and was bordered by sandstone cliffs. Castle Rock, the most prominent, rose one thousand feet above the river. On the western slope of the Continental Divide, the city enjoyed mild winters; the valley's spring wildflowers were already in bloom. Drake thought of Georgiana's cross-stitching. So wrapped up in the woman and what would please her, he knew she'd appreciate the colors of the red Indian paintbrush, white rock and sand lilies, and bluebells.

"Looky there," Hardy pointed to the rear platform on Georgiana's private car.

"Well, I'll be damned!" Drake swore, his gaze never leaving Beeton's back when he exited the train and started down the street. "Did Georgiana dump you too, stepbrother?" he said tersely, the sight of the man even a hundred feet away making his stomach turn.

"Why don't you go to Georgiana? I need somethin' to wash the trail dust away." Hardy nodded toward Beeton who was walking down Green Street toward Fat Jack's Saloon and Hall.

Hardy tracked Beeton through the back alleys and dust-filled streets, his sense of smell bombarded by City Bakery, with its aromas of fresh breads, pies and cakes. His stomach growled. He'd only had a cup of coffee on the trail this morning before reaching Green River City.

He kept his eyes trained on the Englishman's back as he weaved in and out around the myriad buildings of commerce that made up the town's main street. When Beeton finally stopped, it wasn't at a saloon, but at Freud and Brothers, the largest gunsmith in town.

Hardy waited out back in the alley, but minutes passed and the viscount didn't come out. Anxious to confront the man about his attempts to have Drake killed, Hardy started toward the building. Just then the train whistle sounded, giving the passengers a five-minute warning for boarding.

"My. My. My. They allow any sort of riffraff to stand around on city streets." Beeton stood in the doorway, arms akimbo, puffing away at his cigar.

"I want to talk with you Beeton," Hardy growled, tipping his hat back with his knuckle and placing his other hand directly over his holster.

"This is hardly the place for social discourse. You'll excuse me. I have a train to catch." The stout man pushed his way around Hardy.

"We'll both go. I told Drake I wouldn't tell him about who was trying to kill him until I was real sure of the bastard. On this long ride somethin' Yancy told me has been rollin' around in my head. Somethin' about two railroad workers and a certain Englishman. Could they have been the same varmints who tried to blow Drake to kingdom come? Could they be the men who need some trainin' when it comes to handling a team of horses?" Hardy pulled his revolver, settling the long barrel against the man's spine. "Now why don't we mosey on over to the marshall's office."

"You don't have any proof, Anderson," Beeton slowed and turned to talk to Hardy.

"As soon as I locate those two men, I'll have enough to hang you with." Hardy kept nudging Beeton's back with his gun as they walked away from the back of the gunsmith store, then along the side of the building. Before they reached the front boardwalk, the train whistle again gave its warning. The Englishman stopped dead in his tracks, his hand moving close to his inside breast pocket.

"Easy does it there, Mr. Viscount." Hardy pushed his gun tighter against the man's back.

"My cigar has burned out. I need a light."

"Okay. But do it slow and easy like."

That was exactly how it happened. Slow and easy. A noise behind them in the alley caused a split-second distraction, and that was all the time Beeton needed.

Pulling a derringer from his pocket, he took aim at Hardy's chest. Between one heartbeat and the next, Hardy's reflexes kicked in and he lifted his arm sharply, trying to deflect the shot. Grappling with each other, the men staggered in a deadly dance. Hardy lay on the ground, his blood pooling under his body, watching helplessly as Beeton hurried away.

CHAPTER 12

"She won't see you, Drake." Siobhan stood guard outside the door of Georgiana's car. Arms firmly crossed, she kept her balance as the train increased its speed and the platform bumped up and down under her feet.

"After riding seventy miles through this territory, do you think you can stop me?" he growled.

A shadow of alarm touched her pale face. He hadn't meant to frighten her, but during the trek he'd made an important decision. He was not returning to Bear River City without Georgiana.

I love you, Georgiana. When I know the truth about who my father was I'll have to tell you about being a bastard, but given time you'll grow to love me as much as I do you.

In order to confide his feelings to the woman he loved, he must get through her guardian angel.

He'd never harmed a woman in his life, though he'd been tempted after Amelia's suggestion that marriage had been out of the question because of his tainted blood. Amelia had done him a favor. Without her rejection he would have been tied to a miserable life with her. He would never have met Georgiana and discovered the strength and beauty of her love.

"You're crazy, Drake Lassiter," Siobhan chided him.

"That may be true. I'm not going to stand here and argue with you. Let me in." He lowered his voice, a rasp of entreaty suffusing his words. "Please, I want to talk to her."

His plea must have softened her. She didn't offer an argument and the knot eased in his belly.

"If you can get past the galley where Washington is packing away his stores, she's in her bedroom. Be gentle with her," she advised, moving aside at the door so he could enter.

As he passed Siobhan, he grabbed her by the shoulders and kissed her on the cheek. "Thank you."

He found the porter in the galley, dispatched the man quickly to the other end of the car, shuffled him out the door, and locked it securely. He didn't want any interruptions when he started his powwow with Georgiana.

The thick carpeting muffled the sound of his boots as he rushed down the length of the long companionway. A few feet before he reached the third doorway, he halted. He pushed his palm against the wood-paneled wall, the quick thought that she would refuse him leaving him more shaken than at any other time in his life. He dug deep under his overwhelming apprehension and uncovered the confidence he needed to go to the woman he loved.

He stopped in midstride, halfway through the doorway. Georgiana sat at her dressing table, her arm raised as she held a brush, instantly aware of his intrusion, astonishment touching her pale face.

"What are you doing here?" she demanded quietly, never stopping the motion of brushing her long hair. "Where's Siobhan?"

Entering the room, he said, "I sent her to another car because I wanted to talk privately with you."

"Why? I've never kept my business dealings from Siobhan." Their eyes met in the looking glass. "That's why you're here. Isn't it? You must have run out of money to buy timber for your precious railroad."

NIGHT TRAIN

"No. There's thousands of ties floating on the Green River right out there under your nose." He jerked his head toward the window so she could look for herself at the river, awash with logs as far and as wide as the eye could see.

"Then it must be something else. Maybe you're unable to meet a payroll. Or the shipment of nitro for your blasting has been held up for payment. I'm sure there must be hundreds of reasons why you traveled all this way to see me." She dropped her hands to her lap and her body stiffened. "And they all revolve around the rails. Leave me alone, Drake," she said, her voice firm, final.

Every curve of her body spoke defiance as she tossed her hair across her shoulders, the pulse at her neck thumping erratically. Her full, high breasts rose and fell swiftly, the white linen shirt tight against her taut nipples.

As he had done so many times in the past, he lifted his hand to touch her, to boldy bring her into his arms. But when her eyes darkened to an indigo blue, he moved to the window instead, challenging his own rampant need for her with unhurried purpose.

"Drake . . . please. What do you want?" she asked in a rush.

Like a steep mountainside that needed careful grading, Georgiana required very unique treatment. He smoothed his hands across his two-day growth of beard and wrenched himself away from his ridiculous comparison of the chores involved in laying rails and the woman he loved. He weighed his capacity for straightforward thinking while a cynical inner voice cut through his thoughts, reminding him once again of their differences.

"If only my brother, Michael, were here," he groaned aloud. "He'd be able to help me. He knows how to treat a lady properly. He knows all the fancy words."

The heavy lashes that shadowed her cheeks flew up. "I've never complained about how you treated me, Drake. Just the opposite." She met his gaze, a tear slipping down her cheek. "I'll always cherish our time together." Her voice faded to a hushed stillness. "I'll nurture each word you've spoken to me until the moment I no longer breathe."

"Then why are you running away from me?"

Georgiana floundered in an agonizing maelstrom. A stab of guilt lay buried in her breast. Could she tell him she couldn't compete with his dream of finishing the railroad? Would she tell him that he'd never once told her he loved her? Fighting a deep despair of loneliness for the future without him, she felt weakened and resigned herself to tell him some truth.

"I'm going home to England where I belong. There is no future for us."

"You fool!" He drew her to her feet, wiping at the tears that framed her eyes. He shook his head vehemently. "You beautiful fool. I won't let you go," he whispered in her ear. "You're mine, Georgiana." His voice broke with huskiness.

Yes, I am. I will always be yours.

She pushed at his chest. "You don't know what you're saying." She felt the tears burn at the back of her eyes. She pressed her palms against the hard muscles of his shoulders, trying in vain to move a man who could be an unmovable force when he so desired.

"Listen to me!" He grabbed her wrists, raised them above her head, and chained both hands with one of his. Her breasts thrust against his chest, her heart thumped uncomfortably under the strain.

"Why? So you can lie to me?" She didn't want him to see into her eyes, to see the hurt mirrored there. Instinctively, he lifted her tilted chin with his palm. "Don't . . . I want to leave America with some bit of pride. We were lovers, Drake, but we never spoke of love." *In my heart, yes, but only silently.* She steadfastly refused to open her eyes.

"I know. It's something that needed to be done. That's why I've tracked you down. We have some serious talking that needs to be done."

What was he trying to tell her? She repeated his words in her mind. At first she had thought he was speaking of a job he had to do. She knew how much demand was placed upon him by the railroad. Then why wasn't he back at Bear River City, or at a construction camp seeing to the building of the rails?

Slowly she lifted her eyelids. A hot ache rose in her heart. *Don't let it be a lie. Please!*

He released her wrists. His eyes were deep and unfathomable with no signs of light. She tenderly touched his jawline with her fingertip and over his bottom lip. He nipped at it with his teeth. When she said simply, "Say it," a blaze of emotion flashed through the bleakness.

He whispered, "I love you," and his mouth covered hers, her breath catching in her lungs.

Tonight there would be no shadows across her heart, for she was blissfully happy, fully alive. She held onto Drake's broad shoulders as he swept her, weightless, into his arms. He buried his face against her neck and she was jolted from the encompassing emotions when the brim of his hat tapped her forehead. She seized his Stetson and sent it flying. It crashed into the porcelain bottles on her dressing table.

Her body tingled when he touched her and soon they were both naked in the middle of the bed, his hips pressed into hers. He thrust deep, claiming her again on a journey of body, mind and spirit to the highest peak of ecstasy.

Once sated, the train's clicky-clack sounds intruded through the floor of the railcar, rousing them from the languid afterglow. Drake rested against the headboard and pulled Georgiana up onto his chest. She rested her head on his shoulder while he tenderly stroked her hip with the palm of his hand. "I'll have your car changed over at Rawlins. We'll be back in Bear River City tomorrow night. As soon as the railroad is completed we can be married."

"You haven't asked if I want to return, or if I want to marry you."

"I assumed . . ."

She'd never seen Drake Lassiter flustered and at a loss for words. She savored the moment, for she knew it might never happen again. She looked up into his eyes, speaking to him of her love and approval with the stars that she knew shined in hers. But she still spoke the word. "Yes."

"Yes, you'll go back with me? Or yes, you'll marry me?"

"Let me see," she lowered her voice, being purposefully mysterious. "I should make a logical choice based on clear thinking."

"I forgot. You're not like the women in New York. You're too damn independent."

"Will that be a problem?"

"No. You're like the women of the West. Independent, free-thinkers. Unlike a prim, well-bred debutante of New York with her practiced nuances." He kissed her forehead, gently smoothing her hair back off her forehead. "It's what I love about you, Georgiana."

"Then I'm not what Queen Victoria has called members of my social class? 'The wretched, ignorant, highborn beings who live only to kill time?' "

"God, no!" Drake chuckled and planted a kiss as tender and light as a summer breeze on her lips. "You're the only woman I've ever known who was interested in my work. And the only woman to scold me about some of the trestles on this line. The day I got caught in that blast, Hardy and I were coming back from checking on a bridge at Devil's Gate."

"You believed me when I spoke of the unsafe conditions on the line?"

"You gave me something to think about. The new bridge at Devil's Gate had developed a problem. I've ordered it fixed, as well as an investigation of all the other trestles along the route."

She was shocked. No man but her father had ever acknowledged that she, too, could assess problems and determine their solutions. Georgiana knew there would never be another man for her. Siobhan had cautioned her on finding a man who would love her despite her fortune. Drake helped her discover what had been buried inside her body and mind and that knowledge was more precious than gold and silver.

Her heart overflowed with emotions and sentiments. She wanted to tell him about them, but his lips descended on hers, blocking any other form of communication except the heated hunger of his kisses.

Minutes later, his lips hovered over hers, his face full of strength, no shadows obscuring his love for her. "Your bed is very comfortable, sweetheart. I've not been gentle with you. You must think I'm an animal making love to you on the hard floor of a cave. On a cot."

She captured his face in her hands, seeing regret in his eyes. "Each time we've been together, darling, is special. And you are a wonderful lover. You'll make a marvelous husband."

He lifted his brows and sheepishly grinned at her. "A smart businesswoman wouldn't make that assumption without any knowledge of the competition's assets."

"Oh, I think I know enough about your assets, Mr. Lassiter," she purred, sliding her hands over his shoulders, across his broad muscled chest and down below his waist. "I don't want anyone else," she stated simply, her voice low, husky with devotion for him. "You're mine."

His features glowed when he rolled her over on her back. Their bodies melded, her long silky hair twisting magically around his arms, holding him prisoner as surely as metal shackles.

"And you, my love, belong exclusively to me," he affirmed, a kiss on the swell of her right breast sealing the bargain. He kept his hands busy skimming across her hips and thighs, staking a claim with his heated touch.

"You won't change your mind because of my money?" she asked anxiously, her breathing harsh and uneven.

He smoothed his knuckle across her flushed cheek. "Sweetheart, your money or lack of it isn't important. I have more money in a bank account in New York than I could ever spend in a lifetime. Maybe a few lifetimes." He chuckled, the sound deep and pleasurable. "But what I've never had until now is someone who loved me. You've given me that. And what's more important, it doesn't matter to you that I'm on the frontier building a railroad."

She clung to his shoulders and for a moment relief washed through her. She'd fallen in love with a frontiersman. She'd never considered his wealth or lack of it. His rugged individualism, his tough determination and his open approach to life meant more to her than his bank account balance. But she needed to know about his life before the railroad. "Tell me about your life before the War." *Tell me who hurt you, darling.*

She smoothed her palms down his back, coaxing him gently to respond to her request. Her head turned on his shoulder and she stared up at his jaw as she waited. After a brief hesitation, he began slowly to tell her the story. "My family is nouveau riche. Too bourgeois for old New York money—making too much money, too fast. My father . . . Clinton, invested a portion of his inheritance in the Rock Island Railroad. He worked on its construction, made a fortune and then opened an engineering company in New York."

"Another Brassey."

"Yes, you could say that, but on a smaller scale."

"He had a vision like Thomas."

"Clinton always shared his visions with me. He saw the need for a transcontinental railroad fifteen years ago. We'd talk for hours about the expansion of this nation into uncharted and primitive areas. We always knew a railroad was needed to keep civilization just a step behind westward expansion. When I was old enough to make a decision about my future I told Clinton I wanted to be an engineer just like him."

His reference to his father by name was peculiar. "You never say 'Father' when you speak of him. Why?"

He considered her for a moment, a shadow of agony in his eyes. "Calling him Clinton is easier."

She noticed his rigid expression as well as the tone of his

voice. What was so wrong with his New York life that he couldn't share it with her? She touched his eyebrow, her fingertips gliding along the ridge of hard bone, the firm planes of his face.

Whenever he held her in his arms, thoughts of the rest of the world, the world outside this railcar, ceased to exist. "Don't you find this bed too soft?" she laughed, forgetting everything but the man she loved.

"Soft, huh, we'll have to see what can be done about that." He twisted his hips and tugged her over on top of him. She moaned, "I love you." Her senses reeled. She lost her rhythm for a moment, clutching his shoulders so she wouldn't fall off the top of the world. He pulled her face down to his, planting kisses all over her mouth. Shifting his hips higher off the bed, he took her to greater heights of ecstasy with his deep penetration.

"We're not leaving this bed all night," he groaned.

She couldn't agree more. Whispering her total cooperation, she nibbled on his earlobe. He growled his approval and spun them into a magical exclusive world for lovers where the outside world ceases to exist.

The train's whistle awakened Georgiana at dawn, the sunrise chasing them as the train sped across the Wyoming Territory's landscape. She felt the train slow down and the car rattle, gathering momentum again after the change of speed. She slid closer, her back against Drake's wall of heat. The bedroom was chilly. The stove had burned down during the night, but Drake could take care of that when he awoke.

"Mmmmmm," he murmured against the soft skin of her nape, his hand tantalizingly fondling her left breast.

Pressed against him, she felt the proof of his growing awareness of morning and her.

"You're nice and warm." She moved his hand from her breast to her lips and smothered his knuckles and fingers with kisses.

"And I'm going to stay that way." His breath was an

erotic whisper against her ear. He tugged her even closer, stroking his long hair-roughened legs along her smooth curvy limbs.

Through the haze of sexual pleasures, a spark of reality intruded. It was dawn and Washington was always in the galley, preparing food for the day's meals. There weren't any sounds coming from there now. "What did you do with Washington and Siobhan?"

He mumbled, "I locked them in the front car. I wanted you all to myself."

Inching away from Drake, she caught her robe in her hand and sat on the edge of the bed.

"You're not going anywhere," he grumbled, sliding close to her and grabbing her around the waist.

"But this is Washington and Siobhan's home. They can't have spent a comfortable night up there."

"They can wait."

"Drake Lassiter! How can you be so unconcerned for their welfare?"

"In a few minutes. I'm only thinking about you and how I just want to hold you a little longer before the day intrudes." He eased his hold on her and lifted his hand to her right breast. "Come back to bed, sweetheart." His casual stroking left her breathless. His touches could still disorient her this morning after making love most of the night. Just the thought of how they had loved found her body awash with a sexual flush.

She couldn't deny his request. She was sure Washington could make himself comfortable for at least another hour or so. And Siobhan would understand.

She dropped her wrapper on the floor. Looking back at him sprawled on the bed roused her passion, but touching him sent a raw sensuousness into her being. When she looked into his eyes, she recognized his kindred response to her explorations.

"You don't give a man time to gather his strength."

"Oh, I think you're doing just fine," she whispered close

to his ear. She slid her hand higher on his rock-hard thigh, teasing him with short forays toward the hardening flesh between his legs.

The noise of the train whistle jarred her for a moment. Even with Drake's heated body pressed against her back, she still felt a chill down her spine at the shrill and lonely sound. Her hand clenched against Drake's leg when the sound was joined with another eerier discord.

"What's wrong?" he asked, his palm resting on her knuckles.

"The sound. It's very disturbing."

"We're near Bitter Creek. The trains always slow down over the gorge. The pine timber trestle bridge groans a bit." He sat up next to her on the edge of the bed, their hands still touching.

The brakes squealed and the train swayed as it slowed to take the deep slope of the mountain range. Bottles on her dresser rattled and the doors to her wardrobe flew open, shoes and hats scattering on the floor. Moments later the car was moving at a normal pace again.

Drake smiled reassuringly. Letting go of her hand, he pulled her against him for a kiss just as the railcar jerked and tilted on a steep angle. The brakes and the steel undercarriage screeched, making an unearthly sound. Drake grabbed Georgiana's shoulders and held her as the bed started to break away from the wall and shift across the floor. Abruptly he jumped from the bed, pulling on his trousers.

"Get something on. Now."

As if to punctuate his words, the railcar screeched and twisted. Attempting to put on her nightgown and robe, Georgiana fell against the side of the bed. She screamed. Drake picked her up, threw on her robe, tied it at the waist and started moving with her to the door. Again the floor rocked under them and they were thrown against the wall near the doorway.

"Georgiana, hold on to my waist and don't let go," Drake

hollered to her over the clamorous sounds that surrounded them.

She locked her arms around his waist, tucking her head against his shoulder. One moment they were standing up against the wall, the next instant Drake slammed the door shut, locked it, and held on to the doorknob as the floor flipped over and became the ceiling. Her heart slamming against her chest, his heartbeats resonating through her body, they tumbled, the topsy-turvy movement of the car throwing them into the middle of the room and against the bed. When the railcar finally shuddered and screeched to a halt, the room's contents rained down on top of Drake and Georgiana.

Adrift in a deep dark tunnel, Drake heard someone screaming Georgiana's name. He opened his heavy eyelids and attempted to focus. Streams of the morning sun filtered through the gap in the roof of the car. Steam rose from the warm stove. Thank God there wasn't a newly set fire in it, they'd be in the middle of a fire, the flames destroying them. Dust and dirt mingled with the breeze that blew through the gaping hole. Through one of the broken windows he saw the grading embankment rise high above his vision. Nearby he heard the sound of rushing water.

Damn, they were at the bottom of the gorge!

Georgiana was pinned under him against the metal undercarriage of the railcar. Clearing his face of debris and pieces of the white counterpane from Georgiana's bed, he tentatively moved his arms and legs. Good, nothing broken. If he was in working order he could help Georgiana out from under the rubble that was piled high around them.

"Sweetheart. Open your eyes," he commanded in a harsh voice, fear taking the place of tenderness.

Her eyelids fluttered briefly and he held his breath until he saw her eyes. He wanted to howl at the moon when he saw the pain shadowed in them.

"Drake? What . . . happened?" She moved under him.

He picked up a lock of her hair and caressed it gently, then moved his hand to push the streaming mass back from her forehead, trying to calm her. "I don't know, sweetheart. Don't move yet. You know how I love to be on top of you, but . . ." He tried to keep her mind from the accident.

Next to her, free from debris, there was an open space where he could crawl, but he wasn't sure what would fall on top of her once he moved. He had to move her out from under him first.

"Sweetheart, can you move your head for me?"

She dropped her eyelids and opened them again, nodding her head just a fraction.

"Turn to your left. See that spot next to us?" She slowly turned her head and answered with a slight nod. "When I lift up off you I want you to roll out from under me over to that spot. Do you understand?"

He asked her again, for her eyelids kept fluttering. Did she understand? He must get her to safety. Above the car he could hear rocks and pebbles sliding down. For the first time since his childhood and his church-going days, he prayed. There must be people alive in the other cars who could come rescue them before it was too late. Until then he was responsible for her.

"When I say the word, roll out."

Adding another prayer he hoped that his shoulders' strength would be strong enough against the pile of wreckage. Drawing on energy and power that he'd never known he possessed, he planted his palms on the floor above Georgiana's shoulders and strained against the weight on top of him. Metal clanged, wood cracked and glass shattered and tinkled. Georgiana's eyes flew open and she stared at him, a scream stuck in her throat.

"Now!" he shouted at her.

With his last ounce of stamina, he held himself up above her while she attempted to roll away. Unable to move, she whimpered in pain. He pushed her over with one arm, then eased down flat against the floor again. He was still a prisoner. Thank God Georgiana was clear.

She turned her head, her gaze warm and loving. She grimaced in pain when she lifted her hand and touched his cheek, wiping away a trickle of moisture and blood that had collected there. "My Atlas holding up the world," she whispered and dropped her hand.

When her breathing grew heavy and she didn't move, he yelled, "Georgiana!" until his throat was raw and dry and only a raspy whisper escaped.

Above where the railcar had tumbled down the steep incline he heard another voice calling clearly. "Georgiana!" Then he heard someone call his name. "Drake! Where are you?" Could it be Siobhan's voice? Or was he hallucinating?

"In here." He closed his eyes, relief flooding him. He shouted and then found a piece of wood and started banging on the exposed metal, hoping they would hear the noise. "Hurry!"

Georgiana awoke from her terrible nightmare. In it their train was falling down a deep gorge. Drake held her hand while he stroked her head with his other palm. *Just like in Siobhan's vision.* But there was something wrong. His eyes were closed, his face stark, frozen in some sort of macabre mask. The room was lighted with a small lamp in the corner.

Everything seemed normal. She could feel the movement of the train through the floor under her bed. They'd been making love but then . . .

She fought through the cloud that covered her mind. Nightmares. A train wreck. Drake lifting the world to save her. She was confused.

"Drake," she rasped, her voice a weak and tremulous whisper.

He opened his dark eyes, a relieved expression on his face.

"Thank God! You're finally awake."

"Where . . . What happened . . . ?" *Why can't I speak coherently? I'm floating. My limbs are like lead weights. What is wrong with me?*

"A train wreck." He calmly stroked his hand across her forehead and down along the smooth skin on her cheekbone. "Thomas Durant sent another car and I'm taking you to Omaha for medical treatment." But as he spoke, telling her of the accident, his hands moved down to her shoulders. "Try to move your legs, Georgiana. Take it easy. The doctor had to drug you because of the pain. You've been in and out of consciousness for the last two days." His grasp was hard, his voice raspy and tight. She could feel his anger flow like a tidal wave through his fingers.

Train wreck? Drugs? Two days? She fought through the cobwebs of her cotton-filled sleep. Why couldn't she remember what had happened? She attempted to move her legs and discovered they were useless.

"Drake." She grasped his hands. "I can't move my legs." She sought to prove her words, tugging her hands from his to run them along the length of her legs.

Gently he touched her chin, lifting her face for his perusal. She studied him as well, noting the strain in the lines around his mouth and eyes. His hair was disheveled. He wore a two-day stubble. And the light had gone out in his eyes. They were darkened with an unfamiliar emotion that made her shiver.

"You'll be fine. I'll take care of you." He repeated those words like a litany as he took her in his arms, rocking her back and forth.

CHAPTER 13

Omaha, Nebraska
Sounding like the wail of a lonesome coyote, the far off train whistle roused Drake. The little bit of light in the bedroom enabled him to read the time on the pillar and scroll shelf clock on the wall. It was 6:00 A.M. in Georgiana's hospital room in Omaha. He'd been by her side both day and night until fatigue had finally won out, pushing him into sleep. She rested peacefully now, but for the past twenty-four hours she'd been in and out of consciousness, sedated most of the time with laudanum for the pain in her legs. Yet even in sleep she clung to his hand.

His own body felt battered and weary, his strength and endurance tested when he'd pushed himself up against the wreckage in the railroad car. His back was as twisted as the iron rails that had fallen on top of their car from sitting in the uncomfortable chair all night. Stitches might pull at the skin on his shoulder, the resulting scar might be a constant reminder of their terrible ordeal, but his real pain lay in the thought of how close he'd come to losing Georgiana. After the accident the doctor had sewn him up and sent him on his way. Drake had refused pain medication, for how could he have accepted a few hours of oblivion when

Georgiana lay in a tent, unable to move her legs as they waited for another car to transport her to Omaha for medical care?

Gazing at Georgiana as she lay broken and pale, Drake felt utterly miserable because the coupling on the private car had been defective. That, along with the weakened guylines on the bridge, had caused the wreck. *Dammit! It's my fault. I was too late in sending telegrams to the foremen to recheck the bridges.* How could this have happened to his beautiful princess? Why did she have to be the one to be injured and in pain?

He grew angry thinking of her never walking again. His despair was like a shroud over the sun, icy and dark—unlike the times he had basked in Georgiana's glorious sunshine. There must be something he could do. There must be a way.

Drake closed the door to Georgiana's hospital room. Unseeing, he stared past the people as they walked up and down the hallway.

"How is she this morning?"

Drake turned to find Siobhan standing against the opposite wall of the corridor, her arms piled high with packages. She looked too calm to be a miracle worker.

If Georgiana was alive, it was because Siobhan and Washington had organized railroad workers and passengers in the undamaged cars to help locate them. After hours of digging through the wreckage, they'd brought them to higher ground on the other side of the trestle.

The last few days he'd stayed by Georgiana's bedside, hoping for her sweet, sunny and warm personality to show itself. But she was hidden behind a cloud bank too deep and too high for him to climb over.

"About the same," he finally answered Siobhan. "She was restless through the night, but she's resting peacefully now. She won't see the specialist Thomas Durant has sent to examine her. She won't eat the food sent to her. She won't . . ." His gaze lowered as did his voice. He washed his palm over his face, feeling the heavy growth of stubble. He hadn't been to his hotel room for more than thirty-six hours.

"Why don't you go clean up, eat something and get some sleep? I'll stay with her until you return." When he hesitated, she chided him. "Go ahead. You can't help her if you're lying in a hospital bed, too. Do you wish to scare her when she awakens?"

"Thank you for being her friend. And for being mine," he said, his voice, though deep, was crisp and clear. Siobhan touched his forearm; he rested his palm over her hand.

Her eyes caught and held his. "What blarney is this? Thanking me for friendship? I've never heard such nonsense." Then she gave him a conspiratorial wink. "Go on with you."

He managed to shrug and say offhandedly, "All right. But I'll be back before dark." A raw and primitive grief almost overwhelmed him. "She has too many nightmares at night."

Siobhan squeezed her eyelids tightly. "Then she'll need all your strength. Go rest." She shooed him down the hallway, stood up straighter and opened the door.

"Go away. I don't want to see anyone." With a grim expression, Georgiana turned her head away from the door.

"But I'm not anyone," Siobhan admonished her, setting her packages on a set of pine side chairs by the door.

Seeing the rumpled bedding, Siobhan worked her way around the bed. She held Georgiana's back while she smoothed out the sheets, fluffed her pillows and tucked the coverlet in around the mattress.

"Now. Isn't that more comfortable?" Siobhan asked. "Aren't you interested in what I've brought with me?" She gazed back over her shoulder at the neat pile of small boxes on the table. "The workers found some of your personal items when they salvaged the railcar."

Georgiana studied the walnut table, her breath coming out in a harsh, uneven rhythm. "My cross-stitching box?" Slowly she sat higher in the bed.

"Yes. It's a miracle. There're also a few newspapers to read, a box of chocolates, a number of telegrams—"

"The box," she interrupted with a quick intake of breath, holding her hand out.

Georgiana accepted the Morocco case, her heavy lashes closing as tightly as her fingers on the rich wood. When she opened her eyes, her hands trembled. The lock was still intact. Evidently its ride through the train wreck had been a smooth one. Unlike her own.

She unlocked the lid, lifted it and was momentarily speechless with surprise. Touching the piece of cross-stitching, she dug deeper within the material's folds against the silk and velvet lining. "They're safe . . ." her voice broke in mid-sentence. "They're safe," she repeated.

She clenched her sewing and the diamond and ruby brooch in her fist and dropped her hand against her heart. Until now she had been unwilling to cry over her affliction. Clutching the keepsakes of the two most important men in her life, she felt her heart near to bursting.

Georgiana heard the scrape of a chair next to her bed. A tense silence enveloped the room as she sought to erect a wall of defense against Siobhan. She rubbed her hands up and down her legs, praying she would feel the pressure or that she would feel something when she pinched herself.

She felt some pain, exactly what the doctors had told her to expect. If there was pain, they said, then eventually there might be feeling and movement. But now her limbs were dead. And her heart and soul were within a breath of dying along with her legs. Drake was her dream, her love, her strength, yet every time he entered her room, the shadows of fear in his dark eyes frightened her. The tight knot within her begged for release.

"I want to rest alone. Don't stay with me, Siobhan."

"And where would I be going? You tell me. If I was in that bed would you leave? Would you let me shout at you and break your heart? God in heaven, would you?" Georgiana knew she would break down at any moment, but she was able to hold a firm control on her emotions.

"Don't . . ." Georgiana spoke, her voice calmer than she had anticipated after lying in bed full of dread for so many days. "You're right. I would never leave you if you were hurt."

Siobhan lifted a happier face to Georgiana and nodded. "Then let's stop feeling sorry for ourselves. You're a businesswoman. Add up the assets and liabilities and then let's determine what we can work with," Siobhan said.

"The doctors—"

"Yes, yes, I know what the doctors have said about your injuries. There is a very slim chance you may walk. Durant wants you to be examined by a specialist." Poised now with determination, Siobhan robbed Georgiana of the material and brooch, put them back for safekeeping in the case and walked around the small stuffy room, pushing back the heavy curtains that kept out the light. Omaha's bright spring day blazed through the windows. "Now, if it was me in that bed, I'd want to do everything possible to be able to get up in the morning and walk away from it."

"I'm afraid."

"Of what?"

"Of not being able to walk again. Of becoming a cripple like my mother. I watched how everyone pitied her . . . and those who loved her cared for her. I *won't* be a burden to Drake. I can't risk him ever looking at me with pity. What will I do if Drake ever looks at me like that?"

Siobhan had never seen Georgiana in such a state. Even after they had lost John she had pulled herself together and personally taken care of the funeral arrangements. But the young woman's lower lip trembled, her cheeks flushed against the ghostly pale color of her skin. She had dark purple smudges under her eyes. Her hair was dull and lifeless. She was a shadow of the vibrant young woman Siobhan had always respected and admired.

"We aren't certain you're going to be an invalid. And

worrying about it won't help a bit anyhow. Let me help you with your toilette and fix your hair. You'll feel better. I sent Drake to the hotel to rest a bit. You want to be pretty when he returns. There's a new nightgown and wrapper in one of these packages. It's blue, your favorite color."

Georgiana dropped her eyelids and nodded slowly. "I love him so much, Siobhan. What am I going to do? He asked me to marry him before the accident. I can't. Not now. Not like this."

"By all that is holy, what am I going to do with you?" Siobhan grabbed Georgiana by the shoulders, glared into her eyes and shook her gently. "John Radcliffe, may God rest his soul, asked me to take care of you if anything happened to him. His request was never an imposition because you're like one of my sisters." She tightened her grip and forced Georgiana's wayward gaze back to her face. "But if you allow this adversity to destroy what is good and gentle and wonderful in you, I'll have no choice but to walk away."

Please, God. Don't let Georgiana know how much I'm trembling or that I've lied about leaving her.

Without waiting for Georgiana's recriminations, Siobhan pushed up the sleeves on her linen blouse and went to work.

As the sun set over the river, Drake walked along the hospital corridor, his nerves calmer after a good meal, a bath and a few hours sleep.

He opened the door and eased into the room. While Georgiana worked on her cross-stitching, Siobhan sat next to her pouring tea. The British and their damn tea parties! But the ritual was a godsend. This was not the same woman he'd left this morning, comatose and pale.

"Drake," Georgiana said, her voice sounding startled.

"The specialist examined Georgiana this afternoon," Siobhan spoke, lifting her head from her task.

Georgiana tucked the sewing into the box, eyeing him cautiously as Siobhan kept up the conversation, offering her chair to Drake and pouring him a cup of tea. "He was very encouraging. Wasn't he, Georgie?"

He closed to Georgiana's side of the bed and saw that her eyes were remote, unlike the night before their accident. Then she had been a loving creature of the night, making him forget that he was a bastard who should walk away and never touch her again.

"He told me it would take time. If I rest and take care of myself. Maybe I'll—"

"Exactly what I thought," he interjected. There was no maybe in his thoughts about her walking. The important word was *when* not if. She would walk again. He jumped to his feet, almost spilling the tea. "I checked with the staff and you'll be discharged tomorrow. I've rented a suite at the Herndon House for you and Siobhan."

"Drake, I don't know . . ." Georgiana started to object in a weak voice.

"Don't shut me out, sweetheart."

Drake set the saucer on the nearest table and seized her hand, hoping that she would gather some strength from his own. He heard the door close silently and realized Siobhan had left them alone. He couldn't stop looking at Georgiana. Her skin was translucent—a freckle or two showed on the bridge of her nose from being out in the sun. Her eyes were dull pools of blue, her lips parted in surprise. Her appearance chilled him: Where was his vibrant princess? Right now he needed the warmth of one of her smiles.

"Drake, I'm tired." Her voice dropped off. Her chin spilled to her chest and her eyelids fluttered a few times before closing over her haunted eyes. He waited guiltily for a few minutes to see if she had any discomfort, but she slept peacefully.

All he wanted to do was to take her in his arms and hold her. He paced the room, but he always came back to her side. Her covers needed attention and instead of calling Siobhan, he stood over Georgiana and tucked in the counterpane.

His knuckle grazed a box against her side. She stirred, but did not waken. He pulled the case out and found a spot on the tabletop. His hands touched the lid and lifted it. Her cross-stitching! Intrigued at the skeins of threads woven through the material, he turned it over.

His hands shook. It was the piece of work he'd seen in her bedroom the day the doctor told him he could go back to work. The colors of the fiery bonfires and the trees had been completed. But what affected him the most was staring at his likeness: the hair was dark with a widow's peak, the deep-set eyes gray, a strong chin, angular bones in the face . . . her detail was perfect. He tightened his hold on his response, his legs as soft as an old pair of leather chaps.

She'd been too distant since the accident, saying she was tired when he'd entered her room. She'd been enjoying a tea party with Siobhan. *Georgiana, you're a fool. A fake. And the most wonderful woman in the world.*

He would bide his time, for she needed to heal. And he would be by her side. Sooner or later, regardless of her health or her disability, he'd ask her again to marry him. He had no choice. Without Georgiana in his life, there was no sunshine.

Drake turned the key in the lock and opened the door to Georgiana's hotel suite. For the first time since her discharge from the hospital, he'd missed supper with her and now the rooms were quiet at this late hour. Because of the accident and Georgiana's hospitalization, he'd taken a short leave from his duties with the Union Pacific. Once he'd ensconced her in the hotel, he'd paid a daily visit to an office that had been loaned to him. Caught up in reading the reports sent to him from Superintendent Reed and noting any changes to be sent back to the end-of-track, he'd forgotten the hour.

Running his hand across the back of his stiff neck, he couldn't leave behind the disturbing news in one of the dispatches. Hardy had disappeared. Telegrams had been sent

NIGHT TRAIN

out to all the line foremen between here and Bear River City, but no one had seen his partner. Drake would bet his best Stetson that Beeton had something to do with Hardy's disappearance.

Damn! He couldn't leave Georgiana now and search for his friend. She still was experiencing too much pain in her legs. Most nights he stayed with her, watching over her, praying for her recovery and his own salvation.

A lamp burned brightly enough to show him the way across the sitting room. Once near Georgiana's room, he slipped out of his waistcoat and hung it on the chair next to her door. He worked off the shirt's cuffs, pulled at the collar, and lay the stiff pieces on the cushion.

He breathed deeply, expanding his lungs and purging his mind of the clutter of his daily activities. He needed all of his faculties to grapple with his growing fears that Georgiana wasn't getting better. Siobhan's door opened and Drake turned to greet her. She shushed him and beckoned him across the room with her index finger.

"How is she?" he whispered, fear grinding inside his belly.

"The same. She missed you at supper," she softly rebuked him.

"There was a pile of dispatches on my desk..." His words drifted off. He didn't want to tell her Hardy was missing and worry her needlessly.

"Are you planning to sit with her again all night?" Her face was full of strength, shining with a steadfast and serene peace. "You're the only one who can keep those nightmares of the wreck at bay for her."

You know as well as I that I don't sit with her, Siobhan. I hold her all night long.

"I won't leave her alone," he promised with quiet assurance.

Drake cracked the door to Georgiana's bedroom and slipped in. The curtains on the French doors were pulled back, the moonlight illuminating her as she lay in a half-tester canopy bed with a pure white counterpane. He walked to her side, his expression grim.

Her face was still paler than normal but a subtle splash of pink tinted her cheeks and her forehead, perhaps a sign that she was getting better and this ordeal would soon be behind them. Her affliction affected him equally. He'd awakened too many nights with phantom pains in his own legs.

Her even breaths softly escaped her lips. For a moment his heart pitched convulsively when she turned her head and moaned in her sleep, the sound reminding him of the intimate sounds she made when he held her in his arms. Tricks. That's what his mind was playing with him.

He removed his clothing—all but his trousers—and slipped in beside her, his arms gathering her against him, her body instinctively curving against the hard planes of his body. He rested his head on the pillows, preoccupied with her provocative scent that clung to the sheets. He closed his eyes, savoring the wonderful fragrance of wildflowers he'd come to recognize as her essence.

He wasn't aware he'd fallen asleep until he heard her whimpers for help as she wrapped her arms around his waist, pulling closer and closer to him. He placed his lips close to her ear and whispered words of comfort and love, warding off the trembling from her nightmares.

Her eyes flew open, misty and terror-filled.

"Sweetheart, you're safe. I'll help you. Nothing is going to ever hurt you again." He held her, his heartbeats slamming against his chest, beseeching her to trust him. "Nothing."

"A dream. Car . . . twisted . . . afraid . . . tumbling." She gulped some air, lifted her chin and offered a tremulous smile. "Then you appeared."

"Remember you called me your cavalier. I'll always be here for you." He kissed her forehead, smoothing the twisted strands of hair back from her eyes. *Even if you don't want me once you learn I'm a bastard, I'll always love and protect you.*

Georgiana didn't want to move. Drake's touch had a definite calming effect. Her breathing settled into a simple rhythm as she cuddled into his loving embrace. For a long time he just held her, soothing her with words and light kisses on her forehead, cheek, eyelids.

But that lull was ruptured when pain radiated from the end of her spine down both her legs. Biting down on her bottom lip until she felt the coppery taste of blood, she held out as long as possible before she sobbed out with pain.

"Do you want your laudanum?"

"No!" she almost shrieked. "I don't like losing control of my faculties. And the drug makes me stick to my stomach."

"I know, sweetheart." His expression stilled and grew serious. "I've got another idea that will help."

He quickly withdrew from her arms, moved out the bedroom door and returned with a small jar of balm that the doctor had given her to use on her legs to keep them supple. Slowly so as not to jerk her body, he turned her on her stomach and tossed the pillows aside as if they were balloons dashed about by the wind.

The pain halted for a moment as did her breathing when he lifted the hem of her simple linen nightgown, eased her hips away from the material, and tucked it above her waist. When he sat on the edge of the bed, she could hear his labored breathing as if he had run up the four flights of steps to the top floor of the hotel. She stole a glance at him. His eyes were deep and dark, the color of iron rails across the plains. Briefly she thought she sensed the fragrance of the prairie wind but it was only the scent of him.

"This will help," he confided to her when he knelt next to her and leaned over her back.

His touch was warm, strong and very familiar as he massaged the area on both sides of her spine just above the injury site, kneading his knuckles into the muscles and rubbing gently with his palms. She was astonished at the sense of peace flowing from Drake's roughened hands to her sensitive skin. Sensations burst throughout her body. Though she was unable to move her legs she could sense when his palms massaged up and down each calf, soothing the knots in her tight muscles.

She was not just naked; she was weak and vulnerable to his touch.

"Mmmmmm," she sighed when he progressed up her spine again, his large palms splaying out across her entire back, his thumbs exerting gentle pressure on certain spots. She was melting into the soft mattress.

"Feel good? I hope so, sweetheart. I can't stop touching you," he growled against her earlobe, his long fingers gently grazing the plump underside of her breasts.

Another moan escaped and without warming, he slowly flipped her over onto her back, his hands cupping her breasts. Then he ran his thumbs deliciously up and down her nipples. Even in her present condition his appeal was devastating. The lusty look in his eyes pronounced he was having no difficulty making love to an invalid.

She eyed him closely. The idea of his eagerness excited her, yet the thought that she could not be the lover that he desired left her bereft. The pain blended with loneliness and bitterness when she thought of being confined to an invalid's chair for the rest of her life.

She looked at him, disoriented. Tears pooled in her eyes and without any control over her emotions she wept.

Confused at her outbreak, Drake dropped down on the bed beside her and pulled her into his arms. She heard his voice, muted and sharp at the same time as he planted kisses on her cheeks and forehead, his soft caresses disturbing yet exciting.

"I'm sorry, sweetheart. You're beautiful and I want you so badly."

He whispered roughly that her disability didn't matter. They would find a way to share the joy of an intimate relationship. He continued to kiss her, his hungry caresses spiraling out of control. The physical pain, her constant companion, tormented her. Now it was compounded with her

NIGHT TRAIN

rising desire to consummate their lovemaking, but knowing in her condition she could not. What had begun minutes ago as a therapeutic massage had turned into a bewildering emotional strain.

"I can't, Drake," she cried out just as his lips pressed against her mouth.

"All right." He drew away from her, his stare intense in the dark room, the only light the moonbeams floating across the center of her bed. "Are you in pain again?"

Yes! My heart aches for us, she thought. She shook her head in answer, that little bit of movement making her head swirl with doubts. She needed more time to erase the mental bruising. She shriveled a little at his grave expression of concern. Instead of love, uneasiness shadowed his depths now. Once more she had to ask the question—could their love survive her disability?

"Then you need to sleep. I'll stay and hold you."

Without the strength to argue, and exhausted from her emotional upheaval, she lay quietly on her side as he gathered her in his arms, her mind knowing it was time to make a decision. Staying in America only offered heartache. For her and Drake.

The heat of Drake's body coursed down the entire length of hers as she fell asleep in his arms. If only that warmth would seep into her heart where a massive piece of ice had taken hold.

Thankfully, when Georgiana awoke early the next morning Drake was not in bed. He had told her he did not want Siobhan to discover him sleeping with her. As if Siobhan didn't know what was going on in the other bedroom of the suite. Still, she thought he was lovable and sweet for thinking about her reputation.

"Good, you're awake." Siobhan charged into the room. "Are you ready for breakfast?"

"My mouth is watering for a big slice of Washington's cornbread. I miss him."

"If you're wishing for food you must be feeling better this morning?"

"Yes. I am. I have a purpose again in life."

"And what would that be?"

"I've decided to leave America. We'll have to cancel the trip to Suez. It doesn't matter anymore. I've decided to place the additional investment in the Union Pacific. I don't think it will be more than a few weeks before the rails are joined."

"That's fine. Are you going to tell me the real reason we're running away?"

"You're supposed to be my companion, not my mother."

"I've had to be both. You can get away with lying to me but don't lie to yourself."

"I won't allow Drake to throw away his life looking after an invalid."

"Well, now that's interesting. In all the conversations I've had with the man, he never once mentioned that he resented being with you. Quite the contrary. He loves you, Georgie. What do you think he'll do when he finds out you're leaving?"

"He's not going to know when I leave."

Dr. Joseph Carroll, the specialist Durant had brought in from St. Louis, shook his head in exasperation when Georgiana asked him about traveling to England. The tall thin man with white hair and a pleasant smile looked at her askance.

"Young woman." He tore his spectacles from his face and stared down at her, his face puckered in annoyance. "If you insist upon this arduous journey at this time during your recuperation, I can say most assuredly that you will never walk again. You must allow the compression in your spine to heal."

"But what about the pain?"

"That is a good sign. Where there is pain there is feeling."

She had to agree, for last night she'd detected some sensations in her legs when Drake had massaged her calves.

That had been the first time since her accident. Maybe there was hope that she would walk again.

"Yes, Doctor. Only last night I could feel . . ."

She couldn't blurt out that Drake's gentle touch had proved to her there might be hope that she would walk again. Until the day she could walk into his arms without any assistance, she needed time away from his influence. But if she couldn't go home to England where could she find a retreat away from Drake and the conflicting emotions that continued to baffle and bewilder her?

CHAPTER 14

Georgiana watched Drake drag his fingertips gently over the Morocco box, her opal earbobs, a single black leather glove and an assortment of bottles and a vase, the items neatly arranged on the rosewood bureau's marble top. The sight of his calloused, dark-skinned fingers fondling her delicate personal belongings left her light-headed. So many times those strong hands had passionately seduced and sometimes playfully coaxed impassioned responses from her that she hadn't realized were within her.

When he raised his chin, his reflection in the looking glass stunned her. She knew he was determined, forceful, even arrogant on occasion, but his appearance since their accident was of a man at odds with himself and the world around him. As in the days after he'd been shot, he now acted like a caged animal in need of his freedom. He hadn't dealt very well with being away from his work with the railroad then and now he was affected similarly.

"Congress has settled on Promontory Point, Utah Territory, for the meeting of the rails," he blurted out, twisting quickly toward her, his words magically coinciding with her very thoughts.

Talk of the railroad cleared the shadows of doubt from his

face, replacing his features with animation. His voice held a vibrancy she hadn't heard since before her accident. In days past he'd been like a roped steer waiting to be branded. She watched in fascination when he knocked over a small opaque white glass vase with his large hand and then motionlessly stood it back up, unbroken. He was a big man, a man of the wide-open plains, but she had never noticed until now how out of place he was in a room cluttered with women's bric-a-brac. He most certainly had something on his mind.

"You're needed there. When are you leaving?" she asked cautiously.

He pulled a mahogany side chair with an ivory and gold cushion close to the bed and straddled it. His eyes had a burning, faraway look in them. His heart might be here with her but his soul was nine hundred and ninety five miles west of Omaha. Her heart fluttered wildly in her breast. His nearness was overwhelming. He was so very good-looking, the span of his shoulders and the length of his thighs accentuated by his gray waistcoat and black trousers. Cloaked in the trappings of civilization, he was still the strong, powerful frontiersman with whom she had fallen in love.

"I won't leave you." For an instant his glance sharpened, then grew gentle and contemplative. "You're very important to me, Georgiana." For emphasis he leaned over the chair's back, gently grasped her chin between his thumb and index finger and kissed her lips.

She wanted to melt into his arms, but had to fight her own battle of restraint. If her injuries did not heal she would be an invalid the rest of her life. Mastery of the limits imposed on her by her physical condition would encompass her entire life. She couldn't see beyond that.

The probable destruction of her own independence was terrible, but how could she ask Drake to sacrifice his freedom by attending to every whim of her confinement. It would kill his spirit.

Looking at him, she felt an aching sense of loss. She

NIGHT TRAIN 199

wanted to ride side by side with him on the plains, her hair unencumbered and tossed about by the wind. She wanted to enjoy another picnic and run through the tall prairie grass without shoes, to dance the night away under an ebony sky with only the dazzling light of the moon and stars to guide them. Then they could go back to the cave so she might teach him so many things about the woman who loved him.

She wanted to give him children.

She yearned for all those things, but she could not chain such a virile man to a wife unable to walk.

She'd been worried about how to divert his attentions from her and her condition. She had the tools at hand. The railroad was his life.

"Thomas must want you back immediately."

His gray eyes darkened to the color of slate as he held her gaze. "I sent him a telegram when the accident happened. He's aware of my other responsibilities."

"Don't do this, Drake. At the end-of-track is where you belong. You can't give up your dream of finishing the railroad because of my accident."

He leapt to his feet. He came close, looking down at her intensely. "How the hell do you think I could do my job? I'd worry about you night and day." His voice sounded tired. His strong jaw looked fragile. For a moment, his shoulders sagged.

Seeing a man such as Drake Lassiter reduced to this tore her apart, yet she was so close to breaking down and asking him to stay. Without him how would she get through the long days? The lonely nights? He had shared his strength with her when she had been near exhaustion. As weak as she had become when her feelings for Drake were in jeopardy, how could she influence him to walk out of her hotel room and take the first train westward?

His dream of building the transcontinental railroad was his life. She was quite familiar with men with visions and destinies to fulfill.

"Drake. You can't quit. The men I have known—my

father and Thomas Brassey—they never shied away from their duties or a challenge. You've walked in their footsteps. Don't falter now. You're so close to the end of your journey."

Suddenly she found him sitting on the edge of her bed, the heat of his body enveloping her. He leaned toward her, exhaling with agitation. She returned his glare.

"Why?" He took a moment to catch his breath. "Why are you so intent on me leaving? I know there's another reason you want me to go. Have you learned about my family in New York?" He sighed heavily, his voice filled with anguish. "Is that why you're getting rid of me? You found you can no longer love me?"

She looked away, knowing no more about his life in New York than what he'd told her before the accident, yet something in his tone indicated that here was the way she could convince him to leave. "I need time to think Drake. Surely you can grant me that."

"You want to be alone?"

"You have forgotten that I have Siobhan with me and Thomas has asked me if he could send Washington to help out if necessary. Siobhan thinks it a wonderful idea to have Washington prepare my meals and help with the chores. Dr. Carroll says I'm doing well. I don't have as much pain. And I am sleeping much better at night." *Stop babbling! He'll see through your lies. God, forgive me for telling him Washington is coming.*

His expression was like someone who had been struck in the face. Silent a moment while he stared at her, he finally sighed and said, "All right. I won't fight you. But I'll be gone no more than a week. Promise me you won't go back to England. I won't leave you without knowing you'll be here when I return."

Thank God, he didn't ask for a promise not to leave Omaha!

He took her hands in his, turning them over to place a kiss in the center of each palm. Crushing her hair at the nape of her neck, he pressed his lips to hers, the kiss like the soldering heat that joins metals.

"Do you promise?" His soft breath puffed against the tiny wisps of hair around her ear. "You won't leave?"

His lips brushed her brow tenderly while she cuddled close to him for what could be the last time. Grabbing at his muscled forearms so hard that she creased the black wool coat, she knew if she lifted her head she'd break down in tears. Her lips moved quietly, telling him she loved him, but when he pressed her again for her promise she had to answer his demand.

Nodding her reply, she whispered, "Yes." She clung to him, her balance tenuous for she was buffeted by emotional currents as strong as the warm, dry chinook winds of the plains. But that couldn't be. Her heart felt like a large chip of ice.

After a long and troubled night of soul searching, Georgiana asked Siobhan to sit with her. She refused to be tied to her bed indefinitely. Other arrangements would need to be made.

"Doctor Carroll suggested that I purchase an invalid's chair. At first I said no, but the hotel suite is large enough for me to move around in it. That way I won't be dependent upon you every hour of the day."

"That's never been a problem." Siobhan's face lit with a big smile. "But I was waiting for you to fight back."

"We must find someplace for me to recuperate."

"Not England. The doctor said a long trip was out of the question."

"I know. We must find something closer."

"Yet far away from Drake." It was a statement, not a question.

"Oh, Siobhan, can't you see it must be this way?"

Siobhan stood, then moved the chair with the ivory and gold cushion—the one that Drake had straddled yesterday—

back against the wall. "When do you want your massage?" Siobhan asked.

Something else to remind me of Drake, Georgiana agonized, telling Siobhan she could begin her treatment immediately. The activity would help her relax. Something she had been unfamiliar with since her accident.

With her massage completed, Georgiana felt like taking a nap and not up to the adventure that Siobhan had planned for the rest of the afternoon. Attempting to shake off the lethargy that flowed through her upper body, she refinished buttoning her linen blouse when she heard the sound of boot heels in the sitting room. Drake! But she thought he had left for Utah on this morning's train. But when Lawrence walked through her bedroom doorway, she took a quick breath of utter astonishment.

"Lawrence!" She drew in a sharp breath. "My God, where did you come from? You left the train in Green River without any word."

"I had to attend to some personal business." His expression was grim as he watched her. "I didn't mean to alarm you." He took a few steps closer to her and studied her thoughtfully for a moment. "Is Lassiter here?"

"No, he's gone."

Briefly Lawrence's eyes widened, surprise and then relief touching his face. "Are you feeling unwell, my dear? You're very pale."

"I'm better now. The doctors are more encouraging now than immediately after the train crash."

"What are you talking about?" His dark eyes pierced the distance between them.

She realized he mustn't have heard about her accident. "My railcar was destroyed."

"Good God! How?"

He tossed his tall black hat onto the marble-topped bureau, tipping over and breaking the opaque white glass vase that Drake had so gently picked up and replaced only yesterday. Drake had always treated her and her personal belongings with respect, while Lawrence cared only for himself.

"A trestle over Bitter Creek gave way. Durant's car and the caboose were the only pieces of stock damaged."

He paced the room, staying clear of the doorway but continually shifting his gaze to that area as if expecting someone to walk in on them at any moment. Dressed in a frock coat with a black waistcoat, silk cravat and wide tubular trousers, Lawrence was de rigueur thousands of miles away from a society that encouraged extravagant clothing and unproductive lives. How unlike Drake's simple, everyday clothes of boots, trousers, cambric shirt and rawhide vest that allowed him the freedom to continue his worthwhile work.

"Where was your Mr. Lassiter during this whole episode?"

"He was in the car with me and pushed me to safety until the rescue workers could dig us out."

"The man is indestructible," he murmured satirically.

Strange and disquieting thoughts began to race through her mind. Did he wish Drake had died in the crash? It seemed an absurdity, yet she was still bewildered by his change in mood since he had entered her room. With all the planning that needed to be done to leave Omaha without Drake's knowledge, she crammed her concern over the two men's enmity into a corner of her mind.

"When are we leaving for home?" He finally halted his movements, standing over her at the side of the bed."

"I'm unable to travel that distance."

"Then we'll go to my ranch. You can recuperate there. I'll make special travel arrangements for you. It's only two days by train to Cheyenne and then a short carriage ride outside of the city."

Her mouth dropped open. He was an ever-changing mystery, his solicitation about her well-being and convalescence almost heartwarming. She'd never seen this side of Lawrence. When she had made the decision to leave Omaha she had never once thought of Lawrence's ranch. But why not? It was close, yet far enough away and definitely not England. She had only promised Drake not to return to her home. Lawrence's ranch was the perfect solution until her condition stabilized or until she could walk into Drake's arms again.

"Are you sure your head wasn't injured instead of your legs?" Siobhan pranced around the room, her arms raised in supplication to the heavens. "You have lost your mind if you plan on going with Lawrence."

"It's the perfect opportunity for me to leave Omaha before Drake returns." Her hands shook when she mentioned Drake's name. How was she to persevere with her decision to allow Drake his freedom if the mere mention of his name provoked her body to rebellion? "It will only be until I can walk again. You'll be with me. Won't you?"

Siobhan whipped around and glared at her. "Just you try to go anywhere with that man without me by your side."

"He has offered me a retreat and has recently been a perfect gentleman."

"Maybe you can forgive him for his unfriendly antics but I don't trust the man. There's something about his eyes," Siobhan whispered, her fists tightly held at her side. "They always make me feel as if death is stalking me."

"I know in the past that you and Lawrence have had differences, but going to his ranch is the last resort. He's offered his hospitality and I am going to accept it temporarily."

"Then I'd better start packing for the trip." Siobhan offered a forgiving smile and began to empty a few of the bureau drawers.

Drake looked down over the town of Echo City, Utah, that had been a small Mormon farming community until the arrival of the railroad. For many years, stagecoaches had made this a regular stop and even a pony express station—a stone building—still stood at the foot of Pulpit Rock.

Riding past a sod-roofed homestead with five women tending the garden and feeding the animals, he shook his head in wonder. How could one man live with five wives? Most men had a problem finding and keeping one woman happy.

He'd found the woman with whom he would spend the rest of his life, but their happiness was jeopardized because of her foolhardy determination not to saddle him with an invalid. She had gotten the thought into her mind that if her legs were permanently paralyzed he would only pity her. Damn fool woman! He didn't fall in love with her because of her legs. He loved her because for the first time in eight years he felt whole and alive.

Drake hunkered down next to the rails, his palm resting on the warm surface. He felt the vibrancy and the passion flow through his hands much like when his hands caressed Georgiana's supple skin.

He looked off into the distance, the locomotive but a dot on the horizon, miles from the city. Yet the vibration of the rails of the westbound train was a reminder that Georgiana was at the other end of those tracks, nearly a thousand miles away. For the first time since coming West four years ago, his eyes strayed eastward. Back to the woman he loved.

Georgiana, whether you walk or not, when I return to Omaha you're going to agree to marry me.

Climbing atop Jake, Drake allowed the stallion his head, the horse eager to race with the powerful locomotive. Drake rode into camp northeast of Great Salt Lake, a long, slate-blue streak against the distant horizon that was covered by immense flocks of wild geese and ducks. Swans mingled among the thousands of birds, their white plumage giving the impression of snow-capped ice floating on the water.

The Union Pacific's "Big Trestle" was in progress. He'd heard from some of the men in Echo City that Leonard Eicholtz, their bridge engineer, had been ordered to build the four-hundred-and-five-foot span across the ravine immediately east of Promontory Point through the black lime.

After dismounting, a short walk among the men filled him in on what he'd missed since the accident. He then joined the tall, dark-headed Samuel Reed, the Union Pacific's general superintendent of construction as he stood near the parallel grading where both work crews cut across the far side of the ravine.

"Sam. How goes the war?"

"It's hell as usual, Lassiter. Great news, though. All the track work has been done. We only have one serious obstacle left." Reed jerked his head toward the problem area as they shook hands. "I heard you were in Omaha. I was sorry to hear about Miss Radcliffe's injuries in the wreck."

"Thanks, Sam. She's lucky to be alive, but she's recuperating nicely." *Or she will be when I can hightail it back to her.*

"While I was writing my wife about the decision to build the 'Big Trestle,' I told her of Miss Radcliffe's terrible crash." Reed was known among his crew as being devoted to his wife and rumors always abounded about what he had written in his "Dear Jennie" letter this week. Now Drake knew Georgiana had been his topic of discussion.

"How long will it take Leonard to complete the bridge?"

"About fifteen days."

"You can't build a bridge that long and that high in such a short period of time. It's ludicrous. And damn unsafe." Drake's voice hardened; he was madder than hell about the way the railroad was building bridges.

"I understand your concern, Lassiter. But the word has come down from the top. The bridge goes up. Crews will work day and night to complete it."

Drake stood aside, gazing from the east side of the Promontory Mountains and seeing the magnificent panoramic view of the Wasatch Mountains. In such a natural beauty how could anyone build a hazardous structure and allow human lives to be at risk? He swallowed hard. The question was a double-edged sword pointing directly back to him. For hadn't he had a similar conversation with Georgiana the day of their picnic? Then he'd been an unlovable, arrogant, bitter, hostile bastard with a single mission that controlled his life. He'd imagined that building the transcontinental railroad would help mend the deep wounds from the War. In some ways, it had accomplished the goal, for men from both sides had set aside guns and taken up picks, shovels and hammers to construct fourteen hundred miles of rail. Their accomplishment had changed the country forever.

Georgiana had warned him about the trestles, but because of his stubborn male pride, he had refused to take heed. Now he understood and sympathized with her concerns—though too late—but then he had thought she was interfering with his life's work.

He knew she loved him unequivocally, but would that feeling remain once she had the knowledge he had still withheld from her regarding his family?

"Looks like I'll need to stay a few days and keep watch on the progress on the 'Big Trestle.' I have an understanding with Eicholtz when it comes to extra timbers and guylines on his trestles."

"Are you sure you want to stay? Thomas told me you might not be back to finish the job. We'll do this trestle no differently than the others, Lassiter."

"Just to be safe, I'll stay awhile. I'm concerned about becoming a victim of one of our fine bridges again."

Reed never answered. A foreman reached him and needed orders for a work crew. Drake mounted Jake's back, forgetting the railroad and the chores associated with his job.

His mind was on only one thing. Dammit! He couldn't leave now and return to Omaha. Riding to the other side of the work camp to look for Eicholtz, Drake stopped just over the ridge, the sun disappearing behind a layer of clouds and throwing gray shadows over the landscape.

He was tired of dark clouds lurking over his shoulders.

Georgiana had changed all that. She was the fresh breeze after a storm, the sunshine on a dark day, the light of a thousand candles in a dark cavern, the light of his life, the smartest and most beautiful woman in the world. And as soon as he reminded the bridge builder of his responsibility to the safety of the passengers who would use the railroad, he'd hightail it back to Omaha and Georgiana.

CHAPTER 15

Drake worked off his excess energy by pacing the length of the hotel suite's sitting room, his anger rising faster than the sun on the edge of the horizon. When he had arrived in Omaha last night, he'd learned that Georgiana had checked out of the hotel. First Hardy disappeared, now Siobhan and Georgiana.

Damn! He'd been trained to build and construct. But his life the last few months had been nothing short of a catastrophe. What a goddamned life he'd created for himself!

Drake took three quick strides across the long room and answered the knock at the suite's door. He expected John Sinclair from the U.P.R.R. office with information about Hardy, Siobhan and Georgiana, but instead found a man with classically handsome—and oh so familiar—features.

"Michael!" Drake thundered as he shook hands with his brother. "What the hell are you doing here?"

"Why don't you ask me in so we can talk privately?"

"Come in." Drake moved aside to allow him entry.

Michael strolled through the doorway, planted his bowler hat on the sideboard's marble top, and walked over to the settee. "It's been a long time, Drake." He made himself comfortable on the needlework cushions by unbuttoning his frock coat and pushing it back over his hips. Leisurely he stretched his long legs out in front of him. "Much too long."

"Yes, it has. Eight years." Shocked to see his brother, Drake sat in the carved rosewood side chair, fighting a gnawing premonition that Michael's visit was not a social one. "What brings you to Omaha?"

"Mother sent me," he said, his voice suddenly hushed and almost too quiet.

Drake frowned. "You can go back and tell her I'm not coming home."

Michael's congenial expression instantly changed. Just like that summer on Long Island. Drake had run away, seeking the security of their treehouse after an argument with Clinton about which academy he would be attending in the fall. Mother had sent Michael to bring Drake home, but he refused to come down from The Citadel and pulled the ladder up onto the higher branches above his younger brother's reach. But Michael, twenty pounds lighter and very agile, climbed the oak tree like a monkey. He'd hauled off and with a perfect bull's-eye gave Drake the first shiner of his life.

Out of sheer amazement and then grudging admiration, Drake had gone home with his brother, but he'd no intention of doing so again.

"How did you know where to find me?"

"Dad has always kept up with your whereabouts over the years. Recently, Thomas Durant has been helpful in keeping us apprised of your activities. Father spent a weekend recently on Durant's boat."

"Go home, Michael."

"I will. But first I have something for you." He tugged an envelope from his coat's inside pocket and held it up for Drake to take.

"What is it?"

"A letter from Mother."

"No." Drake eyed the paper like it was a snake that would strike at any moment and took a step back.

Michael sat up straighter and pushed the missive closer to Drake's hand. The anger of moments ago was gone and in its place was distress, pure and simple. What the devil was wrong in New York that Michael would travel this distance to personally deliver a letter from Mother?

"Take it, Drake. She would have wanted you to have it."

"*Would* have?" he asked, responding to the odd note in his brother's voice.

"She's dead, Drake. We lost her the seventeenth of February."

Drake gripped the sides of his chair, feeling cold inside. He needed distance, a moment to reorient himself. A mist rose in his eyes and clung to his lashes while bile churned in his stomach. No! He would never see her sweet smile, smell the scent of the lilac water that clung to her skin and clothes, reminding him of his boyhood. He'd buried that part of his life when he walked out on her. Then why did it hurt so much to hear about her death?

"What happened?" He rose and solicited information: he had to know all the particulars. Then with the knowledge he could flay himself for the fool that he had been not to have returned home sooner.

"You know how she helped out at the orphanage. One night she stayed late and was caught in a storm. She developed a cough and then pneumonia. Her last thoughts were of you and she pleaded with me to deliver this to you." Michael held the piece of paper out to him. "Take it, Drake."

Michael's tone was relatively civil in spite of the grief and bitterness on his face. Dammit! He could not fight his brother over a letter.

Drake grabbed the paper. Privacy was out of the question, but he could at least put distance between himself and Michael. He stood at the large window overlooking Omaha's busy main street, the post-dawn light making a lamp unnecessary. He tore the seal on the envelope and unfolded the paper. His mother's flowing script tugged at him.

> My Son,
> I ask your forgiveness. I will not apologize for loving Jason Lassiter. Only know that I loved him above all else in life and when he returned that love I was the happiest of women.
>
> The Lassiter family were friends of my parents, and I grew up with Jason and Clinton. Jason and I discovered love when we were very young. And when I was of age, Jason asked for my hand. Before we could wed, he died in a boating accident. Because I found myself with child within a week after the funeral, Clinton agreed to marry me and give his brother's child a name. Until the Van Dykes paid a former servant for that information, I thought no one except Clinton knew Jason was your father.
>
> After you were born, Clinton finally told me he had always loved me. But because his older brother asked for my hand, he had stepped aside, knowing my feelings for Jason.
>
> Know that until the day I died, I loved Clinton. He was my husband, my friend. And he loves you and Michael equally.

Struck dumb with the identity of his natural father, Drake crushed the pages of the letter in his fist, holding them close to his heart. *Clinton's brother is my father. My uncle. My father.* His inner voice continued in a litany, back and forth. Then he smoothed the crumpled sheets and read the rest of the letter.

> Drake, my darling, Clinton and I always wanted to tell you about Jason, but fear kept us prisoners. As a child, many thought you to be cold and uncaring, but I knew that you had a depth, a calmness that would

help you later in life. Even at a young age I saw how intense you were, logic a very important part of your personality.

When the Van Dykes told you about my indiscretion, you were compelled to run. Clinton and I were heartbroken but we understood. Throughout the last eight years of your exile, he told me of your achievements in the army and with the railroad. Knowing where you were during those years kept me from going mad. My last wish is that you will reconcile with your father. He loves you very much.

Good-bye, darling. I'll always love you.

Mother

Drake held the letter against his chest, his breathing harsh and loud. For eight years he'd stayed away from home, disallowing his mother an opportunity to tell him about his father. He'd been no better than the Van Dykes who shunned her. How could he have been so cruel?

Mother would not have allowed Jason Lassiter to compromise her unless she had loved him dearly. Much like Georgiana's love for him. He'd shut himself off from feelings and the emotional intricacies that developed with love. Until Georgiana had come into his life.

He moaned as his chaotic thoughts tangled with his sanity. Georgiana had loved him without consideration for her reputation. Without consideration to the possibility of her being with child. Without consideration for a future for them together.

As quickly as the granite slabs of rock that he'd learned to destroy with nitroglycerine charges, the hatred that he had carried in his heart for eight years exploded and shattered. He was free for the first time in eight years, all because a beautiful, intelligent woman with hair the color of fool's gold had loved him. Still loved him, he prayed, even though she had disappeared. Now if he could only find her so he could tell her over and over how much she meant to him.

"Drake." The level of Michael's voice told Drake his brother was near, not across the room any longer.

"Give me a minute, Michael."

Understanding what Drake needed, Michael nodded. Drake turned his back, facing the window and the sunshine that shone through the glass and drapes. Darkness had been purged from him. And never again would he feel its harsh frigid fingers around his soul and his heart. Georgiana was his sunshine and his warmth.

Drake swung around and hauled Michael into a bear hug. They clasped each other, two giant men, two loving brothers in the clutch of emotion unseen by the outside world. Words came in half whispers. Incomplete sentences of wrongdoing. Visages of the past. Shiny words of a future. But they both understood.

Johanna Lassiter had left a legacy of love and understanding. And two sons who would continue to love and remember her until they were gone from this world.

"Hey, little brother," Drake broke down and spoke his first coherent words since Michael gave him the letter.

"What is this 'little brother' stuff? I could still whop your arse any time." Quickly, Michael's words changed from quietly spoken maudlin sentiments to animated amusement. "It wouldn't be the first time I gave you a shiner."

"No." Drake chuckled. "But it sure as hell would be the last."

"Let's not argue." Michael's tone had a degree of warmth and concern before he said, "At least not until we're home and we can continue our sibling rivalry with a referee in attendance. Father wants you to come home, Drake. He still talks about you joining the firm. He wants your name under his on the front of the building. So do I."

"I should just forget that I have a railroad to build?"

"Is that what you're doing here in this fancy hotel suite?"

Drake instantly sobered. "No, I'm looking for the woman I love."

Michael's expression was that of a man who had just been hit over the head with a bottle. Then he began to chuckle. "You in love? I can't wait to meet this lady. She must be something special if she has taken your heart."

"That's the problem right now..."

Drake spent the next few minutes extolling Georgiana's virtues. Then for more than five minutes he went on a rampage, swearing that when he found her he would lock her away for good so she'd never disappear from his life again.

"It seems to me there is a simple solution to your dilemma."

"Nothing is simple in dealing with Georgiana Radcliffe."

"You'll just have to marry her and bring her home where the three of us can take turns guarding her the next, oh say, forty years or so."

"I'd forgotten what a sense of humor you have, Michael. But I'm not laughing this time."

"No. I guess you're not. This is too serious. Where do you think she may have gone?"

"I'm stymied. When you arrived, I thought you were a man from the railroad office. I'm having their investigators talk to conductors on every train going east or west in the last week."

"Then you don't mind if I make myself at home and wait with you?"

"Not at all. I'll have your bags brought up to the suite," Drake said as he started to pace again.

"I only have one bag and it's in the hallway. I'll get it."

Drake halted his exercise in futility and strode toward Michael. "I'll help you, little brother."

Michael and Drake sparred with each other across the room, a few smashed knickknacks paying the price for their reunion. Drake grabbed the door handle and tugged on it.

A tall, dirty cowboy leaned against the wall on the other side of the corridor.

"Jesus Christ, Hardy. Where the hell have you been?

I've had men looking for you from here to the Pacific Ocean. Couldn't you send a telegram? Disappearing for weeks—"

Hardy stood quietly, his chin resting on his chest, his hat covering his face until he moved his leg and his spurs jingled. "Sorry, Captain," he rasped in a pain-filled voice. He staggered away from the paneled wall and would have fallen on his face if Drake and Michael hadn't caught him.

"Inside. Take him into my room." Drake led the way across the threshold and around the large table in the middle of the room, holding Hardy under his right arm while Michael helped on the other side.

"Talk . . ." Hardy ground out the word urgently and dug his spurs into the Brussels carpet, skidding to a halt. "Before I lose my strength." He lifted his head, his eyes glazed with distress. Drake looked down at his chest and noticed a red stain spreading across it. "Put me on the settee."

Drake squatted down next to Hardy and started to open his partner's shirt. "Now tell me what the hell happened," he demanded, the sight of Hardy's condition like a steel weight on his chest.

Hardy closed his eyes and grabbed Drake by the collar, stopping his inspection. "The Englishman," he said, a faint tremor easing into his voice. "He paid two men to kill you . . . the explosion and the runaway team in Bear River . . . all his doin' . . . when I confronted—" He coughed and went white, grasping at Drake with a hard fist.

Drake and Michael worked as a team to help Hardy down onto the cushions, placing a pillow under his head and lifting his legs to make him comfortable. Michael left the suite when Drake asked him to locate a doctor.

"Hold on, partner. We'll take care of Beeton. I've got a doctor coming to take care of you."

"It's okay." He let go of Drake, took a shallow breath and color flushed across his face again. "The doctors in Green

River City told me I just need to rest. I think I busted the confounded stitches." He looked down and swiped at the crimson stripe on his shirt. "Damn!"

"You'll get all the rest you need with the prettiest nurses taking care of you, partner."

"Damn, Drake. Those doctors had grandmothers takin' care of me. A man can't get better lookin' at an old prune face."

"Partner, you'll be all right." Drake clasped his friend on his good shoulder.

When Doctor Carroll finally arrived, he verified Hardy's injuries and then put him to bed to mend. Drake breathed easier.

Now he could give careful consideration to Hardy's discovery of Beeton's duplicity in the attempts to kill Drake.

The moment the doctor finished with Hardy, Drake pressed him for information about Georgiana and her condition when she left Omaha. Drake felt a bit remorseful at threatening the doctor, but he'd do it again to find Georgiana. The doctor confirmed that he'd warned Georgiana not to do any extensive traveling because of her injuries. She was still in America. But where?

"What do you want to do about this Englishman, Drake?" Michael asked after the doctor left the suite.

"Beeton has to wait. Right now I need those reports about Georgiana's movements." They sat in the parlor, enjoying a couple of glasses of Kentucky's finest. But as the minutes dragged on into an hour, Drake's patience was on a short fuse. "What the hell is taking them so long?"

Drake was ready to charge down to the U.P.R.R. office when there was a knock at the door. "This had best be Sinclair now."

"They told me to rush this over to you right away, Mr. Lassiter." Slicked hair mussed, his brown pants dust-covered and his chest heaving from his run up the four floors to the hotel suite, the myopic office clerk almost fell into the room.

"Have a seat, Sinclair, while I read these reports. I might need to send a wire." He tugged open the canvas pouch. "Get him something to drink, Michael."

"Thank you, sir," the clerk responded.

Drake took a seat at the secretarial desk and cabinet. Cluttered already with line reports and newspapers, Drake pushed them aside and laid out the important documents. He read quickly through sheet after sheet of testimony by the train's conductors. But he stopped shuffling when he found a dispatch for him from Jack Casement regarding the merging of the rails. A joint resolution of Congress placed the meeting point at Promontory Point, Utah. The grading crews had received their orders to stop all work west of Promontory Summit on April 11. The letter further stated that Stanford had ordered all work by the Central Pacific halted east of Blue Creek, the eastern base of the Promontory.

Excitement flooded through him. Joining the rails had been his dream, the essence that made his life worthwhile for these many years. Checking further, he located a letter from Durant demanding Drake's return to end-of-track now that Georgiana was under her stepbrother's care.

"Stepbrother's care? What the hell is he talking about?" Drake ran through the rest of the reports with a renewed zeal. Finally he found it. An employee recalled Georgiana disembarking at the Cheyenne stop because he had to help her off the train in her invalid's chair. He also mentioned a companion, an attractive Irish lass. The words that he read next would haunt his sleep night after night for many years to come. Also accompanying the two ladies was an ill-tempered British aristocrat. Drake balled his fist and slammed it on the hard mahogany surface.

Beeton!

"The Englishman has Georgiana somewhere near Cheyenne." Drake stood, seething with anger that became a scalding fury. "No way in hell am I going to let her stay with that scoundrel."

"Then we know what we got to do, Captain." Hardy leaned against the bedroom's doorjamb, holding his trousers around the waist as he tugged on his shirt with a grimace.

"You've got no sense, Hardy." Drake rushed to his friend's side and helped him up as he started to slip a few inches. "You've got to get back in bed."

"Got to get the lady away from Beeton. Got to get dressed. We'll take the train to Cheyenne. We can beat that misbegotten excuse of a man to a pulp."

"You're not going anywhere," Drake commanded.

"Drake's right, Hardy. You're staying right here. I'm going with him." Both men stared dumbfounded at Michael's announcement.

"This isn't your fight, Michael."

"Like hell it's not. We're talking about my future sister-in-law and any chance I have of nieces and nephews. Would you do less for me under the circumstances?"

He was proud to have his brother by his side. As children they had played as knights in their tree house. There they'd sworn allegiance to a neighbor boy, their feudal lord, and saved the ladies in distress, the girls who lived down the road, who had been locked in the tower by the evil black night.

Michael turned and faced Drake. He drew his imaginary sword and held it out. Drake recognized the familiar salute and followed his brother's lead. When their phantom blades were crossed they spoke the refrain they hadn't forgotten. "Death to the oppressor of the fair maiden."

They were a team again. At stake this time was his soul.

Georgiana had found little solace in the comfortable rooms Lawrence made available to her and Siobhan when they'd reached his ranch a few miles from the city of Cheyenne. After a week of his sheltering concern, Georgiana was ready to scream. Being in an invalid's chair and having Siobhan's hovering presence was enough to cause her madness.

She pushed the chair's wheels and moved to the window. She desperately needed activity, anything to keep her mind busy while she worked on getting her legs moving again. Siobhan had been an absolute jewel, massaging her legs twice a day, moving them back and forth to mimic walking until they were both weak from physical exertion.

Georgiana was making progress. Last night was enough to give her hope for a complete recovery. In the midst of a passionate daydream, Drake's calloused palms had stroked and fondled her back and legs, a hot tingle erupting along the skin as he moved his hands. While she'd scolded herself for such fantasy and attempted to slow her breathing, she'd touched her legs. That's when her skin shivered at the touch of her own fingertips. And when she dug her nails into the skin and felt the normal pain, she stared at the indentations, her heart pounding.

Like a mother willing her child to take that first tentative step, she'd concentrated on transferring her thoughts to her limbs. Then she dropped her legs over the side of the bed. Holding on to the bedpost, she pulled herself up to her feet. She'd cried with joy as she stood for the first time in weeks. She fell back on the bed, exhausted, but elated with her accomplishment.

This morning she couldn't wait for Siobhan to join her so she could see the results of her massages. When was the last time she'd been filled with such enthusiasm? It had been during her childhood, when her father had allowed her to study languages, history, geography, mathematics and classics, instruction usually afforded only a well-educated Englishman. *At least Mother encouraged me and never once complained about my studies being untoward for a woman.* She smiled sadly at the memory of those happy years.

Then Mother died and Father married Edythe. Just as she had suggested that picnics would turn a lady's nose red, she had also offered her opinion that no properly educated lady would take an interest in *those* subjects that held Georgiana's attention. Her tutor dropped her favorite classes. But by then she'd had years of training and clandestinely continued her studies in her room at night by candlelight.

She yearned for those days in the classroom. Learning about the shape of the world, she read the classics and experienced a burning desire to travel. But the most important lessons were her sums. Her father made her responsible for his estate books and he extolled her virtues to Thomas Brassey on his visits. That's when her life changed dramatically. He used her abilities at calculating when she traveled to the Continent and visited a few of the railroad projects in progress. While on site, she helped Thomas compile the papers necessary for building the railroad. Her father and Thomas had opened the world of travel to her and she'd discovered her freedom.

Now that cherished independence offered her only loneliness. She'd give up her home in England, her entire wealth, if only she could walk into Drake's secure arms once again.

Her eyes grew moist as she remembered those years. Her father alive and well. Thomas's yearly visits to their home in Yorkshire. Siobhan loving her like a sister would. Her first trip to America when she first met Drake, naked in a bathhouse. This trip when he wooed her and won her love. His tender care after her accident. If I walk again, will Drake still want me? Will I have the chance to grow whole again in body and heart with the help of his love? Will he finally confide in me the secret of why he thinks no woman would love him?

"What sort of life would I have if I hadn't persisted in my extra studies?" she questioned herself, her voice low, lightheaded with the memories she had evoked.

"You would've been miserable," Siobhan blared out behind her. "Not to mention you most probably would never have met Drake Lassiter." She walked to the table and set a few copies of the local newspaper on it.

Leaving it to Siobhan to find the silver lining in a cloud,

Georgiana thought. Wait until she learns how I stood next to my bed last night.

"What news is there of the progress of the Union Pacific?"

"How are your legs this morning?" Siobhan ignored the question regarding the rails as deftly as she braided Georgiana's long hair.

"I asked first." She squinted, very pleased with herself and revitalized in her determination to return to Drake.

"You don't have to tell me. You're like a wide-eyed child who has just learned to crawl and has discovered a new world."

"You've taken all the fun out of my surprise. Come. Take me into the bedroom. I want to show you something wonderful."

With a dazzling smile plastered on her face, Siobhan wheeled Georgiana into the bedroom and stopped next to her bed.

"Now watch this." She locked the wheels on the chair and grabbed each leg, planting them on the floor one at a time. With all the strength she could gather, she grabbed the bedpost and pulled herself up on her feet.

"Georgie," Siobhan's voice was tinged with reverence and shock. "When . . . how long . . . why didn't you tell me?"

"Last night. Last night. I told you—"

"You're not going to fall down, now, are you?"

Georgiana swayed and would have fallen if Siobhan hadn't grabbed her around the waist and set her back in the wheelchair.

"Sit a spell. It won't do to wear yourself out. This being the first day you're back on your feet." She smiled that big Irish smile of hers that meant she was pleased beyond her capacity to speak at the moment.

It stopped her for just a moment. "There's a great deal of work to do. We must concentrate on getting your strength back. I'll increase your massages to four a day and maybe we'll even practice some walking every day from now on." She shook her head, acknowledging her own statements. Then she looked down at Georgiana, a puzzled look on her face. "Are you having any pain, Georgie?"

"Only a little bit." She smiled to herself, worn out before breakfast with Siobhan's enthusiasm. "But the pain is small payment. Oh Siobhan, do you see what this means? One day soon I can walk back into his life."

CHAPTER 16

"Listen to this, Siobhan." Georgiana held a two-week-old copy of the *Cheyenne Daily Leader* folded in half, excitedly reading Siobhan the headline article. " 'On April 10, a joint resolution of Congress decreed the meeting place for the Union Pacific and the Central Pacific railroads at Promontory Summit, Utah Territory. Last spike made of gold to be driven May 9, 1869.' That's only a fortnight from today," she added in a hushed voice.

Drake had been correct about the area where the railroads would meet! His dream was now easily within his reach. In two weeks he would finish his quest to join the nation with rails.

"Is there any other news of the railroad?" Siobhan asked.

Georgiana quickly glanced through the article, noting the pertinent information that would be of interest to Siobhan. "There are celebrations and parties planned after the official ceremony. I wonder if they will resemble the prairie party Thomas Durant threw when Father and I were on the investors' train." *The party that changed my life forever.* She read further on near the end of the column. "Many dignitaries from the Union Pacific and Central Pacific railroads will be present."

Wistfully, she lifted her gaze out the window, past the ranch's grassland, imagining the end-of-track, the excitement, the history of such an accomplishment. What I wouldn't give to be there with Drake when they strike the blow on the golden spike, she thought with a bittersweet taste in her mouth, for the occasion would indeed be happy and sad.

Papa, how I wish you were here to see this day!

"Are you ready for your exercises this morning?" Siobhan asked.

Georgiana didn't answer immediately. She began to shake, her mind a crazy mixture of hope and fear as she considered the reality of her condition and its affect on her ability to join Drake and share his success.

"Yes. Let's do it now. I want to try to walk across the room without your assistance." She watched Siobhan carefully for a reaction and was delighted to see her shocked expression. "I've been practicing in the evening after dinner by walking back and forth around the bed while holding the bedposts."

"Why didn't you ask for my help? You could have fallen and hurt yourself."

"I wanted . . . needed to do this myself."

She locked the wheels and rose from the chair. Her heart hammered in her ears. She imagined Drake standing a few feet away, dressed in his trail clothes, his Stetson shading his passion-glazed eyes, his arms beckoning her into his powerful embrace. You will walk again, she constantly goaded herself when her legs seemed about to give out under her, the goal of being held within Drake's arms encouraging her step by step.

As her feet moved in front of her in an even line, she held onto Siobhan's shoulder and smiled, knowing that her dream of walking into Drake's arms was almost within her reach.

"Lawrence has refused me the use of a carriage," Siobhan shrieked as she reentered Georgiana's sitting room, a scowl on her face, acerbic sentiments directed at a certain viscount's kin.

"There must be a misunderstanding." Georgiana set her cross-stitching down, folded the newspapers she hadn't yet finished reading and set them on the cushion at the end of the settee. "Why would he do something like that?"

Lawrence appeared in the doorway behind Siobhan. "Ask me when we're alone," he declared, his words loud and harsh in the quiet room.

With a glance in Siobhan's direction, he silently dismissed her as if she were one of his servants. When she stood fast, his face grew livid. His obtrusive manner was intentional and worried Georgiana. In the past she could bring him about with a reminder of family, but his hostile glare strongly alerted her of the sudden change and that she and Siobhan were alone at his isolated ranch. Maybe it was time to return to Omaha, a warning voice whispered.

"Siobhan, would you leave me alone with Lawrence?"

Siobhan nodded slowly and departed, muttering derogatory Gaelic phrases under her breath that brought a blush to Georgiana's cheeks. She needed her wits when she spoke with Lawrence, but his hostility gnawed away at her confidence. He was too close, having moved a chair within a few inches of the settee.

His hand snaked out toward her cross-stitching and the folded newspapers. When he perused the headline in the paper, his expression clouded in anger. "Lassiter!" He spat out Drake's name contemptuously. "Why are you reading this? Aren't you finished with that laborer and this fool idea to invest in the Union Pacific?"

"No. I'm going to marry Drake," she stated simply, the knowledge that she would soon walk unattended a talisman against the infuriated glow in Lawrence's eyes.

Glowering at her, he grabbed her wrist. "Bloody nonsense! Do you think I will allow you to marry that self-seeker?"

Georgiana swallowed hard, trying not to reveal her own

anger. "I don't need your permission to marry. Nothing you can say will change my mind. Siobhan and I will be leaving today." She couldn't stay at his ranch under these circumstances.

He tightened his grip; a burst of pain burned up her arm to her elbow as he twisted and bruised the delicate skin. "You are not going back to your American lover," he said between clenched teeth.

"How dare you!" Her voice wavered, furious at his abuse. "Don't do this. We're related." He'd always reminded her that they were family. Would her appeal quell his irrational actions?

"Only your *step*brother, dear sister," he reminded her. "And that relationship will change very soon."

She blinked, the threatening moisture disappearing in a sweep of dismay. "I don't understand."

"You will. I've waited to have you for too many years. You will marry, but your bridegroom will not be the American."

Incapable of jumping to her feet and running from his restraint, she twisted around and slapped at him, attempted to get free. "This is insane." But she wasn't laughing. Lawrence was obsessed. To what lengths would he go to stop her from leaving the ranch and returning to Drake? "I'll never marry you."

"I think the little surprise Hank has for you will change your mind, dear sister," he said with a significant lifting of his bushy brows.

"I don't love you."

He chuckled. "Who said anything about love? That's not what I want from you, Georgiana."

Visibly trembling Georgiana savored her freedom when Lawrence dropped her hand. As she massaged her wrist, escape was paramount in her mind. She had to locate Siobhan, but without the assistance of her chair, she was fettered to the settee. As her mind whirled, seeking a plan of escape, Lawrence strode to the door.

"Hank!" he hollered for his foreman.

Georgiana gasped when the short, wiry wrangler shoved Siobhan through the door. Her hands were tied behind her back, a checkered bandanna wrapped around her face. There was a bruise on her left cheek. Eyes wide with apprehension, Georgiana saw Siobhan blink and let out a deep sigh. *God help her! She's worried about me instead of herself.*

"What are you doing, Lawrence?" Georgiana shouted, but he ignored her question. As the two men spoke quietly, Georgiana shifted her legs over the edge of the settee. She must help Siobhan. Her friend shook her head, her eyes pleading a warning. Georgiana fell back against the cushion. What could they do against the physical strength of two men? She possessed only mental acuity. "Lawrence, you can't—"

"Shut up! I'll do anything I damn well please. Remember that," he sneered as he stood over her. "And if you don't do what you're told, Miss Ryan will suffer the consequences. Do you understand?"

"Yes," she said, her world crumbling around her with Lawrence's renewed threats to Siobhan.

"Good!" He nodded to his wrangler.

Georgiana kept her eyes on Siobhan as Hank dragged her friend from the sitting room. She bit her lip to stifle an outcry. That wouldn't help either her or Siobhan. She could pray that the floor would open up and swallow Lawrence and his henchman, but she might put her energies to better use. She had to escape using her own wits.

"Now let's talk about the wedding," Lawrence chided her. "Tomorrow a few of the boys will go into town and bring back a preacher."

Needing time to formulate a plan of escape, Georgiana remembered how much Lawrence always kept his distance from Father when he had fallen ill. Knowing he detested being around sick people, she started to cough. Then she turned her leg in an awkward angle until she felt light-headed from the pain.

Holding a handkerchief to her forehead and then against her pale lips, she mumbled from behind the linen, "Lawrence, I'm feeling ill. I must rest."

She waited, eyes tightly closed with the hope that he would immediately withdraw from her sickroom. Determination like a rock inside her, she confidently rejected the idea that she couldn't elude Lawrence's absurd demands. Drake was the one she loved and the only man she would marry. With a pulse-pounding certainty she knew her heart would not be deterred.

Lawrence spoke with quiet firmness, equally sure of himself and his rightful place with her. "My dear, I want you in the best of health when we exchange our vows. Reverend Hall must see how much you love me. You have two days to recuperate. No more," he charged her from over his shoulder as he left the room, leaving Georgiana in a quandary. How would she accomplish her escape without the full use of her legs?

"You're to keep the Irishwoman tied up in her room. I don't trust her with Georgiana," Lawrence warned Hank as they moved silently down the ranch house's second floor hallway to Georgiana's bedroom.

"I don't like this, boss," Hank grumbled. "The woman has money. Friends in high places."

"Stop worrying. When she becomes my wife I'll control her fortune. And I can be very generous with my friends." He rubbed his palms together and stopped between the rooms, his body vibrating with new life. Soon he would have everything he wanted. "She'll settle into the life of a loving wife, or else."

"What are you going to do with the other one?" Hank said in a nasty tone, his dark eyes glittering with impatience.

"Ah, yes, the other one. After the wedding, she's all yours." Lawrence slapped his foreman on the back. "The upper ridge of the ranch is very remote, almost inaccessible.

A man could ride out there with a woman and come back alone."

From their vantage point above Beeton's holdings, Drake and Michael studied the normal workday scene. Buildings used for feed, horses and ranch hands were scattered around the main house. Wranglers corralled horses, supervised livestock and tended the vegetable gardens. What interested Drake most was the imposing residence, a two-story house with a veranda that wrapped around three sides. He could easily enter the second floor through a door or balcony. He watched the ranch house for any signs of activity.

"I think I should ride down and visit Georgiana." Michael affirmed his earlier conversation with Drake.

"I told you it's too dangerous."

"Do you have any other plan? Someone must get into the house and discover if she is safe. You can't go because Beeton knows you. That leaves me."

"Your logic is wonderful," Drake laughed wryly. "Except Beeton could kill you."

"What are the odds that he would kill an emissary from Thomas Durant, Vice-President of the Union Pacific? I've got to go with my instinct. From what little you've told me about Beeton, I don't think he'll refuse my visit."

"I hate to admit it, but you're probably right. Just be careful. Don't leave me to explain our mistakes to Father like you always did when we were kids. Okay?"

Michael paused, checked the chambers of his revolver, reholstered his gun, then nodded and grabbed Drake in a bear hug before mounting his horse and riding down the road.

"You have a visitor, dear sister."

Sitting at the desk rereading the newspapers, Georgiana twisted her head and looked over her shoulder at Lawrence and the visitor. Who was this man? Another one of Lawrence's henchmen?

"Michael Chancellor, ma'am." The handsome stranger lifted her right hand and kissed it. "Thomas Durant said you were lovely. But I had no idea what a pleasant duty this would be."

"Mr. Chancellor, a pleasure to meet you."

Georgiana lifted her eyelids for a quick look at this man; her heart beat like a sledgehammer. *Bless you, Thomas! You've sent me a savior.* She tempered her enthusiasm so Lawrence wouldn't notice anything amiss.

"I'm here in Cheyenne on railroad business. Thomas asked me to look in on you."

She watched Chancellor and how his eyes strayed to certain parts of the room as if verifying the size and location of windows and doors. Fortunately, Lawrence stood behind the man and wasn't aware of his detailed examination of her environment. "You're so kind, Mr. Chancellor." She used gracious inflections in her voice. Lawrence must think this was just a social call.

"Thomas also mentioned your companion. A Miss Ryan?" he questioned as his gaze settled on Lawrence.

"The Irishwoman is indisposed." Lawrence moved distractedly around the room.

"I'm sorry to hear that. Maybe I can return tomorrow and visit you both."

Georgiana attempted to hide her continuing puzzlement at Mr. Chancellor's movements. He walked to the window overlooking a garden and the surrounding hills. He lifted his gaze to the horizon, hesitated briefly, then returned to her side.

"That's not possible. We have a very busy schedule tomorrow. We are to be wed." Lawrence stiffened.

Mr. Chancellor flinched. "Congratulations. Odd, though, Durant said nothing about a wedding."

"Because of Georgiana's recent injuries we have foresworn inviting anyone to the ceremony," Lawrence proudly announced. He came up behind her and planted his palm tightly on her shoulder.

NIGHT TRAIN

Georgiana watched Chancellor, noticing what pains he took to hide his shock. If she didn't know better she'd swear this man knew she didn't want to marry Lawrence. Who was he? She studied his features. His eyes were gray like Drake's. When he forced a smile, her heart lurched. It was so familiar. Could this be Drake's brother? She rubbed her hands across the maple secretary desk, her fingers catching on the edge of the newspaper. Dare she write a note asking for help?

Good fortune shined down, for Hank entered the room, asking to speak with Lawrence. While her stepbrother's attentions were shifted, she picked up her pen, wrote a few words, folded the paper, and handed it to Michael.

He accepted the paper and nodded his head, acknowledging her gift. Then he smiled. Georgiana, fearing that Chancellor would be discovered, knew she had to do something to get him out of there. When Lawrence returned and stood again next to her chair, she moved her head as if to swoon as she moved restlessly in her chair. "I'm very tired. The accident, you know. Thank you so much for coming." All she could hope was that Lawrence would assume she was feeling ill. She stared at Lawrence and lifted her hand for Michael's good-bye. "Please tell Thomas I appreciate his concern."

"You've been wonderful taking the time to see me. I wish you the best and I know you'll feel much better very, very soon." Chancellor's lips lingered on her hand, his gentle grip one of concern and comfort.

When her visitor left the room followed by Lawrence and Hank, Georgiana rolled her chair toward the French doors and out onto the veranda. She looked to the hills. In her heart she knew Drake was close. She wrapped her arms around her waist. Freedom. Soon.

"My love. Hurry!" she silently pleaded, praying that it was Drake who would read the message on the newspaper.

"Help! I'm being held prisoner." Drake read Georgiana's words and crumpled the paper. Jumping up from the large boulder, he stared down at Beeton's ranch house. He recognized Georgiana sitting on the veranda in her wheelchair, her blonde hair like the glow of firelight in the pre-sunset hour. She was a siren calling to a cold, hungry traveler.

"I've got to get her out of there," Drake cried out as he strode to the tethered horses.

Michael ran to Drake's side and grabbed his reins. He shouted, "Think, Drake! Beeton might hurt Georgiana. And if you're dead you won't be much help to her."

Drake knew Michael was right. Rushing into Beeton's lair in broad daylight wasn't smart. Georgiana could get injured again or even killed.

He walked away from his horse back to the crumpled newspaper that lay in the dirt. He lifted it and smoothed out the section where Georgiana had written. His fingers rubbed against those words as he stared down at the ranch house. "All right. We'll get the law to take care of Beeton. We've got enough on him now: the plan to have me killed, the attempt on Hardy's life and the note from Georgiana asking for help. Ride into town and bring Sheriff Forbes. I met him in late '67 when our tracking crew reached Cheyenne. He's a good man. It'll be dark soon and I'll wait here out of sight."

The plan was good and Drake watched the descending night's shadows swallow Michael and his horse as they rode south toward Cheyenne. Finding a flat spot on a boulder sheltered by low tree branches, Drake settled down.

The moon rose, hovering over the roof of the ranch house. The stars shimmered in the dark Wyoming sky, reminding him of the night he and Georgiana had spent in the cave. The spring breeze wafted up the incline, bringing with it the smell of sagebrush, alkali, pasture grass, livestock and wildflowers. Georgiana's scent.

What was keeping Michael? He should have been back by now! Restlessness spiked his resolve. Knowing Georgiana was Beeton's prisoner, Drake couldn't wait any longer. He packed his gear and concealed his horse in a

NIGHT TRAIN

dense copse of trees. Checking his revolver, he pulled out his bowie knife from his saddlebags and tucked it in his boot.

Beeton must be confident, Drake thought as he stalked the house and the outbuildings. There was only one guard on duty, sleeping on a rocker next to the front door. Recalling the position of Georgiana's room as he had watched her prepare for bed earlier, Drake easily found a trellis with small vines climbing the side of the house. He mounted the crisscrossing wood and grabbed the balcony's railing, pulling himself up onto the veranda.

He stopped at the window, listening for any movement from within Georgiana's room. All was quiet. He entered quickly, his eyes adjusting to the dark before he saw her peacefully asleep on the bed. He breathed in sharply, moving closer. For the rest of his days, he would cherish that exquisite sight. She was an ethereal vision, her long golden hair enveloping her shoulders like a lover's arms.

As he sat on the edge of the bed, he gently brushed the hair from her face and kissed her lips. She whimpered and shifted to her back, her lips moving spontaneously under his tender assault. "Wake up, sweetheart," he whispered against her mouth.

Her eyes opened, stark disbelief and then relief shadowed in their depths. She said his name, "Drake," and pulled him closer, his lips a mere breath away from hers. "Oh, darling, you came." Her voice sent the pit of his stomach into a wild swirl. He reclaimed her lips, and crushed her to him. Burying his face in her neck, she breathed a kiss there.

"Michael has gone for the sheriff. I couldn't stay away another minute, not knowing if you were safe with Beeton."

"Then Michael is—"

"My brother." Drake smiled and lifted her into his lap, keeping her near as he gently stroked her back, hips and thighs. His determination to see her safely away from Beeton dampened any rising desire. "I'm going to help you dress and then we're getting out of here. I don't want you in this house when the sheriff arrives. Beeton will be desperate then."

He quietly told her about Beeton's duplicity in the accidents that had plagued him for months. Georgiana dropped her hands to his upper arms, tightening her grip when he said, "Siobhan can help you dress. Is she sleeping next door?"

"Siobhan's a prisoner. One of the men is guarding her."

"Damn the bastard!" Drake swore quietly.

"You took the words right out of my mouth, Lassiter. Can *you* tell Georgiana who your father is?"

Before Drake could draw his weapon, Lawrence entered the bedroom, a revolver steady in his hand and pointed at Georgiana. Drake rubbed the back of his neck, sensing someone else was with Beeton. His gaze swept the room until he located a man entering from the veranda, his gun also drawn and trained on Georgiana.

Siobhan had allowed the man guarding her to think she slept. But the moment she heard his footfalls on the wood planks of the veranda, she opened her eyes, jumped from the bed and stood at the open window, listening for his return. Voices rose from Georgiana's room.

Realizing this was her chance to escape, Siobhan twisted her head from side to side, looking for something she could use to help her free herself.

The pitcher and bowl! If she broke the porcelain, she could use the sharp edge to saw through her bindings. Swiftly she reached the table and twisted around so her fingers could curve on the handle. Ready to drop it on the floor, she paused. She recognized the sounds of a struggle emanating from Georgiana's room. The noise muffled the breaking of the pitcher.

With the shard held tightly in her fingers she pressed it against the ropes and moved her wrists back and forth. She held back a scream when she stuck her skin for the third time, a trail of blood making her fingers sticky. Refusing to give up now, she tugged at her bindings until she felt them loosen. One last cut and she yanked her wrists free. She inspected her slashed wrist, but the cuts weren't deep. Tearing the bandanna from her mouth, she wrapped her hand. As she was wondering how to dispose of the piece of porcelain, she heard Georgiana scream. Siobhan hurried along the veranda toward the window leading to Georgiana's room.

With her back tightly against the side of the house, Siobhan watched in horror as Lawrence pulled Georgiana from her bed, and tugged her against his chest, his arm around her midriff holding her up. Lawrence pressed his gun against her temple, scolding her for loving a bastard.

"I don't care about Drake's father," Georgiana shouted angrily.

Drake went for his gun, but Hank's was already drawn and he clipped Drake on the back of the head. Drake flipped off the bed and onto the floor on his stomach. Hank commandeered his gun.

"You're the bastard." Georgiana spat at Lawrence as she twisted, attempting to get away from his hold. Clamping his arm at her neck, Lawrence tightened it against her windpipe.

Drake groggily lifted his head, dragging his hand across the back of his neck. He moaned. "Don't fight him, sweetheart. I don't want him to hurt you."

"He won't hurt me." She tried to wrestle away from Lawrence's hold, scraping her fingernails across his hand.

"You bitch!" He pulled back just as he was going to slap her. "Don't push me too far."

Georgiana had a comeback ready as she stared down at Drake. Concern was written all over her face. "Without me he has nothing. If I die he'll never see the money."

"How astute, dear sister." Siobhan saw Lawrence signal Hank with his eyes and head. "But that doesn't go for your American lover." Hank pushed the muzzle of his revolver against the back of Drake's head. "Now are you going to behave?"

"You won't kill Drake. I'll never cooperate with you if anything happens to him."

"Don't push me, Georgiana. You're just like your father. He thought he could control me when I threatened to tell about him and that Irish slut of his."

Siobhan edged closer to the window, leaning behind the thin layer of curtains that moved in the evening breeze. His slur was irksome, but at this moment words could not hurt her. Only the demented man's actions would harm any of them. She listened carefully as Beeton continued.

"He meant to divorce my mother and marry that Irish whore. He thought my words were only an idle threat, but he learned differently when I held the pillow over his face."

Hearing Georgiana's gasp of surprise, Siobhan stopped breathing. Before his trip to America, John had pledged his love, but she refused his proposal of marriage. When he returned he had been a different man. Talking to her about America, he'd asked her again to marry him. In his weakened condition she couldn't refuse, for she loved him beyond all reason and social conditions, and they'd begun to make plans. Then two days later John was dead. Murdered by Lawrence.

The blood of her forefathers—the mighty Celtic warriors—rushed like fire through her veins.

Lawrence's shrill voice added fuel to the raging inferno. "Oh, you're wondering why I tell you all this when you can go to the authorities with the news of your father's murder?" His face broke into a smile of a madman. "I'll tell anyone who questions me that you are mad. If you warm my bed without complaining I may allow you to live. One way or the other I'll control your money."

"Why would I marry you if you're going to kill me?" Georgiana demanded.

"If you refuse now, Lassiter dies."

Outside, near the window, Siobhan heard the snick of a gun being cocked.

No! Siobhan thought to herself. Lawrence would not get

away with a second murder. Clenching the porcelain in her hand, praying to the saints, she crept into the room, behind Lawrence. Hopefully, she could disarm him.

Lawrence moved away from Georgiana and stood near the window. As if a sign from heaven he faced the room. Siobhan snuck up behind him and, before he was aware of her presence, she swiped at his gun hand with the broken shard.

Out of the corner of his eye, Drake glimpsed a movement on the veranda. Had Michael finally returned or was it just an illusion? His stomach rolled with nausea from his head wound, but he gathered every last bit of strength to do battle.

Just then Lawrence cursed. Jerking back against the window frame, he dropped his gun to grab a woman by the nape of her neck. As he pulled her by the hair, Drake saw a flash of red. Siobhan!

Siobhan struck at Lawrence like a wildcat. She bit at his hands and arms when he slapped her repeatedly across the face. She spit at him. She clawed at his face and neck when he pulled her closer to control her. For a split second Hank looked over at the fight. Drake dove for the gun only a few feet away on the floor. Before his fingers wrapped around the butt, Hank kicked the gun under the bed.

Angered, Drake smashed into Hank's legs, tumbling the man to the floor. As they grappled for control of the weapon they rolled around and around, knocking over small tables and chairs. When the gun fired, both men jerked.

Drake lay on the floor alongside the bed. Pushing at Hank's dead body, he started to get up. His hand skimmed across the gun that lay on the carpet near his hand. He touched the butt, ready to shoot Lawrence. But the Englishman was no fool.

Siobhan lay in a heap at the foot of the bed, an occasional moan and movement attesting to her survival. Lawrence held Georgiana in front of him like a shield with Drake's

Colt as his weapon. If Drake shot from this angle he might hit Georgiana.

"Get up," Lawrence barked. "Over there." He indicated the clear area before the window.

Drake staggered to his feet, his body tensed for what was to come. Beeton had no choice now. Perhaps he could still afford to keep Georgiana alive, but Drake and Siobhan were expendable.

Looking lovingly into Georgiana's misty eyes, Drake wanted to tell her so much.

"Time to say good-bye to Mr. Lassiter, dear sister. I find that keeping him alive is too tedious." Lawrence lifted the gun and took aim.

With the coming sunrise, Drake heard the clatter of hooves and the shouts from men at the front of the house. Lawrence shifted his gaze for a split second. Taking a deep breath and willing his limbs to move, Drake leapt at Lawrence and his gun. Fear struck at him when he heard the gun being fired and then Georgiana dropped to the floor like a sack of potatoes.

Drake dug out from under the weight of Lawrence's body and swiftly crawled to Georgiana's side. He knelt over her, moving his gaze and hands over her, certain he would find a wound. She groaned, opened her eyes, and he lifted her into the cradle of his arms. She relaxed, sinking into his cushioning embrace.

"Are you hurt?" they asked simultaneously.

"No," they both whispered. Drake kissed her, needing the succor of her sweet mouth desperately.

Preoccupied with the events of the last few minutes, he'd forgotten the riders outside, but he now heard a banging and then a crash at the front door. He stared back at Beeton's body, a large puddle of blood seeping from under him. A few feet away, Siobhan sat on the floor, her hair hanging in her eyes, a smoking gun held in her two hands. Tears seeped from her lashes. She spoke to the spirit of John Radcliffe,

NIGHT TRAIN

proclaiming her vengeance for his murder. Dropping the gun on the floor, she held her head with her hands and cried.

"I'm fine. See to Siobhan," Georgiana told Drake.

He went and took the woman in his arms, holding her while she continued to weep. Finally, she glanced over at Georgiana, accepting her love and understanding for the deed she had done. She patted Drake's forearm and said, "Thank you." She took a deep breath and wiped the tears from her cheeks.

Drake kissed her on the cheek, got up, and marched through the doorway to the second-floor railing. He looked down at the men as they started up the stairs.

"Michael! Over here," Drake called to his brother.

Turning to rejoin Georgiana and Siobhan, he stopped just inside the room. He squinted, unable to believe his eyes. Georgiana was walking toward him, a triumphant smile shining on her face. He held out his arms, grinned and watched her take a few slow steps.

CHAPTER 17

Cheyenne, Wyoming Territory

"There's a special train due in one hour." Through the window of the station, the small, gray-haired stationmaster slowly answered Drake's question about the next westbound train. "But it won't be stopping here or along the line. The mucky-mucks are heading for Promontory for the big shindig planned." He read the schedule of trains, his cap shading his eyes from Drake's perusal.

Relief filled him. He hadn't missed the joining of the rails. Rescuing Georgiana had been of the utmost importance, but now that she was safe and back in his arms, he still might be able to finish his job. He had to join up with that train.

"It will stop. You're going to flag it down."

The man's head jerked up and their eyes met. "Now listen here, mister. I don't know who you are, but there are regulations that must be followed. I can't—"

"Drake Lassiter."

"What did you say?"

"The name's Drake Lassiter. Get your fingers busy on that key. Reed will vouch for me."

"The superintendent?"

"Yeah." Drake pushed his hat back and settled his hand on his holster, then on second though wrapped his fingers firmly around the butt. Wouldn't do any harm to hurry the man about his business, Drake assured himself. "What are you waiting for?"

The flustered man dropped his gaze to Drake's revolver. "Yes, sir. I'll get to it right now." He left the window, settled at a desk and sent the message.

While waiting with Michael for the operator to bring them a reply, Drake watched Georgiana and Siobhan where he'd settled them out of the noonday sun. They sat patiently in the little room available for travelers. He'd carried Georgiana to the bench as her legs were still too weak to walk any long distances.

It was a healing time also for Siobhan. After Sheriff Forbes had listened to the explanation of events that led to Siobhan shooting Lawrence, the lawman had agreed there would be no charges against her. Neither had he charged Drake for Hank's death.

Relieved and desperate to put distance between themselves and the ranch, Georgiana refused to stay another day on the property. It wasn't until their arrival at the station that she mentioned Promontory and how much she wanted to see the joining of the rails.

But her bright blue eyes had told him much more than her words ever could. She looked over at him now, her gaze bright and cheery and his heart swelled. The sunshine had come back into his life. God, he loved her! As soon as they could be alone he wanted to show her how much she meant to him. Locking the world away, he'd lay her down in the middle of a big four-poster bed, with plenty of room to move around on and then—

"Mr. Lassiter, sir." The railroad employee broke into Drake's pleasure-seeking thoughts. "I apologize for the inconvenience. Use my office to make yourself comfortable. I'll flag the train for you."

Drake twisted around and faced the exuberant man, quite

a difference from the man who had greeted him ten minutes ago. "We're fine where we are. Just don't miss flagging that train."

"No, sir, Mr. Lassiter," the railroad employee assured Drake.

Pulled by locomotive No. 119, a wood burner with a standard straight stack, the train came to a halt. Drake and Michael were waiting on the platform, suitcases and steamer trunks piled high on a four-wheeled cart nearby. A uniformed conductor jumped down. The engine hissed, a cloud of steam rising around the platform like dragon smoke.

As Drake began a heated discussion with the conductor, Thomas Durant appeared on the observation deck. Dressed in a slouch hat, a fitted velvet sackcoat and vest, corduroy breeches, and top boots, he leaned over the railing and hollered, "Drake! Michael? What the hell is going on?"

"Looks like I picked the right train." In high spirits, Drake hailed Thomas.

"Don't just stand there, jump aboard. We've got a date with destiny, son." Thomas motioned to the conductor to start the train rolling again.

"Wait. Stow this baggage. I'll be right back." Drake ran back to the waiting room and scooped Georgiana up in his arms. Siobhan hurried along behind them, a small portmanteau held in her uninjured hand.

Drake strode back toward the train and then through the railcar's door, directing a few ladies to vacate the settee. He gently placed Georgiana down amidst a handful of passengers, their eyes wide in astonishment and their mouths pursed, ready to condemn his actions. Silencing them with an icy glare, he made Georgiana comfortable with a few pillows commandeered from two of the bedrooms and left her with a kiss and a promise to return to her side soon.

Thomas Clark Durant, former assistant professor of surgery, past trader of commodity futures and a businessman known for his acumen, stood in the open doorway of his car, his eyes caustic and impatient. The passengers milled around mumbling in the far corner of the compartment. Then Thomas's face broke into a smile.

"Now that Mr. Drake and his party have joined us we can continue our celebration."

Loud acknowledgments broke out and normal sounds of conversation resumed. After a few words of instruction to the conductor to get the train moving, Thomas closed the door and shook Drake's hand. "I assured Hardy that somehow you'd not miss this momentous occasion." Drake jerked around. Hardy, looking a little pale, but grinning nevertheless, sat on the far side of the room. Drake gave his partner a mock salute with two fingers and returned to his conversation with Thomas. "You're the man that's always in the middle of the fray. With the joining of the rails our fighting is over, Drake."

Fighting is over. How good that sounded. But was it? Lawrence had intimated to Georgiana that Drake was a bastard. Would she accept his past? Would she silence the raging conflict in his personal life? He needed to speak with her before they reached Promontory. She was the only one who could assure him peace in his life and somehow he needed to accomplish that before the last spike was driven on the transcontinental railroad.

Whistle shrieking, the train jumped to life again as they departed the station. Drake rejoined Georgiana and, as he sat next to her on the settee, Thomas introduced everyone. Holding Georgiana's hand, he told Thomas briefly what had happened at Beeton's ranch; everyone in the car was riveted by the appalling story.

After a few minutes, Drake left Georgiana in Siobhan's capable hands. As he joined Thomas, he heard Mrs. Samuel Reed and her daughter, Anna, discussing the landscape and the perils of traveling through the open frontier with Georgiana and Siobhan.

Sidney Dillon, John Duff and Grenville Dodge, Directors of the U.P.R.R., stood on the observation deck, enjoying

NIGHT TRAIN

cigars and champagne, deep in conversation about the ceremonies and the festivities planned for after the joining of the rails. They welcomed Thomas and Drake as the train gathered speed, rushing toward Promontory Point. Drake's gaze strayed into the compartment as he sought Georgiana. Magically, she looked at him. Sipping at her champagne goblet, she mouthed silently, "I love you," as sunshine poured from her smile.

That's all he needed, for her smile warmed his heart.

Stepping away from the conversation, he stood at the brass rail and studied the track, two thin lines of iron joining a country devastated by the war. During that conflict he'd shunned his home, his family. Peace had come to the nation. Only Georgiana held the special balm to heal his wounds, for if she refused his love when she learned about his mother's indiscretion he would never see home again. There was no home without Georgiana.

As the train neared the Piedmont station around noontime, Drake marveled at a large contingent of railroad workers surrounding the tracks. The train had stopped along the line for telegrams. Drake was aware the eastern line was near its conclusion with only a few hundred men left to complete the mile and a half necessary to join the rails. The large camps were being broken up and abandoned. "Thomas. Come and see this. There must be nearly five hundred men outside." Drake moved aside as Thomas joined him at the window.

"What the hell?" Thomas grumbled.

The conductor joined the crowd, spoke briefly to four men and angrily returned to the train, flagging the engineer to start through the swarm of workers. When the train moved, Drake rushed to the door with Thomas. There was something wrong. The private car stood dead on the tracks. The men had loosened the pin and the car was detached.

The conductor opened the door followed by the same four

men he had spoken to previously. They were goading him with drawn guns.

"What is the meaning of this?" Thomas demanded.

"We're looking for Durant," the man at the front of the riffraff charged, his voice deep with an Irish brogue.

"I'm Durant," Thomas said coolly.

"I've been elected as chairman of these delegates to put our demands to you."

"Demands! I don't have time for this sort of thing. This train must be in Promontory tomorrow morning."

"Not possible. We want our money. Some of us haven't been paid for five months."

"Blasted idiot!" Thomas charged, but Drake noticed the Vice-President's expression. He was chewing something over in his mind. Then he said, "All right, the money is coming. I'll pay you when we come back through here tomorrow."

"Not good enough, gent. I've got a few contractors and five hundred workers who want their money now." The disgruntled worker lifted his gun barrel and pointed to the outside where the angry men milled around, their braggadocio wafting through the walls of the car.

"You can't do this," Drake yelled at the man. He'd attempted to keep quiet but was unable, knowing Georgiana's well-being was at risk.

"Just watch me," the man exploded, leaving the car in the hands of his three armed companions.

Within an hour the occupants were divested of their weapons and the private car was placed on the side track and the wheels were chained, preventing any movement.

The leader returned. "We've taken possession of the telegraph office. Our operator will only send messages about finances. Nothing else. Until you wire for our money you're our prisoners."

A day and a half later, before dawn, Drake sat alone with Georgiana in the back of the parlor. The passengers had slept little during the standoff with most of the men grouchy and Mrs. Reed and her daughter registering constant complaints. Georgiana appeared wan, though she continued in good spirits. She held his hand in her lap, relaxing back against the velvet cushion on the settee. She looked slyly up at him, her eyes a deep sky blue, and moistened her lips.

"I thought after we escaped Lawrence we'd be together. Safe. But now I wonder . . ." she trailed off, her grip on his hand tightening.

"Hardy's on a first-name basis with at least a score of the workers and he has learned there is a trainload of troops expected along the line in the next twelve hours. We'll be free soon." He lifted her face, his hand strong and firm around her chin. "We're going to make it. I won't let anything happen to you."

With a pang, she realized that they very well might not survive what was happening around them. If she had only a few hours to be with Drake she wanted to spend them in a place where she had felt so much joy. She swallowed with difficulty and found her voice. "I know this may not be a prudent request, but I want to go outside on the observation deck," she blurted out, scarcely aware of her own voice. "The night is so dark and the stars the brightest I've seen." Her eyes strayed to the velvet draperies that hid the night from view. When she turned her gaze back, she stroked her fingertips along the hard line of his cheek.

The stern warning she expected never came. He grabbed her hand, pressed a kiss in its palm, and held her gaze with his heated stare. "I love you so much."

She lifted her face and kissed him gently on the lips. "I want you to tell me about your life in New York before the War," she directed him when she was in his arms as he carried her across the parlor to the outside door. "I think Lawrence's mayhem is mild compared to the torture you've experienced since before the War."

His gray eyes were as dark as the night sky, the light in his soul unable to shine through the morass of troubles he held in his heart. "I told you about Clinton and the engineering business," he offered when they were settled against the iron railing.

"I know you did, darling, but I want to know who hurt you so terribly that you were afraid of my love." She nodded, slowly blinking her eyes to edge him on. "There's nothing you can tell me that would change the way I feel about you."

Strange and disquieting thoughts began to race through her mind. She wrapped her arms around his neck, holding tightly to him. If he wasn't holding her would he flee her questions?

"There's nothing—"

"Nothing?" she interjected, her face only inches from his. "Look at me, Drake."

A few night fires burned in the camp set up next to the coach and the light threw Drake's tormented expression in relief. He lifted his gaze.

He tenderly kissed her on the cheek and then took a deep breath. "I'm a bastard," he sighed heavily, his voice filled with anguish. "My mother was not married to my father. He died before they were married . . . ."

Swallowing the sob that rose in her throat, she looked up, but he rushed on without giving her the opportunity to react to his confession. A suffocating sensation tightened her throat. Oh, dear God. Now she knew all this time he'd been concerned about what she would think when she learned the truth about his family.

Georgiana listened, her heart aching with pain for the man she loved as he told her how he'd renounced his family and his home. He'd endured so much pain. Throughout their lifetime together she would shower him with love to soothe the effect of those tormented years.

Hugging him closely, she offered solace as he continued. His speech faltered briefly when he told her of the news of his mother's death. She stared at him with more love than she thought existed in the world.

The hurt he'd carried with him during the War and through the Great Plains as he built the railroad lay naked in his eyes. A spark of hope stirred in her and she said, "I'd like very much to meet Clinton, your father." Overcome with emotion and with tears running down her cheeks, she said, "I love him very much. He took care of the man I love."

She felt the relief sweep through his body as he wrapped her in a cocoon of euphoria.

"You can't imagine how happy you've made me."

"I can see the happiness in your eyes. They're no longer clouded by the grief of a tormented man. I see a silvery glow of peace and contentment."

"Do you remember that day on the observation deck when you told me I needed something else to believe in? Not just the railroad?"

"Yes," she said quietly, the tears coming again into her eyes.

"You've given me that something. And you're never getting away from me," he swore to her when he kissed her, sealing their love for the rest of their lives.

On Saturday morning, May 9, the day on which the last spike was to have been struck at Promontory Point, Thomas Durant submitted to his persecutors and wired for funds. He and his guests were liberated when he paid his tormentors $253,000.

"It's done."

Drake's husky voice startled Georgiana. She should be jealous of his heavy breathing and the excited beat of his heart. But he wasn't interested in another woman. He was watching the striking hammers unite the last rail for the transcontinental railroad.

She meshed her fingers tighter within his grasp. Should she have stayed in the private car away from the intense crush of people? Daily her legs were growing stronger, though she could not walk yet without support. She'd stubbornly refused to use the wheelchair, and leaned against

Drake, safe and secure, his power and strength evident in the hard muscles that transversed his body.

She'd been aware of the importance of this event from her very first trip to America. On this clear, cold afternoon of May 10, 1869, before a crowd that included barmaids from the nearby railroad camps, train crews, Irish and Chinese workmen, the 21st Infantry and its regimental band, a couple of Mormon bishops, and an assortment of dignitaries, Leland Stanford, the President of the Central Pacific Railroad, had taken in hand a sledgehammer of silver. Driving the spike of gold through a tie of laurel, he had ceremoniously connected the Central Pacific to the Union Pacific.

"Now we can go home, Georgiana," Drake murmured and pulled her tighter against his side. "I want you to meet my father." He didn't hesitate anymore when he said the word father. Her heart was joyful for the healthy look on Drake's face.

The future was clear and strong. They had something to believe in—their love and the force of it in their lives.

EPILOGUE

Drake eased his body into the warm bathwater, sighing as he stretched his tall frame out in the generously oversized tub. He raised his right arm, lifted a glass to his lips, and two fingers of his father's expensive brandy disappeared, washing away the taste of the road. Next time Clinton wanted a new site reconnoitered, he could do it himself. On second thought, Drake knew he had a solution. He'd give Hardy a promotion and send him out to do the preliminary work. The road was no place for an old married man.

Drake repositioned himself. The layers of dirt slid from his flesh, leaving mud in the bottom of the tub. Steam rose from his bath, mingling silently with the music that drifted through the wood plank floor of the bathroom.

Georgiana didn't expect him until tomorrow. He'd decided to surprise her by arriving early. But the applause of the audience of guests in his large brownstone home listening to a musical recital shattered his thoughts of some private time with his wife.

"Ahhhh," he sighed, his voice loud in the bathroom. He refilled his glass, relishing the fire and warmth that spread through him, a needed balm to soothe his weary body. A box of fine Havanas sat nearby and he pulled one out, snipped the end and lit it, puffing energetically.

He rolled his shoulders, stiff from his lengthy train trip and then carriage ride. Now all he needed was a hearty meal and a soft woman. The thought of a certain lady's curvy, feminine flesh pressed against his rough frame gripped the lower part of his body with a new rigidness. He smiled. He'd have no trouble finding the woman he desired.

His mouth was dry from just the thought of seeing her again after his long absence. He swallowed the last of his liquor, leaned over, and picked up the bottle sitting on the small marble-topped table next to the tub. With his attention on pouring another drink, he didn't lift his head as he heard the door to the bedroom open and then close silently.

"Can't a man get privacy? I told you I'd take care of dressing myself," he chastised Giles, his valet, and banged the empty bottle on the table. In the process of lifting the refilled glass to his lips, his gaze shifted to the door and he sucked in his breath.

She stood there, tall and regal, dressed in an evening gown of pink-coral grosgrain, the color heightening her skin's own soft tint. She leaned against the wall, her eyes half closed as she attempted to catch her breath, gain control over her emotions and, at the same time, discover where the voice had come from in the semidarkness. A small light near the door gave him the advantage. She held her chin high. He held his breath as she locked the door. Her skirts swished as she spun around.

"Who are you running from now?" Drake's amused words broke the silence.

"I'm running to you," she answered quickly, her hand pressed against her throat, his memory of her quickened pulse setting him on fire.

Her words amused him and deep in his chest Drake felt a chuckle, ready to explode from his lips. She sashayed across the bathroom, her blonde curls swinging across her alabaster skin, the sound of her slippers muffled in the deep-pile Persian carpet. "Darling, I have a letter I want to read to you."

"Later. I have a more important message for you down here." He splashed the water near his waist.

"We'll get to that. Soon." She looked at him, the double meaning of her gaze obvious as she admired his wet chest and shoulders. She leaned over and planted a lazy kiss on his eager lips.

"The letter's from Siobhan."

He smiled and rested back against the tub. "How is your guardian angel?"

"Edythe has remarried and moved into her husband's home, and Siobhan is quite happy. She misses us both, but not this 'godforsaken country.' "

"And what do you want to do with the property?"

"I'd like to give it to Siobhan."

"I think that's a splendid idea. But I don't think she'll accept. Why don't you ask her to stay on and look after everything for you? That way she can't say no and she'll have a home for as long as she lives. Or until she marries."

Amusement and joy flooded her face. "Excellent idea. Drake, you're so clever."

"It's easy once you understand the feminine mind."

"Do you understand my mind right now?"

"Only too well, madam. What about your guests?"

She elevated her chin and glanced toward Drake, his naked body shrouded by the water in the partial darkness. "Under the circumstances I prefer your company, husband."

She stood only inches away from him now, the color of her eyes turning deep indigo with desire. His nostrils, so used to the smell of sweat, horses, dust and pine forests, drew in the fresh, clean scent of her body. Her unbound hair fell across one shoulder, thick and luxuriant.

His thoughts filtered back to the first night they'd met. He knew she remembered, too, for the knowledge was in the twinkle in her eyes when she lifted her chin. Her lambent gaze touched his naked skin, warming his heart and searing his soul.

"It seems I'm overdressed for this party," she said, then

bent over the tub and tugged on the closures at the back of her dress, her swelling breasts mere inches from his lips.

His mouth went slack at the sight of her hardened nipples and their darkened color. The cigar dropped into the bath water, sizzling as hotly as his nerve endings.

He rose from the tub, stretched for a moment, and ran his hands through his hair, squeezing the water from the strands. Water drizzled and splattered down his body and over the front of Georgiana's beautiful dress. She jumped back.

"Oh, Drake. Look what you've done to my new dress."

"Buy another one, sweetheart."

"Thank you, I will. And I'll use the money from your bank account. After all, it's only fair, since you destroyed my gown."

"Buy yourself a dozen new ones." He lifted his hand high in a grandiose manner as he stepped over the side of the tub. "Just as long as you take them off only for me."

The room was shadowed, but her face was bright with sunshine while she continued to undress. He grabbed a towel, but before he could dry himself he felt her eyes burning a path down his spine and across his buttocks.

He wrapped the towel around his waist, but her hand stayed him. She touched the knot on the towel to verify its sureness. Her eyes widened with delight at how easy it was to be with him.

Above her neckline, her pulse pounded erratically. Her lashes flickered. He took a step closer. Briefly she lowered her lashes, but a moment later she looked at him and clearly studied his almost naked body until flags of crimson whipped at her cheeks. He grinned, knowing she was enjoying her little teasing session.

He felt a familiar ache that demanded the soothing touch of his wife. Pure instinct took over. He tightened his rough palms on her softly rounded shoulders and eased her closer. He breathed in her scent, a blanket of prairie wildflowers that reminded him of the trek across a wilderness and the only way he survived was finding her. He felt her relax as he slipped his hands down her arms and hesitated a moment at her elbow where his fingers tangled in a loose strand of silken hair.

"Are you going to be a perfect gentleman? Or do I get to play with my rascal of a husband tonight?" She made a slow inventory of his body above the waist, her gaze a warm caress. Impatient with his response, she turned toward the bedroom, her wide skirts swishing across his ankles.

"Time is a-wasting, Mr. Lassiter," she spoke over her shoulder in a very prim voice. The diamond and sapphire earbobs he'd given her as a wedding present swayed, brushing across her shoulders.

But suddenly her demeanor changed. Briefly, mystery shimmered, excitement flared in her eyes. Before she took two more steps, he grabbed her and swung her up in his arms, forgetting the towel wrapped around his waist. It dropped.

Georgiana snuggled into his embrace, her arms winding around his neck and playing with the wet hair at his neck.

"Rascal," she purred in his ear.

"I have a present for you."

"I know," she whispered, and continued passing her tongue across the skin of his neck.

"Besides that." He set her back on her feet and raked his gaze over her body, then lifted an envelope from the table next to the tub. He handed it to her.

"I don't need any presents. I have your love."

"This is . . . You've given me so much. You've unlocked my heart and soul."

Drake twisted around, sitting on the edge of the tub to gain control over his escalating passion while she studied the papers he'd handed her.

She stared, wordlessly, and then burst into tears.

"I didn't think a trip to Suez would elicit such a response," he said.

"That you would leave your family so soon after being

reconciled and take me to the opening of the Suez Canal. I don't know what to say—"

"You don't need to say it. I only want your happiness, sweetheart."

Georgiana was still dressed; he was naked. This equation was wrong. Edging his fingers along the back of her dress, he found the closures. Usually adept at divesting her of her clothes, he was all thumbs tonight.

"Here, let me help," she offered, and wiggled her arms back to work on her dress.

Drake's pulse quickened as he speculated just how long it would take for Georgiana to peel off her petticoats so he could feast his eyes on the white flesh of her soft thighs. Her nearness always affected him and he knew he would go to his grave a happy man after being married to her for forty or fifty years.

The muted noise of the music recital floated delightfully on the night. Leaning back, he rested his forearms against the gold-flocked wall and took deep soothing drags of her scent.

His impatience almost destroyed the night. Not wanting to wait any longer for her undressing, he tugged at the filmy material and heard a ripping sound. Georgiana gasped, twisted in his arms and lost her balance. She slid quite naturally from his lap into the tub, spurting and flailing once she hit the water.

"You brigand," she yelped from her knees in the tub. "You're hopeless."

"That's why I married you, sweetheart." He leaned over her, grasped her under the arms and lifted her to her feet. "I needed something to believe in and I found you."

Tears pooled in her eyes. "Why do you do that all the time? Say such nice things. It makes me cry."

"Oh, darling, I love you."

"I look like a drowned rat." She saw them together in the large looking glass that hung on the wall. Her arms were wrapped around his broad shoulders, his hands caressing her bosom.

"Never! You're always beautiful," he growled, his palms rubbing against her hardened nipples on display for him under the sodden material.

Still standing in the tub, she was so quick he never saw the mischievous glint in her eyes. In a frenzy she tore at her dress, the material disappearing before his eyes. Soon she was as naked as he. If her dressmaker could only see Georgiana now. There would definitely be a scandal.

He wanted her desperately. No other woman would ever make him feel the way she did. Like a damn god. As a wedding present, she'd given the management of her entire fortune over to him. What the hell did he ever do in life to deserve her trust and love? For the rest of their lives he'd make sure every day that she knew how much he loved her for her beauty of soul, her warmth and the sunshine she brought to him.

He lingered over the soft skin under her breasts, the feel of it against his calloused palms creating an all too familiar ache deep, deep in his soul. He'd finally found the peace in his being that only the fair princess had been able to deliver.

"Georgiana, sweetheart. Let me take you to bed. A gentleman owes that much to his lady."

"I had something else in mind. Do you remember the cave and hot spring?"

"How could I forget?"

"Then make sure you take a deep breath because we are in for some water play tonight."

She knelt in the water at his feet and held up her arms, a goddess calling to her slave who heeded the call of love.

On the flocked wall, hanging above her head was the cross-stitching Georgiana had sewn as a reminder of the night they met on the Nebraska prairie. His eyes must be going bad because he could have sworn the face of his likeness was happy, exuberant. He didn't remember seeing such an expression when he'd peeked at it a few times before its completion.

"Georgie." He'd taken to calling her by Siobhan's pet name. "There's something wrong with your cross-stitching."

"What, darling?" She stood, the water running in diamond-studded trails down her supple body.

"Did you change any stitches?"

"Very observant, Mr. Lassiter. I took it down while you were gone, I added a smile to your dark face."

"You'll always be my sunshine. All the sunny smiles I have belong to you, sweetheart. Along with the sun, moon and the stars, you've given me something to believe in."

"And what it that, my darling?" she whispered, moving closer to him.

"Love." He smiled, pulled her wet body against his, and pressed a kiss against her mouth. Inching away from her lips, he said, "You've given me the sunshine of your love."

Diamond Wildflower Romance

A breathtaking new line of spectacular novels set in the untamed frontier of the American West. Every month, Diamond Wildflower brings you new adventures where passionate men and women dare to embrace their boldest dreams. Finally, romances that capture the very spirit and passion of the wild frontier.

___WARRIOR'S TOUCH by Deborah James
    1-55773-988-9/$4.99
___RUNAWAY BRIDE by Ann Carberry
    0-7865-0002-6/$4.99
___TEXAS ANGEL by Linda Francis Lee
    0-7865-0007-7/$4.99
___FRONTIER HEAT by Peggy Stoks
    0-7865-0012-3/$4.99
___RECKLESS RIVER by Teresa Southwick
    0-7865-0018-2/$4.99
___LIGHTNING STRIKES by Jean Wilson
    0-7865-0024-7/$4.99
___TENDER OUTLAW by Deborah James
    0-7865-0043-3/$4.99
___MY DESPERADO by Lois Greiman
    0-7865-0048-4/$4.99
___NIGHT TRAIN by Maryann O'Brien
    0-7865-0058-1/$4.99
___WILD HEARTS by Linda Francis Lee
    0-7865-0062-X/$4.99 (December)

Payable in U.S. funds. No cash orders accepted. Postage & handling: $1.75 for one book, 75¢ for each additional. Maximum postage $5.50. Prices, postage and handling charges may change without notice. Visa, Amex, MasterCard call 1-800-788-6262, ext. 1, refer to ad # 406

Or, check above books	Bill my: ☐ Visa ☐ MasterCard ☐ Amex	
and send this order form to:		(expires)
The Berkley Publishing Group	Card#_____	
390 Murray Hill Pkwy., Dept. B		($15 minimum)
East Rutherford, NJ 07073	Signature_____	
Please allow 6 weeks for delivery.	Or enclosed is my: ☐ check ☐ money order	
Name_____	Book Total	$_____
Address_____	Postage & Handling	$_____
City_____	Applicable Sales Tax (NY, NJ, PA, CA, GST Can.)	$_____
State/ZIP_____	Total Amount Due	$_____

If you enjoyed this book, take advantage of this special offer. Subscribe now and get a

FREE
Historical Romance

No Obligation (a $4.50 value)

Each month the editors of True Value select the four *very best* novels from America's leading publishers of romantic fiction. Preview them in your home *Free* for 10 days. With the first four books you receive, we'll send you a FREE book as our introductory gift. No Obligation!

If for any reason you decide not to keep them, just return them and owe nothing. If you like them as much as we think you will, you'll pay just $4.00 each and save at *least* $.50 each off the cover price. (Your savings are *guaranteed* to be at least $2.00 each month.) There is NO postage and handling – or other hidden charges. There are no minimum number of books to buy and you may cancel at any time.

Send in the Coupon Below

To get your FREE historical romance fill out the coupon below and mail it today. As soon as we receive it we'll send you your FREE Book along with your first month's selections.

Mail To: **True Value Home Subscription Services, Inc., P.O. Box 5235 120 Brighton Road, Clifton, New Jersey 07015-5235**

YES! I want to start previewing the very best historical romances being published today. Send me my FREE book along with the first month's selections. I understand that I may look them over FREE for 10 days. If I'm not absolutely delighted I may return them and owe nothing. Otherwise I will pay the low price of just $4.00 each: a total $16.00 (at least an $18.00 value) and save at least $2.00. Then each month I will receive four brand new novels to preview as soon as they are published for the same low price. I can always return a shipment and I may cancel this subscription at any time with no obligation to buy even a single book. In any event the FREE book is mine to keep regardless.

Name

Street Address ..... Apt. No.

City ..... State ..... Zip

Telephone

Signature
(if under 18 parent or guardian must sign)

Terms and prices subject to change. Orders subject to acceptance by True Value Home Subscription Services, Inc.

0058-1